HARAPPA - 1

LURE OF SOMA

SHANKAR N. KASHYAP

INDUS PUBLISHING GROUP
Bengaluru-560 003.

LURE OF SOMA

Author :
Shankar N. Kashyap

Publisher :
Indus Publishing Group
C/o. Smt. Rajeshwari Nagaraj,
#38, 4th Cross, ITI Layout,
New BEL Road, Bengaluru - 560 054.
Karnataka, India.
Phone: 99725 98632

Revised Edition : 2017
ISBN: 978-81-931714-5-5
Price : ₹499/-
Pages : 240 + 12 = 252
Copies : 1,000

Cover Design :
Sri G.K. Shivanna

Graphics Design :
Smt. Sujatha S.

Acknowledgements

For Geetha who has stood by me through it all and Shamanthi, Sushma and Tejas for they have been such a big support.

I would like to thank my publisher C Aruna, whose untiring work has culminated in a master piece.

I can not forget the inimitable G.K. Shivanna whose artwork has to be seen to be appreciated.

Shinjini Mukherjee who kept the narrative in the straight and narrow and has been of invaluable help through out.

The girls in the office, Yashoda and Sujatha who have put in enormous number of hours to bring the Lure of Soma out into open.

Other Books of Trilogy

Harappa 2 : FALL OF SHURUPPAK

Harappa 3 : BATTLE OF TEN KINGS

Reviews

"This is the story of his life and love which intermingles with politics of the day and the final armed conflict between the Avestans and Harappans. It has several characters from the Rigveda – including Shunahotra, Vishwamitra, Vasishta, Grtsamada, Medathiti. There are short, but concise descriptions of the life styles, religion, education and commerce of the time"

Niraj Mohanka,
Author of Royal Chronology of India

"Dr Shankar Kashyap's Harappan series is an extraordinary work based on the Indus Valley Civilization during the third millennium BCE. The author has brought to life the Indus Valley civilization and the episodes in Rigveda.""Dr Kashyap is a great storyteller and his first book, Harappa: Lure of Soma is a gripping tale set against the backdrop of an ancient civilization."

Meera Bharadwaj,
New Indian Express.

Preface

Half-way through the third millennium BC lay the golden era of the Indus Valley Civilization or Harappan Civilization. It stretched from the river Indus and Hindu Kush mountains in the west to the Ganges-Yamuna doab in the east, Himalayas in the north and the Arabian Sea in the south. The area was over a million square miles and it was the biggest empire of the time, bigger than the Sumerian and Egyptian civilisations put together.

After the Last Glacial Maximum about 13,000 years ago, the Himalayan glaciers receded just far enough north to leave a vast fertile alluvial plain between the Hindukush mountains in the north-west and the Aravalli hills in the east. This area was flooded every year like clock work by the river Indus. This vast land was fed by the waters of seven great rivers – Sindhu (Indus), Parushni (Ravi), Vitasta (Jhelum), Vipasa (Beas), Sutudri (Sutlej), Asikni (Chenab) and Saraswathi (Gaggar-Hakra).

The Indus Valley Civilisation was at the peak of development in the middle of third millenium BCE and had several large urban centres such as Mohenjodaro, Harappa, Kalibangan, Dholavira and Rupar. The excavations show uniform developments across the area, suggesting area-wide communications, and exchange of ideas & resources across the vast land. Harappan seals have been discovered as far away as Mesopotamia & Egypt in the west and in places at the southern tip of the Indian sub-continent, suggesting travel and communications over vast distances. This vast civilisation appears to have disappeared around 1900 BCE. There are several theories for its demise.

Who these people were is a question that has been asked for centuries. Not many subscribe to the "Aryan Invasion" theory anymore. It is now generally accepted that the population of Indus Valley Civilisation was made up of indigenous people and there was a gradual migration and integration of their races with people speaking the Indo-European language, hailing from Central Asia. During the nineteenth and twentieth centuries, it was probably difficult for scholars to accept that such an advanced civilisation could have pre-dated a population which they considered lacking in cultural development. The conclusion that there was an "invasion" by Aryans from the steppes of Central Asia was drawn based on tenuous philological evidence.

Archaeological evidence of horses and chariots from the Yamnaya culture and the ensuing Sintashta culture has given rise to the speculation of an Aryan Invasion, and has long been considered the pre-cursor of the Vedic Civilisation. There has been no evidence so far to suggest a mass destruction or warfare, among the ruins that have been excavated till date, to support the possibility of an invasion. There is, however, a grain of truth in the view that wars were fought on battlefields rather than cities being attacked or ransacked during the pre-historic period.

There are still thousands of Harappan sites waiting to be excavated. The excavations so far have revealed a highly advanced civilisation with well-developed city planning including roads, engineering, water supply and drainage. Some of the discoveries show that the system of drainage could be compared to that of the modern day. The Indus Valley script still defies our experts and remains a mystery. Very little was known about the people who lived in these cities until recently. Thanks to archaeology, we now know what they looked like, what kind of clothes they wore, their jewellery, their food habits and religious practices to some extent.

All the cities of Indus Valley Civilisation show an extremely high standard of engineering and mathematical skills not seen in any other contemporary civilisation elsewhere on the globe. For example, all the high streets of the large cities such as Harappa and Mohenjodaro were set along major cardinal axes. For such an achievement, a sound knowledge of astronomy and mathematics

along with engineering skills was essential. Mathematical texts 'written' by eminent sages such a Baudhayana, Apastambha, Manava and Katyana have been placed between 800 BCE and 200 BCE. The dating again is based purely on linguistic evidence when compared with other contemp rary texts. Apasthambha described both the Pythogarean theorem and the concept of Pythogarean triples dating at least 200 years before Pythogaras.

There is a school of thought, which subscribes to the idea that the Vedas were composed by the Harappans or the Meluhhans as the Mesopotamians called them. Rig Veda is the oldest of the Vedas and has been dated to have been composed around 1700 BCE. Niraj Mohanka of New Dharma takes it even further to 4000 BCE as the timeline for Rigveda. There was no archaeological evidence to suggest the dating of the Vedas until recently. This was based purely on linguistic and philological evidence. The evidence hence is within the books themselves. However evidence is emerging now that the Vedas might have been written a long time ago during the Bronze Age dating back to third millennium BCE. There are now both archaeological and textual evidence emerging which show that both the Vedas and Harappans might have belonged to the same time period. One of the grammar texts - Rigveda Pratisakya - used for analysis and understanding of Rigveda has been dated back to between 3100 and 800 BCE. New evidence is emerging all the time which is putting our history further and further back. It will not be long before the Indus script is unravelled and we may get an answer to the question whether the Harappans wrote the Vedas.

Rig Veda is the oldest of four Vedas which includes Sama, Yajur and Atharvana. It is organised into ten books or 'Mandalas' and consists of 1028 hymns. Numbering of the books is rather arbitrary and again based on linguistics. For example, the first book of Rigveda in considered much younger than the second. The language of the Vedas was considered 'archaic' as long ago as the time of the great grammarian, Panini, who has been dated to have lived around sixth century BCE. Dr David Frawley suggests that the positioning of vernal equinox in the Vedic scriptures suggest that the authors were from 6000 BCE. Astronomical configurations shown in the Vedas and Bramhanas suggest that these were

written well before 3000 BCE. I recommend a visit to www.Indiahistoryonline.com. It has an excellent link to an extremely well-researched chronology of history, of not only the Vedic people but also other reliogions of the world. Rigveda is essentially a Bronze age document when the mighty river Sarasvati "flowed from the mountains to the ocean." The river started to dry up towards late third millennium BCE and was reduced to minor seasonal streams Gaggar and Hakra by 1700 BCE. This by inference, puts the date of creation of Rigveda during the third millennium BCE.

Zarathustra (Zoroaster) is considered to be the author of the religious text of the Avestans, Yasna Haptanghaiti. This has been dated to around the middle of the second millennium BCE. The geography of Ariana is quite clear in the book and puts it squarely in present day Iran and to some extent Afghanistan and north-west Pakistan. There is very little known about people who lived in these parts before Zoroaster. According to the Avestan Gathas, he teaches the Avestan King Vishtaspa and overcomes obstacles placed by other priests and ruling classes. The dating of both these individuals has been severely contested, some placing Zoroaster from 700 BCE to as far back as 7000 BCE. The language used in the Yasna Haptanghaiti is old Avestan and the date of the language is still contested.

There is archaeological evidence to show that there were significant tectonic activity in the area and several of the rivers were diverted during the second and third millennium BCE. Diversion of several major rivers left parts of the country barren and unlivable. Even now, Greater Iran shows seismic activity with regular earthquakes.

It is in this context that the lives and trials and tribulations of people living in the Indus valley during the middle of third millennium BCE are described in this book. I have used existing archaeological evidence along with known historical evidence in writing this book. I have used some poetic license to accommodate the dates and times of various individuals and events to suit the story telling. The book tries to portray the life of ordinary people during the period of Harappans, while trying to tell the tales of the priestly kings, Magi, Rishis and Sages of the great Indus Valley Civilisation during the middle of third millennium BCE. This is the story of our hero, Upaas, a trainee physician from Harappa. It is the story of a young man growing up, falling in love, getting involved in adventures and finally fighting for the city he loves most – Harappa. The story shows the human elements of people around him. He faces friendship, love, hate, jealousy, treachery and deceit in day-to-day life. There is a generous sprinkling of magic and sorcery. As the country of Ariana west of Hindukush dries up, the Avestans faced with near-extinction take up arms against their neighbours to obtain the precious Soma. The tactics used include deceit, sorcery and finally a war between the Meluhhans and Avestans.

The Soma plant has been the centre piece of several hymns in Vedic scriptures. It is a plant that is still not accurately recognized. The Vedic people revered it as a God, drank the extract from the stalk of the plant, used the plant for medicinal purposes and it is supposed to have magical properties. The Avestans had a similar plant and called it Haoma and their scriptures also revered the plant for its spiritual properties. Vedas describe it as growing in a sacred mountain around a sacred lake (Mount Mujavant and lake Sharynavat). Avestan scriptures describe a similar sacred mountain and a sacred lake in Sistan where the Haoma plant grew. Quite similar to the Soma of the Indus Valley, we still do not know exactly what this plant was as it disappeared at the same time as the Harappans.

Shankar N. Kashyap
Newcastle upon Tyne

The Kings, Sages and Places:

Upaas	- Trainee Physician
Pindaara	- Cart driver
Pradipaka	- Council lamplighter
Nivya	- Upaas's younger sister
Lopa	- Avisthu's daughter
Vidhayaka	- Upaas's elder brother
Satakrutu	- Upaas's younger brother
Shushun	- The Elamite prince
Parthava	- Upaas's friend
Ubhaya	- Trainee physician

Council of Elders :

Sage Shunahotra	- Chief Priest of Harappa
Master Kapila	- Chief Architcct and Upaas's Father
Master Ashwin	- Chief Physician
Ganeral Nahusha	- Army Commander
Master Kodhandaki	- Chief Priest of Temple
Master Adhvadipa	- Commander of Defence
Master Audyogica	- Chief Engineer

Index:

Chapter 1

THE CITY OF GOLD

Chopping wood all afternoon had exhausted me. I slowly put down the heavy axe, pulled off the towel that I had tied round my head and mopped the sweat off my face. It was peak summer and the days were hot. The sun was a bright crimson ball in the west, suffusing the sky with shades of red and tinging the clouds with a golden hue. A gentle breeze now and then cooled the sultry summer air at this height, rustled the leaves at my feet and brought with it the distinct wet earthy fragrance of the first summer rain from somewhere in the distant hills. Crows cawed loudly as they returned to their nests and I could hear cowbells, and cattle calling out 'ambaa' as Pindaara hustled them home. Towering oak trees all but obscured the mountains of the north behind me and coloured the landscape green as far as the eye could see. In the distance, the snowy peaks gleamed like pearls and narrow streams of fresh water flowing down from the melting snow shone like mirror shards in the slanting rays of the sun.

The city was spread out before me on the plains. A change of guard was taking place at the western gate. The gates were manned by the elite group of guards commanded by Master Nahusha. These guards were specially chosen for their alertness and skill with arms and had to undergo two years of rigorous training before they were posted at the gates and on the walls. All of them wore bronze shields and carried tall brass tipped spears, which made patterns of dancing stars on the walls in the evening light.

Many bullock carts were waiting at the gate to enter the city before they closed the doors at nightfall. The dock just off the gate was quiet – all the boats had moored down for the night. The river Parushni kissed the city wall just south of the gate, flowed gently southwards along the western wall and again turned southwest past the city disappearing into dense forests. As it neared the great river Saraswathi, two days ride away, Parushni became a raging torrent, swollen with several streams that joined it on the way. I spotted a lone boat hurrying on towards the dock, eager to be moored before dusk melted into the darkness of the night. The fisherman manoeuvred the boat deftly toward the moorings and threw the rope to a guard who had stepped forward to help; he steadied it against the dock wall and then helped to tie it down to an anchoring stump.

With in the walls, the muted light shone off the copper and bronze plates and finials on the walls and doors and turned the city golden. No wonder they called it the 'City of Gold.' Behind the towering, flag bedecked walls was the imposing Temple with its great, gleaming copper and gold dome that dwarfed everything else in sight, even the large Gurukul beside it. It was this magnificent Temple, rather than its immense walls, which gave the city its sense of invincibility and power, I thought. It certainly gave me a sense of safety and belonging.

The upper town was a little smaller than the lower town and obviously more prosperous. All the houses there were large two storied structures and belonged mainly to the priests and the Elders of the Council. Past the Temple towards the east, the small flat roofed houses of the lower town crowded together in a huddle of perfect order. The prosperity and safety of the city attracted men from far and beyond and there were people from Dravida Kingdom, Elam, Sumer and Median living alongside native Harappans in the Lower Town. As a result, it had nearly doubled in size over the last ten years.

Just past the eastern gate was the massive Peepal tree on top of the hillock, which marked the start of a deep forest beyond it. I could not see the northern gate as it lay behind the large houses of the middle town, where all the rich merchants and some of the senior officers of the army resided. Beyond the city, on all sides, the countryside was lush and green with large expanses of barley fields interspersed with tall trees gently swaying in the breeze. A thin line wound through the trees: it was the road starting at the southern gate and going down all the way to Sindhu, only a few days ride away.

I turned with a sigh to the neat pile of logs I had chopped down over the past four hours, enough for both my Master's and our house for the month. I fetched the donkey a pail of sweet, cool water from the shallow stream that came all the way down from the Shivalik Mountains. The sun was going down rapidly and I would have to hurry. It was hard to get the guards to open the gates once they had been shut for the night. It did not take me long to reach the bottom of the hill.

There was a crowd of travellers and foreign merchants at the western gate. Those who could not find a place to stay within the city had camped outside the gate, close to the walls, so that the guards were near enough for their security. I counted at least fifteen wagons, heavy with goods, parked in a circle in the field just across the gates. Small fires had been lit and I could smell their cooking.

Some were from as far as Sumeria, judging by the smells emanating from their cooking pots. I smelt garlic in the air and that meant Dasyu merchants and their precious gold from the Dravida Kingdom in the far south. There were people sitting around a large campfire right in the middle of the circle of wagons and some men were playing wonderful rhythms on their drums; another musician joined in with a wind instrument and the music became almost bewitching. A couple of men stood up and started to dance. I stood there mesmerised by it all.

"It is beautiful, isn't it?"

The pleasant female voice startled me and I turned to look at her. She had come up from the dark shadows of one of the caravans and stood beside me.

"I have been listening to this music almost every night for the last few weeks. It is enchanting."

She was the most beautiful creature I had seen and I gazed at her in wonder. It was as if in the mellow light of dusk, the moon stood before me!

"Yes. It... it is very beautiful," I stammered, staring at her eyes. They were black as coal and glittered like diamonds.

"I am Lopa, daughter of Avisthu, from the city of Saraswata."

"I am Upaashantha, son of Kapila Angirasa," I managed to say.

"I saw you come down the hills. Do you go up there often?" she asked.

"No, not very often. I had to get firewood for my Master's house."

Someone started to sing a Dasyu song in a deep and gentle voice filled with passion and melancholy.

"Do you know what he is singing?" I asked.

"He is singing about his homeland."

"I can feel how much he misses his home."

"It has been several months since they left their homes. You should hear the songs he sings about his beloved. They are haunting."

"How do you know the language so well?"

"We get a lot of travellers from Dravida, Elam, Sumeria and even Median in our city. They come to my father to learn languages. He is a teacher of languages, you see," she said with a smile. She turned to look at the traffic trickling in through the gate and added, "You better go back into the city before the gates close."

Before I could reply, she disappeared into the darkness around the ring of wagons as quietly as she had come. I stood there for a few minutes trying to figure out what had just happened. Had it been a dream or a vision?

Cowbells tinkled behind me and a voice called out, "Namaste, Master Upaas."

It was Pindaara hurrying through the gates with his large herd of cows, half pushing, half cajoling one of the calves which obviously did not want to go back home. Pindaara was a cheerful, stocky, well-built character and he ambled rather than walked.

"Namaste, Pindaara. I see that Navika is still causing you trouble," I said.

Pindaara loved his cattle and had names for all of them. Navika was born on the day he had met a sailor who was on his way to the port of Saraswata. The sailor had told him of a distant place in the middle of a desert and described the building of large pyramids. Pindaara was impressed and it was his dream to go to this land of the pyramids one day.

"Yes, Master Upaas. But one of these days she will learn that I am the boss," he said, smiling and goading his favourite cow through the gates. "It is already late for the evening feed and I still have to clear up afterwards."

"Master Upaas, you should not stay outside the city walls so late. It is not safe. There have been reports of Avestan attacks in Sindhu. Sage Shunahotra and the Council of Elders are planning to provide accommodation within the city for all travellers," one of the guards called out.

"I lost track of time in the woods," I replied and hurried my donkey on.

As I passed through the gate, I looked up, as I always did, at the sign on the top of the stone column on the left. It read 'Sunset Gate' to mark the western gate. The two large stone columns on either side towered above me to a height of over thirty feet. Each of them was crowned with six large lamps, which were alight at this time of the evening. Brass finials and plates embellished the two massive wooden doors of the gate and shimmered in the light of the burning lamps. These finials were sharp, with points large enough to kill a man if impaled on it. The brass sheets had patterns depicting the emblem of the city a rising sun that also adorned the flags on top of the gates and the walls. No arrow or spear could get through the brass sheets covering the doors. The doors themselves were so thick and heavy that ten people were needed to open or close each one of them. Each door had six heavy brass hinges and three latches, each weighing a few kilos and their edges were covered with bronze strips.

My father was the chief architect of Harappa and he had designed the gates. It had taken more than a year to build them all. When the gates were being built, Father used to go away for several days to the quarry, which was a day's ride from the city, to supervise the stone cutting and I remember going up steep and narrow paths with him on one occasion.

I could hear the bells of the temple as I passed through the gate. The bells got louder as I walked down the street with my donkey and as I neared the Temple, the fragrance of sandal incense wafted on the gentle breeze. I could not see the top of the spire when I was near the Temple it was too high. It was built hundreds of years ago at the time of Lord Indra; its construction was supervised by one of the Sapatarshis, the great Sage Bhrigu, and it was built to the plans designed by the heavenly architect, Vishwakarma.

The streets were completely deserted save for Pradipaka who was going around lighting the street lamps. He carried the torch in one hand and slung the ladder over his left shoulder and looked like Father Time! No one knew how old he was, but he had been lighting the street lamps for as long as I could remember and Father used to say that he was ancient. Though old, he was very steady on his feet and strong as an ox. He never bumped his ladder against any of the bolsters that Father had installed in the corners of the streets to stop carts and chariots from hitting the buildings.

I turned the corner in front of the great Pushkarni and saw the wide-open gates of the Temple. Hands and feet had to be washed in the river before entering the Temple. Inside, the priests were singing Vedic hymns beautifully. It was soothing and gentle and yet powerful enough to lift one's spirits. I had learnt several hymns from the book composed by Sage Vishvamitra Gathinah from Sindhu, and I took pride in reciting them in the proper metre in which they were taught to me.

It was dark by the time I reached Master Ashwin's house. I tied the donkey to the post outside the door, pulled down the two piles of logs off its back and carried them one by one into the courtyard.

"Is that you, Upaas?" Ma Ashwin called out.

"Yes, Ma. I have got you some wood for the house."

She came out and I knelt down and touched her feet.

"Dheergayushman Bhava (May you live long), Upaas. We were running out of wood. The master will be out as soon as he finishes his evening prayers. You should also be at your prayers, Upaas," she said affectionately.

She had lost her son a few years ago to a dreadful illness and now depended on the Master's students for all these chores.

"As soon as I put these logs in the storeroom I will go home and say my prayers," I said.

"Have a jar of cold buttermilk before you go."

A glass of her cold buttermilk at the end of a hot, sweaty day's work was most welcome. She kept the buttermilk in a mud pot, which chilled it, and added just a touch of spices and fresh coriander leaves. It was delicious.

"Thank you, Ma. I am really grateful," I said, as I gulped it down.

"Upaas? It is dark; you should not be out at this time of night especially outside the city walls. It is not safe," said Master Ashwin, as he walked into the courtyard.

I kneeled and touched his feet.

"*Ayushman Bhava.* May God bless you."

"Namaste, Master Ashwin. I do tend to lose track of time when I am out in the woods. I will be more careful next time," I said, as I stood up.

"We must start early tomorrow, we have many patients to see. You had better get home and get some rest. We have a long day ahead of us," Master said.

I was training to be a physician under the tutelage of Master Ashwin after leaving the Gurukul in Sindhu five years ago. He was considered the best physician in Bharata and he chose his apprentices very carefully after several tough tests. It was very hard work, but very gratifying. He was a hard taskmaster and did not take kindly to shirkers or malingerers. There were six apprentices working under him and all of us wanted to impress him with our knowledge, skill and our ability to learn.

"Yes, Master. I will be there early tomorrow. Do you want me to get anything from the forest before we start?" I asked.

"No. I think we have enough stocks of medicine for now. We may need some palm leaves and steatite pencils for writing. I am sure we can buy them from the travelling merchants camped outside the walls. Go to the traveller's camp tomorrow and see if there are any merchants with writing materials. Now, you better hurry back home."

My eyes lit up and my heart gave a leap. There was every chance that I would see that girl again. It was not such a large camp, after all. I would speak to her properly this time. I could still feel her presence near me and her lilting, soft voice echoed in my ears.

"I will go there first thing tomorrow morning, Master," I said quickly, before he could change his mind, and hurried home.

As I walked into the courtyard, my sister, Nivya, called out, "Upaas? It's you at last!"

"Yes. I know it is late. I was in the forest getting wood for Master Ashwin's house."

"Father has been waiting to talk to you," she said, as she poured water for me to wash my hands and feet.

"You know how it is when I am in the woods," I said.

"I know and so does Father. Your habit of getting lost in daydreams worries all of us. You better say your evening prayers and then speak to him."

I changed into fresh clothes and sat down for my prayers. The master had taught me the Gayatri hymn and he had insisted that I should recite it at least five times a day. This would be my fifth one. I really should have recited it at sunset as per the instructions of the great sage Vishvamitra. After my prayers, I went into the hall where Father was sitting and touched his feet.

"How was your day, Upaas?" he asked.

"It was good, father. A little tiring. I had to get some wood for the Master's house today," I replied.

"I am glad that you are serving your Master well. How is your training coming along?"

"Quite well, Father. I am now fairly good at diagnosing many conditions myself. Master often lets me treat patients on my own."

"Have you thought about what you want to do once you finish your training?"

"No, I have not had much opportunity to think about it. My friend, Bhishagvida, went east last year when he finished his training. I believe there is a large city on the banks of the Saraswati where there is a lot of work for people like me. But now I am busy helping Master build up his collection of new drugs,"

"How long do you think that will take? I am sure your mother will not be pleased at the idea of you going away."

"I don't know, Father. People tell me that when his work is finished, Master Ashwin will have the largest collection of medicines in the known world and I, as his apprentice, will be a sought after physician anywhere."

"That is not the only reason why you should move east. Lately, there have been several reports of Avestan attacks on Sindhu and it won't be long before they attack Harappa as well. They were very quiet since Lord Indra destroyed Vratra and his army hundreds of years ago. But now, they have regrouped and have set their eyes on the riches of our Bharata."

"Will they really attack us? We have always welcomed Avestans here. In fact, I have treated several Avestans under my Master."

"That is true. But, you should make sure you are within the city walls before it gets dark. Sage Shunahotra discussed several safety concerns at the meeting of the Council. The reports from Sindhu are not good. The Avestans seem to have raised a well-equipped army and are using the big and very fast Elamite horses to raid outlying farms and steal cattle. They have killed several people in and around Sindhu."

Just then Mother walked in and said, "What is all this talk of war and strife at this auspicious hour? Upaas, you must be tired. Dinner is ready. Come and eat now."

I touched the Mother's feet. For Mother, there is a time and a place for everything. Nothing inauspicious should be discussed or even thought of during "auspicious hours", that is, at sunrise and sunset. She says it is the time when Goddess Lakshmi enters the house and she won't come in if there are inauspicious thoughts or sounds in the house.

"Your mother is right, Upaas. You should have dinner now. It has been a long day," Father said.

My brothers, Vidhaayaka and Satakratu, were already in the dining room. My elder brother, Vidhaayaka, had finished his apprenticeship as an engineer and he worked with the Central Works Department. My younger brother, Satakratu, was to start training in architecture at the university in Sindhu this autumn.

The delicious smell of mother's cooking was all pervading and it made us hungry. Nivya was hovering around the corner, fretting as usual. Father sat at his plate on the floor at the head of the room and we sat on either side of him. He prayed, asking the Lord to bless us and thanking Him for the food we were about to receive. Mother and Nivya served us. They would eat after us, as per tradition. We tucked into the hot rotis and perfectly cooked vegetables and meat. The dessert of barley and the sweetest honey was, as always, delicious.

I went to bed that night content with my life and dreamed of a pair of deep black eyes and a soft lilting voice that called out to me.

The last thing I remember was lying in bed that night, with a smile on my lips and dreaming of laughing jet black eyes and a soft, lilting voice when a sudden jolt jerked me awake in the early hours and I found myself flung down violently on the floor. There was a loud ghostly rumble and the floor heaved up and down. I thought the roof would come crashing down on my head. I was dis-orientated for a minute. I rushed out to the courtyard calling out, "Ma. Are you alright?" Then I ran across to the next room. "Nivya. Are you okay?" Everyone was up and rushing out of the house.

The rumbling and heaving had stopped by the time we came out, but the streets were full of frightened people walking about in a daze. Suddenly, everything became very still. There was deafening silence. It was as if the quake had swallowed up the sound. We could almost hear each other breathe. Then it came, gentle at first and then more powerful - a low-pitched whine that seemed to envelope everything. Instinctively, I turned left - the sky was turning orange and a waist-high, thick mist with ochre edges was creeping down the street.

The whine stopped as suddenly as it had begun and everything went quiet again. The air was still. And there was something else, something missing the 'birds..!' Thousands of birds normally thronged the rooftops of Harappan houses at day break.

They popped and fluttered around raising a cacophony every morning. But the rooftops today were empty, the trees deserted. A thick dust cloud slowly rose up above the mist and streaked across the distant northern sky. Something was wrong.

"That was a very strong quake. We have not had such a strong tremor for a long time," Skanda said. Our neighbour looked at the sky, trying to take in as much of the cosmic chaos as possible. His eyes frowned in worry.

"Yes, I hope there has not been much damage," Father said. "Last time we were lucky and got away without any damage or casualties." Suddenly, a cockerel appeared and announced a belated daybreak. A baby started crying somewhere and the neighbours gathered themselves together and returned to their homes.

"We should get to work and see the extent of damage and if any help is needed," Father said, turning to us.

I had a quick bath, said my morning prayers and rushed to the hospital, hoping that not many injured people needed medical attention. Master Ashwin was already there and a few patients were waiting to be seen. Luckily, the injuries were minor and only one young lad had a broken arm. He looked rather sheepish, as he had actually fallen down when he was going back into the house after the earthquake! I took him into the treatment room and set the arm with bamboo splints and paste. A slow trickle of patients started coming in for minor cuts and bruises and before I knew it, it was noon. The master had to attend a meeting of the Council of Elders and I was left in-charge.

I was now getting used to being in charge of the hospital. I still remembered the first time Master had to go away, when Sage Shunahotra had summoned him urgently. He had called me and said, "Upaas, you have been training to be a physician now for over five years. It is time you started to take some independent decisions about patient management." I had been thrilled and terrified. I did not know if I would be able to treat patients properly without his guidance. What if I made someone worse? What if I got the diagnosis wrong and gave the wrong medicine? What if, God forbid, I killed someone? There had been a million questions and I knew

I would have to find the answers myself. I had bowed my head and said, "Yes Master. I will do my best."

That day had gone by very quickly with an interminable number of patients and numerous problems that had to be handled. Master Ashwin was very pleased with me and I began to manage the hospital on my own in his absence. I did not make any major mistakes. I was quite confident of handling things now.

By lunchtime, we had treated well over a dozen people with minor injuries and I congratulated our team members on their heroic efforts and a job well done. Then all of us took a break for a few minutes. Just as we were patting ourselves on the back, a soldier rushed in and said, "Master Upaas, come quickly. There are problems near the northern wall." The disaster that I had dreaded that morning had ha pened.

The guard had run hard and was out of breath and sweating profusely. "Calm down soldier. Take a deep breath and tell us what the problem is," I said. "A part of the northern wall has collapsed on some neighbouring houses. There are people trapped under the rubble," he said, as soon as he had caught his breath.

"We should take some supplies and get there as soon as possible," I said to Ubhaya and the two junior most trainee physicians, who looked terrified. They just stood there staring at me. I could not have two of my assistants scared out of their wits right now.

"Snap out of it, you two. Get going and gather the supplies. We will need plenty of bamboo sticks, paste, ropes, salves and potions with us. Load a cart and let's go," I said. The authoritarian tone pushed them into action and they rushed around gathering supplies and loading the cart. The soldier helped to load the heavy stuff and we set off towards the northern wall of the city.

Everyone we passed looked worried and tense and my heart filled with dread at the thought of what I would see at the disaster site. Was it only yesterday that I had looked upon this serene city from my favourite place on the hillside?

Chapter 2

THE COUNCIL OF ELDERS (THE SABHA)

The earthquake had caused no damage to the Great Hall. It had stood proud and strong for as long as anyone could remember since antiquity, in fact. Legend had it that it was built, along with the Temple, by Lord Indra to celebrate the victory over Vratra. It had seen some changes since then and the chief of Elders, Sage Shunahotra, had extended the hall to include some side rooms for priests and caretakers to live in. The walls of the Hall were made of several layers of bricks and could withstand far bigger tremors than this one.

There was much activity there at this time of the morning. The priests had just finished the morning prayers; Lord Indra on the central platform of the hall and Pashupathi and Varuna on either side had been decorated and ritual offerings had been made to them. The priests were now waiting to offer the elephants their morning meal, but the earthquake had frightened the animals and the mahouts were calming them down first. It was a miracle that they had not broken off their chains and run amok.

Sage Shunahotra was in his usual seat at the base of the central platform, Master Kapila to his right and Master Ashwin on his left. The other dignitaries of the Council of Elders sat in a rectangle around the Agni Kunda (sacrificial fire altar), which was in the middle. The fire was never allowed to go out in the kunda it was said that the world would end when the fire in the Great Hall died. There were thirteen members of the Council of Elder), which met in the Great Hall once a week; the Great Council (The Samiti) had five Elders. The former dealt with the daily running of the city and the latter made decisions on matters of major importance to life and society in the city. The Great Council was responsible for the security of not only the city but also of the surrounding villages. It controlled foreign trade and made decisions about scriptures. The five Elders of the Great Council were seated cross-legged on mats of thick hemp on either side of the hall along the wall.

Sage Shunahotra, the leader of the Great Council, was a descendant of the great Sage Bhrighu and he had all the good qualities of the Saptarshis. His son, Grtsamada, was my contemporary and extremely clever. He knew the scriptures backwards and could recite almost the entire Rig-Veda in tune. The last time I met him, he was engaged in composing some more hymns to Lord Indra and Lord Agni. Master Kapila was one of the members of the Council, as was Master Ashwin, among others. A Master from Sindhu was always a member of the Council. A Vedic rule made it mandatory for an Elder from a neighbouring city to be part of the Council, so that there would be a balanced perspective on governance. Our own Master Kodhandaki was a member of the Great Council of Girinagara.

Sage Shunahotra began the proceedings. He first welcomed everyone and then recited hymns from the Rig-Veda reminding them that it was their holy duty to keep peace and harmony among all mankind.

"The first item on the agenda today is to find out if the tremors this morning caused any major damage. I pray that there have been no serious injuries or death among our families. Master Kapila, has any major damage been reported?"

Master Kapila had already done a quick round of the city's main districts before coming to the Council. He had sent several engineers to the major structures to assess the damage and order repairs.

He was particularly concerned about the great Pushkarni, which not only cleansed the Harappans for the Yajnas, but was also their main source of water. He had sent an engineer to go round the city walls and another to check the drainage system. He still awaited their reports.

"I have only been able to do a cursory inspection so far. There has been some damage to the eastern drainage system, a little damage to the Pushkarni and several slabs on the eastern road may have to be replaced. But, overall, the damage is not severe. There were reports of damage to the northern wall. I have sent someone to check it out. So far, no building collapse or serious injuries have been reported," he replied.

"I am really glad to hear that. Was there much damage to the Pushkarni?" Sage Shunahotra wanted to know.

'Not much. Our engineers are working on it now and we will soon know the details. Luckily, it does not appear to have affected the water supply at all."

Sage Shunahotra turned to Master Ashwin.

"We have had patients with a few minor injuries at the hospital today. So far, there are no reports of major injuries. And thankfully, no deaths either,"

"Thank you, Master Ashwin. That is a relief," Sage Shunahotra said. "It is still too soon after the quake to be sure, but I hope there is no bad news in the coming hours."

"I won't be surprised if there is. This is the third earthquake this season. It is obvious that Mother Earth is angry with us. This is a warning! We do not follow our scriptures as we should and the Gods are displeased with the way we perform our sacrifices," intervened Master Kodhandaki, who had been waiting impatiently to speak. He was the commander of the famed Gandhari regiment and also in charge of the upkeep and security of the Temple and the organisation of the Yajnas. The Gandhari regiment had the honour of guarding Mount Mujavant and Lake Sharnyavart, where the Soma plants grew. The regiment also protected the installation on the mountain where Somaras (Soma juice) was extracted from the Soma leaves. The Gandharis were a race apart and were renowned for their great magical powers. A detachment of the Gandhari regiment always protected the Temple. Master Kodhandaki was a dour man who rarely smiled. His interpretation of the scriptures was radical and most of the Elders did not agree with it. Nevertheless, he was very good at his job. The Temple had grown in splendour and attendance at the Yajnas and festivals had increased enormously due to his tireless work. But, his extreme ideas, which included sacrifices at the altar during a Yajna, did not make him popular. He interpreted the scriptures in his own way; some said he transliterated them, instead of going by their spirit. He was stubborn; he never let go of an opportunity to advocate his own point of view, as he was doing now.

"Thank you for your observation, Master Kodhandaki. May I remind you of those parts of our scriptures that forbid the route you want to take for our Yajnas? You have always followed the Yajnas as prescribed by the scriptures and we have followed your instructions. Please don't ask us to deviate from our path," Sage Shunahotra replied.

Master Kodhandaki clenched and unclenched his fists as he said angrily, "I believe the interpretation of the scriptures by the Elders has been wrong and we are reaping the fruits of that now."

There was a shocked silence. No one had ever dared to criticise the Elders like this before. It was sacrilege. If such a thing had been uttered in Sindhu, it would have meant imprisonment at the very least or at worst, banishment.

"Master Kodhandaki, I sincerely hope you do not mean that. It is because of our Elders that Bharata has stood strong and proud for thousands of years. It is because of our Elders that our Sanathana Dharma has prospered for so long. We know the Gandharis differ from the rest of us in the interpretation of our scriptures. I, and the rest of the Elders here, have the utmost respect for your capability and your views. However, we understand and abide by the laws laid down by the great Swayambhuva Manu, whatever your views may be. What you have said shall remain confined within these walls."

Sage Shunahotra was very proud of the Elders and of our faith, which he called 'Sanathana Dharma' – the eternal faith. The scriptures had been written by Elders over thousands of years and he believed they were continually evolving. It was said that he could communicate with the Elders of the past through divine thought and with the present Elders, even when they were hundreds of miles away, instantly through divine vision.

Master Kodhandaki started to say something more, but a knock on the door made him pause.

"Enter," said Sage Shunahotra and the doorkeeper walked in warily, hoping that he would not be upbraided for daring to disturb the Elders.

"A thousand apologies to Sage Shunahotra and the Council of Elders," he said with bowed head. "A delegation of travellers is here. They request an urgent audience."

There was an audible sigh of relief from everyone around the room. This welcome distraction would diffuse a situation that was threatening to become rather ugly.

"Please send them in," Sage Shunahotra said.

The doorkeeper withdrew and returned a couple of minutes later with four travellers and Uttarapada, the interpreter. Protocol required that an interpreter be present every time any foreigners were in the Great Hall before the Council, despite the fact that all the Elders could speak several different languages.

The visitors were a motley group. One of them was a Sumerian, his nationality easily identified by the flat cloth cap he wore. He was tall, dark, rather thin and clean-shaven with thick, bushy eyebrows and a long nose. He wore a white robe with full sleeves and wooden sandals with rope thongs, which went clickety clack when he walked. The gown was tied around the waist with a hemp rope with a large gold medallion hanging from its end.

Another was obviously a Dasyu, stocky and well built like a wrestler, with a thick black moustache and a short, pointed beard. He was taller and lighter skinned than most Dasyus seen in Harappa. He wore a wrap-around cloth at his waist and a turban on his head. His chest was covered with a typical Dasyu shawl that he carried over the left shoulder, down under the right armpit and around the body. He had rosary beads and a gold chain with a pendant round his neck. The picture of a female Goddess, very much like our mother Goddess, was etched on the pendant. Not many Dasyus came to Harappa, because there was a long-standing conflict with rogue Dasyu tribes, who regularly raided the far-flung towns of Bharata in the south for as long as one could remember. The Dasyus were reputed to be rough, violent and uncultured, though many who had interacted with them said that the reputation was unwarranted, founded as it was on hearsay and rumours. Those in Harappa were always polite and gentle and their music was lilting and very soothing. It was hard to imagine that any civilisation that produced such music could be violent. Most of the gold in Harappa came from the land of the Dasyus in the deep south, beyond the Vindhya hills.

The third man was different. He was very tall, well built, fair complexioned, with high cheekbones, a long flowing beard and emerald blue eyes. His hair was jet black and curled down his cheeks to his shoulders. He wore a thick short dress with a leather top and a truncated, cone shaped cloth cap with a rope tied around the base. A deep purple cape covered his shoulders and chest and there was a leather belt across his waist. A short ivory handled dagger was tucked in its sheath under the leather belt. He wore sandals made completely of leather. His eyes were bright and piercing, and he held his head high. He had folded his hands under the cape. He did not say much himself, but appeared to be taking in everything that was being said. There was something about him – something mysterious and at the same time loud and bold.

The fourth man was olive skinned, short and rather scruffy. He had an unkempt beard and a graying moustache, which bobbed up and down when he spoke. Thick bushy eyebrows almost covered his eyes.

All this facial hair blurred his features. A distinct stoop made him look even shorter than he was. He was completely wrapped in what appeared to be one sheet of cloth. He carried a long, gnarled oak staff in his left hand and a cloth shoulder bag over his right shoulder. The bag too was worn, tattered and hung down to his knees with the weight of whatever was in it.

Behind him was the interpreter, Uttarapada. Uttarapada bowed his head to Sage Shunahotra and offered obeisance to everyone in the room.

"I am glad you could come, Uttarapada. Not all of us here can understand the languages spoken by our respected visitors," said Sage Shunahotra, modestly. He could speak at least six different languages fluently, including Avestan and Sumerian. Most of the Elders could speak at least four languages.

"Please welcome our respected visitors to our humble city. It will be an honour to assist them in any way that we can."

Uttarapada repeated the Sage's words in four languages to the visitors. All of them nodded their heads and bowed their heads respectfully to everyone in the room. Uttarapada introduced each one of them.

The Sumerian was Shamash, son of Etana from the city of Uruk and he was a merchant trading in steatite and Lapis Lazuli. The Dasyu gentleman was Bhattora, son of Kadambapan from the city of Naridavile deep in the south and he traded in gold and other precious metals. The third gentleman was introduced simply as Shushun from Susa in Elam, trading in oil. The fourth man who had attracted everyone's attention by his uncouth appearance was Hethro, a priest from Median.

Sage Shunahotra smiled and said, "Namaste to all of you. May Lord Indra bestow health, wealth and happiness on you and your families. Welcome to Bharata. What can this humble city do for you?"

The Sumerian took the lead and said through Uttarapada, "I bring greetings from the glorious king Gilgamesh and the people of the magnificent land of Sumer and the city of Uruk to the people of Meluhha." Sumerians called this country Meluhha. He bowed deeply.

"Our humble greetings to your Great King Gilgamesh and to the people of Sumer. We have heard of the great exploits of your king and your people," Sage Shunahotra replied. The legendary stories of King Gilgamesh were well known to the Elders. He had built up his empire almost single handedly, bringing together a large number of tribes who were fighting with each other for generations. He had built the great city of Uruk and reinforced it with strong battlements. Uruk's city wall was considered impregnable.

"We are very concerned about the attacks by Avestan soldiers. There have been several attacks in Sindhu and some of our fellow travellers have been injured or killed. They do not appear to be regular soldiers, as two of the injured merchants were Avestans. They do not follow any rules of war and attack civilians for material gain. We would like sanctuary within the city walls during our stay." He looked worried.

"I am very sorry to hear this. I have been told of the Avestan attacks in Sindhu. You are right, they are not regular Avestan soldiers, but probably rogue bandits dressed up as soldiers. I cannot imagine that the Avestan army would dare attack this far south of their country. The council is already trying to arrange for accommodation for all travellers within the city walls. I have asked Master Abhiyantaa to provide a space inside where you can park your carts. The Council of Elders is also planning to send a delegation to Ariana's capital city, Mundigak, to discuss the issue with the Avestan King. Master Abhiyantaa, how soon can we provide accommodation for the traveller within the city?"

"My engineers are busy clearing the land to the northeast of the city where they will be safe. It will take at least a week before the land is ready for the caravans and bullock carts," Master Abhiyantaa replied.

Uttarapada translated it for each of the travellers. Bhattora, the Dasyu merchant was not satisfied.

"Oh Great Sage, I bring greetings from the people of the Kingdom of Dravida and our Pandyan King, Kadambapan," he said, bowing his head almost all the way down to the floor, the red tail of his turban trailing on the ground. He had a soft, almost musical voice, belying his size and demeanour.

"Our humble greetings to you, sir, and to your great King Kadambapan and his subjects," Sage Shunahotra replied. "We welcome you and assure you that we will do all we can to protect everyone who comes into our city."

"Forgive me, O Great Sage. We have brought our families with us hundreds of yojanas (distance travelled by a cart in one day) from home and it takes several months to reach here. Our concern is not just for our goods, but for the lives of our families, our wives and children." The Dasyus carried gold to trade and they were usually the first ones to be targeted by robbers.

"Pardon the intrusion, oh great Sage Shunahotra," said Master Adhvadipa and turned to the travellers and said, "I have made arrangements for our soldiers to patrol your camp through the night and they will provide any assistance you may require. They will protect you." Turning back to Sage Shunahotra, he said, "I have deployed a platoon of soldiers armed with bows and spears to protect them day and night." He was the commander of the Harappan forces. He had an army of more than one thousand soldiers, one hundred horses, fifty elephants and fifty chariots. He was a very strict task master, but he looked after his soldiers very well and they, in turn, would readily lay down their lives for him.

"Thank you, Master Adhvadipa. We are extremely grateful for your help. As usual you have done your duty before you were asked," Sage Shunahotra said.

The travellers were satisfied.

The gentleman from Elam, who had been quiet all along, said, "I bring offerings and greetings from our glorious King Awan and the people of Haltamti to the land of Meluhha." Uttarapada explained that Elam was called Haltamti in their language. The Sumerian looked rather uncomfortable. The age-old enmity between Elamites and Sumerians was well known. Elamites had only recently regained their independence from the Sumerians who had ruled Elam for the a hundred years from the city of Uruk and had repeatedly suppressed any revolt with brute force and superior power. King Awan had raised a formidable army and fought for freedom. The fast Elamite horses were famous, as were their soldiers for their skills in archery and horse riding.

"Our humble greetings to your great King Awan and your people from Haltamti. We have the greatest respect for your king who fought so valiantly for his people," Sage Shunahotra said. There was a moment's silence and everyone looked at the Sumerian. He had his head down, but his fist was clenched and the knuckles were turning white. Sage Shunahotra looked directly at the Sumerian and appeared to acknowledge his discomfort. The Sumerian felt the Great Sage's eyes on him and lifted his head to look at the Sage.

"Everyone is equal here on the sacred soil of Bharata. No dissent will be tolerated. We have great respect for all civilisations and expect all travellers to respect our laws," he said. His voice was quiet, but carried authority and left no one in any doubt. The Sumerian lowered his eyes, visibly relaxed and unclenched his fist.

"I have been to several countries and have visited many cities. However, this is the friendliest city in the world. I have never been welcomed like this anywhere else. My compliments to the Council of Elders. You have been extremely generous and kind. I wish there was something that we could do for you in return for your generosity," the Elamite, Shushun, said with genuine appreciation.

"That is very kind of you, sir. Our scriptures say, 'A guest is like God' and we try our best to treat our guests as gods. Since you ask, there is something you could do for us during your stay here. You could teach us the ways of your culture and you could teach us how to make oil." Sage Shunahotra said.

Uttarapada quickly translated this.

The Elamite smiled. “I will be glad to teach you the ways of our culture. However, I cannot teach you how to make oil. It is my livelihood. If I teach you how to make oil, you will not need me here.”

Sage Shunahotra laughed and said, “I understand you perfectly. We do not want to jeopardise your livelihood. However, you come to us once a year because of the great distance you have to travel and we often run out of oil long before your return. Besides, we will not be able to make olive oil, since olives do not grow here. But, we could make some oil using our indigenous seeds. That way, it will not affect your livelihood.”

Sage Shunahotra was very keen to get one of the most profitable industries into Harappa. So far, Harappans had only been able to make sesame oil.

“I will teach your people the extraction technique, provided you give me your word that you will not buy olive oil from anyone else,” conceded the Elamite.

“I will have to discuss the proposition with others in the Council before I can give you a reply. But, I am extremely grateful for your offer. Please accept our hospitality and let us know if you need anything else.”

Sage Shunahotra then turned to the Median priest who appeared to be half-asleep. “I hope you are satisfied with the arrangements as well, honourable Priest Hethro.”

He opened his eyes, smiled at Sage Shunahotra and bent his head with his right hand raised palm forwards in the typical Median blessing. He was not young. In fact, he looked ancient. It was hard to imagine that he had travelled this far from Median.

“May the God Baal bless you and the people of the great city of Harappa and the land of Sapta Sindhu,” he said in a surprisingly cultured voice that was completely at odds with his scruffy appearance. Medians and Avestans called Harappa, Sapta Sindhu. “I am only a humble priest. My requirements are small. If the Lord wants to take me today or tomorrow, it matters very little to me. My concern is not only for my fellow travellers, but for all creatures. I have seen the atrocities committed by these attackers. I am here in support of my fellow travellers and beg your assistance in protecting them. From what I have seen here today, I am completely reassured."

It was well said and the Elders were gratified. The stories about Medians being barbaric and uncultured were evidently untrue.

"Thank you for your kind words, O Priest Hethro. You have nothing to fear. I personally would welcome a discourse from you and would like to hear the great scriptures of Median." Sage Shunahotra replied.

"I have learnt some of your scriptures, sire. They are not so different from ours. I know that the great Sage knows our scriptures fully. I have come here to increase my knowledge of your scriptures. I hope by the time I leave this great city, I will have learnt at least a fraction of your great culture'."

"You are too modest, sir. I have heard of the Priest Hethro of Median and his cosmic wisdom. I can tell that you possess great knowledge. I beg you to impart some of your knowledge to us with a discourse," Sage Shunahotra said.

The Priest agreed to give a discourse on the Sun God at the Great Hall the following week. With that, the travellers withdrew from the Great Hall.

As soon as the door was shut behind them, Sage Shunahotra turned to Master Audyogica, who was in charge of industries in Harappa and said, "Master Audyogica, please learn all you can from the Elamite. I want our engineers to build the necessary equipment as soon as possible to extract oil from ground nuts."

"I will certainly do that, Sage Shunahotra. I must compliment you on your diplomacy. The Elamites are not known for their generosity. You managed to strike a bargain with him that is sure to add to our prosperity."

"There is something about this Elamite; I am still unable to put a finger on it. I don't believe he is a simple oil merchant," Sage Shunahotra said, thoughtfully.

There was a murmur of assent from everyone. No one was worried, however, because the Great Sage could use his divine thought to find out all he wanted about the Elamite.

Sage Shunahotra turned to Master Skanda of the Education department and said, "Master Skanda, I would like you to delegate your best student to learn as much about their culture as possible. It is likely that the merchant will be with us for two to three months and we will have to make good use of this opportunity."

"I will send Priyavada, who is the best student we have, to learn from the merchant. I will have to get Uttarapada to help with the language," Master Skanda replied.

"How are we doing with our food production, Master Vaishyakarman?" Sage Shunahotra asked. Master Vaishyakarman was sitting on the left, almost near the door. He was in charge of agriculture. He had introduced several new techniques of crop cultivation and storage, since taking over a few years ago. Thanks to his efforts, Harappa was not only self sufficient in food, but could also distribute food to neighbouring cities and towns and still hold a surplus for trade with foreigners. His innovations had greatly increased the prosperity of the city.

"We are doing very well. The crop this year was bountiful and our storehouses are full. Our farmers have discovered a simple solution to keep grains fresh longer allow some air into the granaries through vents at the top and the grains will last longer. A lot of our grains rotted last year, but that will not happen now," Master Vaishyakarman replied.

"Thank you, Master Vaishyakarman. I am sure the city will be extremely grateful for that. Was there any damage to the granaries during the earthquake?"

"No. These granaries have been built to last. They have been around for hundreds of years and I am sure they will be there for another hundred years."

"We have to beef up the security at the western and southern gates. I need more soldiers and more protection for the soldiers at the gate," Master Nahusha said. He was sitting quietly in the right hand corner of the great hall watching and listening to everything. Nothing escaped his eyes. The safety and security of Harappa depended on him and his select band of security guards. "We need to increase our copper plate production so that we can provide breast plates to every soldier."

"How are the copper foundries doing?" Sage Shunahotra asked Master Audyogica.

"We have increased the production at our foundries. Unfortunately, we have to dig deeper for the copper in our mines. Our engineers are looking at a couple of other sites where there appear to be rich seams not too deep down. But, our process of extraction wastes a lot of the ore. I believe the Sumerians use a technique that causes very little wastage. I wonder if we can learn that process from our Sumerian friend?" Master Audyogica said.

There was laughter all around. They were sure that the Sumerian would not give up any of his secrets. There had been several wars between the Sumerians and the Elamites because of this. Sumeria had knowledge of superior metallurgy, mining and agricultural techniques, but it was impossible to get any help from them. They had strong links with the Egyptians and they had learnt the science of metallurgy from them. They had used their knowledge to build an impressive army and ruled over Elam for a hundred years until King Awan, a minor Elamite chieftain at the time, defeated them. It was rumoured that the Sumerians had left some of their equipment behind and that the Elamites might have knowledge of the latest metal extraction techniques. It was also rumoured that the great Egyptian, Pharaoh Khufu, himself helped the Elamites in their fight for freedom to punish the Sumerians for stealing the technology from Egypt.

"Let us deal with the problems arising from this earthquake first. The travellers will be here for a few months. We will see what we can learn from them..."

There was frantic knocking on the door and everyone turned around in surprise.

"Enter," called out Sage Shunahotra.

The doorkeeper entered with me running in from behind him. He tried to stop me, but failed.

"Upaas?" said Sage Shunahotra and Master Kapila at the same time.

I could not wait for the usual pleasantries of the Council protocol. There were lives at stake. But I did not miss the looks of disapproval and disappointment from father, Master Kapila, as well as Master Ashwin.

But Sage Shunahotra said, "What has happened, Upaas?"

"My most humble obeisance to the great Sage Shunahotra and the Council of Elders. My deepest apologies for bursting into the Great Council and interrupting the meeting of the Elders, but I need help. There is a disaster and if we do not hurry, many lives will be lost. I need my Master Ashwin's help urgently," I blurted out.

"Exceptional circumstances call for exceptional actions. We will discuss the Council's protocol later. Pray, tell us what has happened. We were under the impression that the earthquake had not caused any serious damage?" said Sage Shunahotra.

"Thank you, oh great Sage. The city wall in the northern quarter has collapsed on to some houses and there are people trapped inside. We have pulled out five persons and they are seriously hurt. We need many people to help us clear the rubble and pull others out from underneath. I heard cries and calls for help from deep inside," I said.

"Have you asked any of my engineers to help?" Master Kapila asked.

"Yes, father. Vidhaayaka is already there supervising clearing operations. He has also started to bolster some of the neighbouring buildings to stop them from collapsing. Satakratu is helping, too," I replied.

"Do you have enough medical help? Do we need to get any help from other cities?" Master Ashwin asked.

"My humble apologies to you, Master. I had to do this without your prior approval. I have Ubhaya and two of the apprentices with me and we are struggling to keep up with the load of work. But, I am sure we can manage with your help." It would take at least a few days before any physician from the nearest city, which was Sindhu, could get there, provided the earthquake had not damaged the road. The path to Sindhu went through the mountains and landslides were quite common. If the earthquake had caused even one big landslide, they would have to go round the mountains and would take at least three days to get here.

"My engineers were busy with the aqueduct, which was slightly damaged. I will get them to come along and give a hand," Master Abhiyantaa said. "I am sure they will find a way of reinforcing the structures until they are rebuilt."

"Thank you, Master Abhiyantaa," Sage Shunahotra replied. "Can some of your soldiers help out, Master Adhvadipa?"

"I will arrange for a platoon of our soldiers to reach there immediately."

"Clearly there are matters which need our urgent attention outside the Great Hall," Sage Shunahotra said. "We adjourn our meeting for today. Please stand up for prayers now." With that he stood up and turned towards the deities on the platforms.

"Oh Lord Indra, give us the strength to face these difficulties. Give us the strength to overcome our shortcomings." Sage Shunahotra raised his hands and recited the closing prayers in Sanskrit to Lords Indra, Varuna and Pashupathi and then to Agni, the God of fire. He was an impressive sight, as he stood tall against the blazing sacrificial fire, his long grey hair braided and rolled up on top of his head, his white beard bobbing slowly with his intonations. His broad, raised forehead sported a large white ash mark in the middle and he had piercing brown eyes that missed nothing and seemed to look through people rather than at them.

He carried an aura of authority that made others feel safe with him even while they held him in great awe. No one really knew how old he was. The only thing known was that he had spent several years meditating with Sage Vishwamitra deep in the forests of the Shivalik hills and that he had visited Mount Kailash and been blessed by Lord Pashupati himself. He had untold powers at his command and they had been displayed during the war with the rogue Dasyu tribes from the south several years ago.

Some Dasyus had developed demonic powers and were causing havoc in the forest and on the outlying farms. The way Sage Shunahotra fought and defeated the Dasyus has become part of Harappan folklore. Since then, the Dasyus had given up their demon worship and lived in peace and harmony with everyone.

The two decades that Sage Shunahotra had been the Chief of the Council in Harappa had been years of peace and prosperity for the city. Harappa had become a very rich city indeed.

He finished the prayers and walked past the Elders to the door and they followed him into the bright sunshine outside. As if by magic, priests of the temple appeared at the side door and started to fuss over the deities on the platform. They had a long ritual ahead of them to "put the Gods to sleep".

"I will be at the Temple for the rest of the day. If you need any help from other cities, let me know," he said and turned and walked briskly away.

"Father, I have brought two spare horses for you and Master Ashwin. I thought it would be quicker to get to the northern wall that way," Upaas said, turning to his father.

“That is good thinking, son,” Master Kapila replied. They saw Master Adhvadipa and Master Abhiyantaa rushing off in different directions to get their people moving.

As they rode towards the northern wall to the site of the accident, I appraised them of the situation there. All of us were very anxious and I could see both father and Master Ashwin were in deep concentration. It is never a good idea to disturb either one of them during one of their “trances”

❖

Chapter 3

A TIRED PHYSICIAN

We rushed as fast as the bullock cart could go towards the collapsed wall. The two apprentices rode on the cart and Ubhaya and I were on our horses, following the soldier who had come to call us. As we turned the corner to the northern approach road, we saw a cloud of dust rising into the sky. The road itself was covered in a diffuse brown and grey haze. I could not see very far and soon there was so much dust in the air that breathing became difficult. One of the junior apprentices began to cough and our eyes started to water. At the corner fountain, we stopped to wet our head towels in the water and after wringing them wrapped them round out faces. But, there was nothing we could do to stop our eyes watering.

The site of the collapse was a hive of activity. Many people were trying to help clear the debris. Some were sitting by the wayside and crying. Just as we got there, a man was rescued from under the rubble and we quickly started to work on him. He had broken his leg and was bleeding profusely from a wound. I could see Maya, the junior most apprentice, go white and quickly sit down. She had been in training for less than two years and had seen hardly any serious injuries. I hoped she would not faint. An extra patient was the last thing I needed now.

I asked Ubhaya to unload the salves and splints and quickly used the cloth sheets and a wooden stick to apply a tourniquet around the patient's leg to stop the bleeding. I twisted the cloth sheet with the stick until the pressure increased on the thigh and eventually stopped the bleeding. I knew I had to quickly find the bleeding vessel and stop it spurting with a silk tie. Otherwise, the tourniquet itself would stop the circulation and he would lose his leg.

"I need plenty of water quickly. Can you get a few pails of water please?" I asked the soldier standing by us. He rushed off to the nearest well and came back with two full pails in his hand.

Dhatri, a nurse who had accompanied us, held the leg as I washed the debris off the wounds and found the bleeding vessel. I took a silk thread out of my pouch and tied it around the vessel. I released the tourniquet by untwisting the stick, watching the suture all the time. Luckily, it held and the bleeding stopped. I dressed the wound with a salve and Ubhaya cut some bandages for me to tie around the leg.

"Can you cut some bamboo for splints please, Ubhaya?" I asked, feeling a little annoyed that he had not had the splints ready already.

I had noticed this problem with Ubhaya before: he paid no attention to what was going on around him. His mind was always somewhere else. It was extremely difficult to work with him. Even Master had to ask him to be more attentive and proactive. I was beginning to wonder if had the aptitude to be a physician.

"Can you hold this leg for me while I apply the splint?" I asked again. Dhatri was struggling to hold the leg still. Ubhaya knelt down to hold the man's leg, but by now he had lost consciousness due to the pain. Maya gave me more bandages to tie the splint.

I was concentrating on the job when, a voice said in heavily accented Sanskrit, "It will heal better if you use a mixture of honey and seaweed on the wound before you apply the splint."

I looked up and to my great surprise, an Elamite gentleman was looking down at the man's leg. He was tall and gaunt with bushy eyebrows and a dark, thick moustache. He had the typical truncated conical cap with a rope around its base on his head and all leather sandals on his feet.

"We felt the tremors. Luckily, there was no damage in our camp. But, we saw the dust cloud rising above the city as we came out of the Great Hall and so we came here thinking that we might be able to help," he continued.

"Thank you for your advice. I have heard of that treatment from my Master. It is an Egyptian remedy, Master tells me. Unfortunately, I have neither honey nor seaweed here." I finished tying the splint and stood up. "Namaste. I am Upaas, a physician from the hospital. It is very kind of you to offer your help," I said.

Elamites had learnt advanced medical treatments from their neighbours, the Egyptians, who were known for their elixirs, salves and potions. They guarded their secrets closely and did not share their knowledge with anyone else. However, they were trying to make friends with the Elamites so that they would have a buffer zone between themselves and the Edomites and also to punish the Sumerians for their "treachery". Egypt wanted as many allies as possible, what with Nubians revolting in the south, Hittites in the north and the Edomites to the east. The rumour was that the Pharaoh Khufu had sent his personal physicians to teach medicine to the Elamites in exchange for their fast and strong horses and army support during any conflict.

"I am only too glad to help. I am Shushun, an oil merchant from Haltamti. Your city has welcomed me with open arms and this is the least I can do in return. I have some seaweed in my caravan. I will send my boy to fetch it."

He turned to a young boy who was standing deferentially a few feet behind and said something rapidly in Elamite. He spoke too quickly for me to understand what was being said. I was not very fluent in the Elamite language, but I realised that he did not speak like a commoner. He had a regal bearing about him. The purple cape meant he must be some kind of a soldier. He helped me make the patient as comfortable as possible and with the help of a soldier moved him to a safe place while we dealt with others.

Two more adults and a child about five years old had been pulled out of the rubble. She was crying with shock and fear and I had difficulty keeping her still while I examined her. Luckily, she only had minor bruises on her legs. I applied some liniment and sent a soldier to find her relatives, if they could.

I had turned around to speak to Shushun, the Elamite, when disaster struck and the wall, which was leaning against a house, gave way with a loud thud. The dust nearly blacked out the sun and the ground trembled as if there was another tremor. It had collapsed on the soldiers who were engaged in the rescue operations, burying many of them underneath. As the dust started to settle, I realised the enormity of situation. There were cries of pain from the rubble. We needed help and very quickly. Just the three of us, four, including the Elamite, could hardly deal with this tragedy.

"Where is Ubhaya?" I asked Maya who had stopped whatever she was doing at the sound. She looked much more composed than before. "I want him to go to the Great Hall to fetch the Master."

"I saw him go towards the well a few minutes ago. He has not come back."

I called out to the nearest soldier I could find, "Can I have three of your best horses quickly, please? We need more help here."

The soldier ran across to the other end of the street where the soldiers' horses had been tethered and came back with three reasonably rested and fresh horses.

"Here you are, Master Upaas. Please hurry there are many soldiers also trapped under the debris now," he said urgently. There was no sign of Ubhaya anywhere. I decided to go myself.

"I will go and get my Master from the Council of Elders." I said, trying to hide the panic in my heart.

"Do not worry, Master Upaas. I will manage the injured here while you get help," the Elamite said, calmly. Something in him reassured me that he was quite capable of handling the situation and I could trust him. I looked at Maya and Dhatri, who looked back at me. If I don't do something fast, panic will set in. Without a second thought, I ran to mount my horse and Shushun kneeled down and pulled up his cape to tie around his waist. I was wheeling my horse around when I saw a brief flash as the sun caught the golden ring on a finger of his left hand.

He quickly removed and pouched it before I could see it properly. Was that a royal seal on the ring? I wondered. It did look familiar. Then I forgot all about it and rode fast towards the Great Hall, leading the other two horses along. I intended to bring my father back with me as well as my Master. He would be needed to co-ordinate the rescue effort and reinforce the buildings and the wall. I hurriedly got off my horse at the Great Hall and handed the reins to a soldier at the door to tie the horses to the stakes outside.

"I have to go into the Great Hall. I have an urgent message."

"I am sorry, Master Upaas," said the doorkeeper, who knew who I was. He had come to the hospital with painful knees and I had given him a liniment and dietary advice for his arthritis. "The travellers have just been in to meet the Elders. They took up a lot of time. Uttarapada was also there to translate and the council meeting has already been delayed. I cannot disturb them again without consulting the Captain and he has just gone on his rounds."

"Look here, soldier. This is an emergency. I am sure Sage Shunahotra will understand. In fact, he will be annoyed if he is not informed immediately. Several lives are at stake. If we don't hurry, people will die."

The elderly soldier's eyes widened and he started to fiddle with his spear. He was clearly afraid to break the protocol of the Council and yet, he did not want to be responsible for the death of innocent people.

"All right, Master Upaas. Please follow me," he said finally and opened the large wooden doors of the anteroom of the Great

Hall. He walked fast and I followed him almost at a run until we stopped in front of an ornate wooden door decorated with copper finials all along the frame. Two lamps burning on either side of it made dancing shadows on the walls and reflected off the bronze plaques and copper inlays over the door. The solid brass knocker was in the shape of a lion's head. There was a palpable sense of power emanating from behind the doors. Some of the most powerful men of Bharata were sitting there. There were detailed paintings on the walls on either side depicting the Great War fought by King Divodasa against the Dasyus a long time ago and Lord Indra helping him to defeat the demons from the north. But I was too pre-occupied with the urgency of the situation to notice any of this.

The doorkeeper knocked on the door and Sage Shunahotra said, "Enter."

The soldier opened the door and I could contain myself no longer. I burst into the Great Hall past the soldier, who made a grab to stop me, up to the altar in the distance, and fell on my knees in front of the Great Sage.

It was the first time that I had ever entered the renowned Great Hall, but I hardly noticed anything.

Now, as I made my way back with my Master and Father, it occurred to me that there might be repercussions of my actions of today. I had broken many rules. I had left a stranger, nay, a foreigner, in charge at a disaster site; I had burst into the Great Hall and disturbed the Council of Elders against the set rules of etiquette. There was nothing I could do but await the consequences. Father looked at me as he rode beside me. I was sure he could read my mind at that moment.

"Who have you left in charge of your patients while you came to fetch us?" he asked.

My heart sank. Not because he had asked me a question, but because he had asked me that question. I now realised that it was going to be difficult to explain why I had left a total stranger in charge.

My mind raced to find a way of getting out of this situation, to find a plausible excuse.

Then I remembered what the Great Sage Shunahotra had said to me on the last day of my schooling at the Gurukul: "One thing that will take you far in life is honesty. Be honest with yourself and honest with everyone else. Making a mistake is human and forgiving someone else's mistake is divine."

I knew that it would be best to come clean and tell the truth.

"Father, Master Ashwin. Please accept my apologies. I have left a total stranger in charge of the scene, with Ubhaya assisting him."

"Who is it? What do you know of him?" the Master asked sharply.

"He is an Elamite called Shushun. I believe he was in the Great Hall to speak to the Council of Elders earlier. He looked and behaved with such knowledge of medicine that I felt I could leave him in charge for a short while. I had to make a quick decision in that situation and he appeared reliable. We were clearly overwhelmed and I could hardly ask Ubhaya to go and fetch help." The words came out in a rush.

Master Ashwin and Father exchanged glances and both of them looked a bit worried.

"Yes. He was in the Great Hall a little while ago. Tell me Upaas, what made you have so much faith in him?" Master asked me.

"Well, he appeared to know a lot about medicine and he was offering advice on treating patients when the other part of the wall collapsed. He advised me to use the Egyptian remedy of honey and seaweed that you have wanted to try, Master. He appeared to know much about the treatment of injuries," I said, with some hesitation.

"I hope you have taken the right decision. It takes courage and conviction to make quick decisions during emergencies. I have full faith in you, Upaas. I am sure you have made the right decision." Master was being kind. "Now. Tell me the extent of damage and your estimate of casualties at the northern wall."

"We had helped a few people out of the debris of two houses when the northern wall came down on top of the entire row of houses. There were soldiers and engineers trying to get people out of the debris when it happened. I am sure there are still several people trapped under all that rubble. At a rough estimate, including the six rescuers, there must be around twenty-five people trapped underneath. I am only guessing, Master. I have asked the soldiers to try to find out how many people are still missing. Hopefully, by the time we get there, the soldiers will have a number for us."

"If there are as many as twenty five people needing urgent treatment, we may need assistance from outside Harappa. We need to do a quick assessment and let Sage Shunahotra know as soon as possible," Master said. The rest of the journey was made in silence.

The scene at the north wall was chaotic. There were mounds of debris all over the place and soldiers covered in dust were working hard digging through it and extricating people from under it as fast as they could. Shushun, the Elamite, appeared to have things well under control. He had all the injured arranged in two rows under a shelter. He had managed to commandeer a few of the soldiers to help with cleansing and getting the patients ready for treatment. I could not see Ubhaya anywhere.

Shushun, who was busy with a patient with multiple injuries, stood up and greeted my Master and Father when we got there. His purple cape and white robes were covered in blood and dust. His hands, however, were still spotlessly clean.

"Greetings, Masters. Now that you are here, we should have this mess cleared up in no time."

"Thank you for your help, Master Shushun. It is indeed very kind of you," my Master replied. "What is your assessment of the situation now?"

"The soldiers and engineers have extracted most of the people from underneath the debris. There have been only two fatalities so far.

There are 18 people with injuries who need treatment. My view is that four of them will need hospitalisation,"

I was impressed with his succinct assessment. Ubhaya was nowhere to be seen and I wondered where he was.

"I sent him off to have some rest. He had been working for a long time and looked tired." Shushun said, when I asked. Master was not impressed with that.

"This is no time to rest. He will have plenty of time to rest once all the patients are treated."

He sent a soldier to find Ubhaya and bring him back. Ubhaya returned looking sullen and unhappy.

"I have been working hard for several hours and I only sat down for a minute."

Shushun looked surprised. "But Master Ubhaya, you went away nearly an hour ago!"

"It does not matter. Our priority now is to get all the walking wounded treated and to move the seriously wounded ones to the hospital as soon as possible," Master Ashwin said and turned to the Captain who had just joined us from the rescue operations. "What is your assessment of the situation, Captain?"

"I think we have the situation nearly under control, Master Ashwin. There are four people still missing, including two soldiers. I have men digging out the debris from the damaged houses," he replied.

"How long has it been since the wall collapsed, Captain?"

"I know what you are thinking, Master. It has indeed been a long time since the wall collapsed. But, we cannot give up until we have found them one way or the other."

"I agree, Captain. You find them and let's us see if we can revive them or not. I don't think we should give up until everyone has been found."

I was not as hopeful as the Master about being able to save people who had been crushed for several hours.

Master turned to the Captain again and said, "I want you to send one of your soldiers to my house with a message to my wife and to Master Kodhandaki at the Temple."

The Captain barked out orders to one of the soldiers and when he came, Master Ashwin took him aside and whispered some instructions to him. "And I want you to return as quickly as possible with the supplies from home."

He saw our questioning looks and said, "I have asked him to get some Soma. It is extremely useful in seriously injured patients. Master Kodhandaki is a Gandhari and they are known for their magical healing powers. I need his Gandhari skills in managing some of these injuries."

The soldiers extricated all four buried people, but were too late to save any of them. We were saddened at this loss of lives, but, considering the extent of destruction, we had done pretty well.

That day we saw why Ashwin was the Master of Medicine. His skill at assessing the condition of the patients and treating them appropriately was phenomenal. The seriously injured patients were stabilised and transferred to the hospital in bullock carts. The rest were treated on site and sent home. The Elamite was a surprise as well. He was quick and extremely deft with his hands. The way he guided and supervised the soldiers confirmed again that he was no commoner.

The sun was just beginning to go down by the time we finished. It had been a very tiring and yet, a very satisfying day. I felt relieved that the fatalities had been low, with the death toll limited to nine people three soldiers and six civilians mainly because of Master Ashwin's skill and Shushun's help. The disaster could have been so much worse.

The bodies had been handed over to the relatives and the final rites were to be held that evening before sunset. Sage

Shunahotra would preside over the ceremony, since it was the city's tragedy. The entire procedure was done with extreme dignity and according to Vedic scriptures. A continuous stream of people came to pay respect to the departed and the bodies were moved to the cremation grounds outside the northern gate. That evening was a reminder to all of us of how fragile is the human hold on life.

❖

Chapter 4

THE BLACK MAGUS

It was a moonless night and a sinister, hooded figure, dressed in sll black, walked rapidly through the dark, silent streets. The lamps that Pradipaka had lit at the street corners made little pools of light and shone briefly on a drawn face with a greying beard and moustache, long pointed nose, dark brown eyes, ears pinned back and bushy eyebrows growing close together. Heavy wrinkles under the eyes made him look older than he really was. The man was tall and lanky and his arms very nearly reached his knees and ended in long scrawny fingers. The full sleeves of his long black gown almost covered his fingers; but as he swung his arms they fell back revealing brass bracelets, which shimmered in the streetlight. He walked with a slight limp on the left side and in his right hand he carried a long wooden staff with an oddly carved round knob.

It was a week since the earthquake and the city was still in a sombre mood. Many houses had been damaged and needed repairs and some homes had been completely destroyed. The rebuilding and repair of these had begun. But at that hour, most people were home or already in bed. The night patrol was walking casually along the streets; there was hardly any crime in Sage Shunahotra's Harappa. It had become more of a tradition rather than of purpose as there had not been any trouble in living memory. The man, Matriya the Magus, avoided the patrol by simply slipping into a shadowy lane or melting into a dark doorway when the patrol passed by.

The Magus had waited outside the eastern gate most of the afternoon for the right opportunity to slip into the city. He had set off from Saraswata as soon as he heard about the earthquake and had travelled fast, but it was still three days before he reached Harappa. He had taken every precaution to remain unrecognised he had left his favourite horse behind and had set off well before sunrise; he had stayed off the main roads when he heard other travellers passing by and had stopped only in small villages off the regular route between Saraswata and Harappa.

He knew the roads quite well by now. He had travelled these roads several times over the past year looking for an appropriate place ever since he realised the importance of Harappa for his plans. The road ended at the southern gate of the city where there were too many guards who would ask too many questions that he could not answer. As he had neared the city, he had taken a wide detour through the forest and approached the eastern gate, which was much quieter. It was used mostly by local farmers and occasional travellers. Having done his homework well, he knew that the road to the eastern gate was uphill and the guards often left it unattended and came down to help with the bullock carts, which stru gled to climb up the slope.

He had reached early in the afternoon and waited within the line of trees, out of sight of the guards. It had been a well-chosen site he was in the dark shadows of a very large Peepal tree at the edge of a coconut grove, from where he had been able to see both the eastern approach road and the gate. He had watched farmers coax their bullocks to pull up carts heavily laden with produce from their farms, mostly sacks of barley and rice. There had also been a long line of carts loaded with juicy sugarcane its smell had made him hungry and vegetables and fresh fruits from the local farms. Many farmers were accompanied by their wives and young sons and there had been much chitchat and laughter among them. They had all seemed so happy that the Magus had felt a surge of anger and resentment. Why should their wealth and happiness not be shared with his people? When he closed his eyes, the scenes of emaciated and weak men and women digging in dry, hard land to eke out a living in his country would haunt him.

Ariana, the land of his ancestors with nine rivers, was dry, starving and thirsty. The rivers were now tiny streams and the wells that were dug had more sludge than water. It was as if the Gods had cursed his people and his beloved Sistan. They could not even propitiate the Gods as the sacred Haoma plant - as they called the Soma on Mount Hara had almost dried up without water. The story was much the same across the country and the leaders in Mundigak, the capital, seemed to Matriya to be unable to take any action. Many people had given up the fight, left the city of Sistan and emigrated south and west to Elam and even as far as Sumeria. Some had tried to cross the Pariyatra mountains (the Hindukush) in the east, into the famed land of Meluhha. Most of them died during the harsh mountainous journey. The Magus, Matriya, was one of the few who had successfully gotten through the high passes in summer nearly five years ago and had made his way down south to the port city of Saraswata, where he could disappear among the numerous foreigners in the city.

The drying up of the rivers had begun when he was still a child. He recalled his mother, emaciated from years of poor nutrition and hard labour, struggling to look after his ailing father who had been ill and unable to work since several years. Their land lay fallow as Matriya was too young and his mother too weak to cultivate it. People had begun leaving the town and there were abandoned and dilapidated houses all around them. It would not be long before the city would be reduced to dust.

His father could do nothing but look on at the struggling mother. No one could cure his illness and he could barely get out of the house let alone do any work. The local Magus had fleeced them of everything they had and stopped coming when there was nothing to give. He had also left the city travelling west. His mother often had to beg for food. She fed her husband and son before she ate, which meant that she went without food on most days. Even now, the Magus's heart contracted with pain at the memory. Very few people ever asked after his father or his mother, in case he asked them for help that they were unable to give. Then, just when Matriya was old enough to start working on the land, his father died. With more than half of Sistan deserted, there was no one to help him cremate the body.

The local priest had long gone west in search of greener pastures. So he performed the last rites himself. His mother helped him put the body on the cart and followed it all the way to the burning ghat outside the city. He lit the pyre just as the sun was going down and prayed to Lord Mithra asking him to take his father to heaven. His mother watched dry eyed - her tears had dried out a long time ago. Deep anguish and a burning anger against the Elders of the city, as much as against Mother Nature, filled his whole being. That day, staring into the pyre, he vowed that he would avenge the sorrows that had made their life hell, that he would learn every mantra, do whatever was required to gain control of Mother Nature so that this would never happen again in his country.

They took the ashes in a mud pot to be dispersed in the almost dried up Ustavaiti river (Helmand River), which did not even have enough water for them to bathe after the final rites. Then, just as they set off homewards, the skies darkened; there was thunder and lightning and howling winds and it started raining heavily, as if Mother Nature had taken exception to his vow. But the rain was too little and too late for his father and for much of his country. A soaking wet Matriya had pulled the cart home,with his mother on it, cursing all the Gods that he blamed for his misery.

That day, his mother had suddenly aged many years. It seemed as if her will to live had died with her husband. Matriya had gone to work on their land and also enrolled himself into school to become a Magus. It had been hard work. He attended lessons all day and worked on the land in the evenings. There had been no time for anything else. His mother had watched him silently. There was enough food in the house and wood for cooking since he had started to work the land. He had ensured that his mother ate well, but it made no difference to her health. He had brought physicians and Magi to examine her and had fed her fresh fruit every day. Soon she became too weak to do anything in the house. He had spent more and more time at home cooking, cleaning and nursing her, even getting her potions from a Magus deep in the forest. But nothing helped and soon he was performing her last rites. It was as if his father had taken away her will to live.

His mother's death devastated Matriya. It strengthened his resolve to fight Mother Nature - "the enemy" by gaining full control over her. He soon became a fully-fledged Magus and people started coming to him for help. But the anger and resentment in his heart made him fall out with the city Elders. He believed that they were all against him. They were against his desire for revenge and for control over nature and considered him radical, even a little mad.

It was during one of the summer meetings, when the Council of Elders of Sistan was discussing new ways of getting water to the city, that he suggested that the mighty river Sindhu (Indus) should be made to change its course.

"Is it not true that some of the sages in Bharata are more powerful than the Gods? That the Gods come to them for help? That these Sages can travel vast distances at will and look into the future? Is it not true that they can control the rivers and mountains and all of nature?"

The leader of the Council had said quite gently, "What you say may be true, son. We don't know if they can control nature and move rivers and mountains. These are stories propagated by travellers and storytellers. No one has seen them perform such feats. Don't they also tell you that these sages go through years of strenuous training and hard penitence of such severity that it is impossible for normal mortals? Even if we wanted to, we don't have the Haoma plant necessary for the great Apan Yasht for Goddess Anahita. We don't even have enough Haoma for our daily rituals, let alone for such a powerful Yasht that affects nature. The only place we can find enough Haoma is on Mount Mujavant, which, for all we know, is in Meluhha. The great Pariyatra mountains are impassable and we don't even know where the mountain is. You know how many brave Avestan people have perished trying to cross those mountains."

The Magus Matriya was furious. He had stood up, eyes bright red, waving his hands around, "Are you trying to tell me that we are inferior to the Meluhhans? How are they superior to us? If they can do it, so can we. I will find a way to cross the mountains. Didn't our great Ahura Mazda say that for mortals, where there is a will there is a way? This Council lacks the courage to act. We should take this to King Vishtaspa and let him decide," he had retorted.

The Council of Elders of Sistan had come to terms with their fate and had accepted the inevitability of their situation. But, Matriya was not going to let that happen. He would show them. He stormed out of the Council Chamber and that very night he packed everything he could carry, took his favourite horse and left while the city slept.

He travelled east for days towards the great Pariyatra Mountains and spent a few days hiding in the border town of Haozdar trying to recruit some help for his venture into Bharata. Luckily, it was summer and not the harsh winter when it would be impossible to cross the mountains. He nearly died when his horse missed a foothold going down the mountain pass toward the abandoned city of Sudra (Mehrgarh). As soon as he entered Bharata, he exchanged his Elamite horse for a local one at the border town of Roruka (Nausharo), to avoid suspicion among the locals while travelling. He was in search of a Tantric Yogi said to be living in the mountains, who could teach him magic and the power to control Mother Nature. It had taken him nearly a year to reach the port city of Saraswata.

A coconut dropped to the ground nearby and startled the Magus. He was sitting among the trees in vicinity of the eastern gate since the past two hours waiting for the right opportunity. The shadows were getting longer and he could just about see the men in the fading light at the gate. The sun would set soon and the gates would close. He had to get to the house tonight, the ceremony had to be performed before midnight and time was running out. He hoped that his instructions had been followed and the hearth prepared, the Soma juice brewed according to the secret recipe he had sent, the altar drawn and made according to the scriptures and the devotees taught the hymns. Sixteen people had to chant the hymns together in unison in exact octaves. The type and quality of sound was of paramount importance. Otherwise, it would fail. He patted the thick palm leaf roll he had hidden in the fold of his gown to make sure he had not dropped it somewhere. He might have to risk walking through the gate on his own if nothing came along soon.

Just then he saw what he had been waiting for. A long caravan of bullock carts appeared in the distance hurrying towards the city. They had to hurry to get inside the city before the gate shuts for the night. A farmer was coaxing two bullocks to pull up a heavily laden bullock cart and the farmer's wife, struggling with her head-load of melons, followed it. Others were busy with their own carts and no one paid any attention to the Magus, as he went up to the farmer's wife and said,

"Let me help you. That looks really heavy."

She smiled weakly with gratitude and said, "Thank you, kind sir. I did not know how I would make it up to the gate.'

"It is my duty, sister. I am also going into the city. I will be happy to drop it off wherever you are going," he replied with a smile. "Where do you live?"

"We live on a farm just a yojana from here. We are going to the farmers' camp in lower town tonight and hope to sell our vegetables in the morning. We hope to get some good clothes and jewellery for our daughters in the market tomorrow."

"I am also going into the lower town to my friend Maricha's house," the Magus said. He asked her about her family and farm to keep the conversation going.

"You see our daughters have reached marriageable ages and we are looking for suitable grooms."

She was telling him how hard it was, to get her grown up son to help on the farm when they reached the gate. The two guards came down to help the farmer push the cart through.

"You should not load your cart so heavy farmer. Look at the state of the bullocks! Have some sympathy for them. Next time, I'll have to report you to the Captain," the older of the guards said disapprovingly to the farmer.

The Magus did not say a word and just walked alongside the cart with his head bent as if the load was weighing him down. He had bent at the knees and hunched forward to look short and hoped that the guards had not noticed his real height. He was quite tall - much taller than the Harappans. The guards were too busy reprimanding the farmer and helping him get through the narrow gate to take any notice of this old man with a heavy load on his head, who was chatting with the farmer's wife.

Once they were inside the gate, the farmer turned to him and said, "Thank you, kind sir, for helping my wife. I did tell her not to carry so much weight, but when do women listen to their husbands? She was trying to be kind to the bullocks."

"Not at all. The scriptures say, to help one's fellow man is the same as praying to God," the Magus replied.

The farmer asked him where he was from, what he was doing in Harappa and where he was going. The Magus was immediately wary until he remembered that Harappans were inquisitive people who wanted to know everything about everyone. It was a trait he could not understand.

"I am a traveller from Saraswata. I am on my way to the mountains in search of a Guru who can teach me the ways of penance so that I can try and attain moksha from this earthly bind."

The farmer and his wife were impressed. They had heard of great sages such as Shunahotra doing penance in the deep forest in the mountains, but this was the first time they had actually met someone who was in search of it. He did not tell them that he was, in fact, looking for Mount Mujavant and that he was really seeking the Soma plant.

Night had fallen when they reached the market place where the farmer could park for the night and trade his produce in the morning. Farmers were allowed to bring their carts inside at night as the trading began at sunrise. The vegetables were all sold before the sun was high enough to damage them. The Magus said goodbye and set off towards Maricha's house.

He felt the excitement growing within him as he reached Maricha's house. It was nondescript, just like any other house in the inner quarter of the lower town with no distinguishing features. Only the windows were blacked out by a hemp curtain and the house looked completely deserted. He avoided looking at the door as he went past it. A hundred cubits down the road, he bent down as if to pick up something he had dropped and looked behind him to see if anyone was following. There was not a soul in the dark street. He got up, straightened himself with an elaborate gesture, his eyes darting around to make sure no one was watching. He started walking again, went around the next corner, turned round and stared into the street. Still no one.

Finally, satisfied that he was not being followed, he set off slowly towards the house, his ears alert for the smallest sound. It was very, very important to begin the ceremony tonight. Such an opportunity was unlikely to be repeated in his lifetime. All the signs were there - the moonless night, the stars in the right places and the earthquake showing the displeasure of Mother Earth. The alignment of the stars with the moon was just right and on the full moon day in a fortnight, he would have everything ready for the next stage. It would be the culmination of all those years of effort. He could not have asked for more.

All those experts back home had laughed at him when he had said that he would learn to control the forces of nature with his chants and command the mighty river Sindhu to change course. He had been almost booed out of the assembly in shame and had left town the same night. But, he had not wasted his time. He had spent several years and trekked hundreds of yojanas searching for the right yogi. He had met charlatans who had claimed to be the yogi of his dreams only to be disappointed in the end. He had been lured into the bizarre world of Satanism and Tantrism and had barely escaped with his life from a cave crawling with venomous snakes. He was almost sacrificed to a Goddess in the foothills of Himalayas. He had spent a whole month standing on his head reciting strange hymns taught by a Hata Yogi, only to find that he could not even move a hair, let alone a river. It was years of heartbreaking search and anyone else would have given up.

A chance encounter with a monk in the snowy Himalayas led him to the yogi he had been looking for. He had climbed steep, narrow paths, and at times no paths at all, to the top of a dense forest covered hill. He had fallen into fast flowing streams and had been washed back to where he had started. By the time he reached the top, he was battered and bruised with several cuts on his legs and arms. The yogi was sitting on a flat rock at the edge of a stream under a large oak tree. He looked dirty and unkempt with a wild, flowing beard, which had so completely covered his face that it was impossible to make out any features.

He had his eyes closed and seemed impervious to the Magus's attempt to draw his attention. Matriya stood there for a while feeling rather dejected and was about to start the slow painful trek back down the mountain when suddenly the yogi said without opening his eyes,

"You don't even have the patience to wait for me to finish my prayers. How can you learn yogic powers?"

Matriya was startled, but he recovered quickly and said, "My apologies. But I have been here for a while and I thought I was mistaken."

The yogi continued as if he had not heard Matriya, "If you perfect your intonation of the chants and the stars are in alignment, you can control anything. You can move mountains."

"Can I change the direction of a river?" Matriya asked.

The Yogi opened his eyes and smiled at the Magus. "You can move oceans, change the weather and even make the earth change its direction," he laughed.

Matriya spent a whole year there. He worked very hard, looking after the Yogi's needs, meeting his demands and bearing his scolding and insults. His demands were extreme and often demeaning. He held his temper even when he was treated like a slave.

One day, the yogi said, "My feet are sore. Come and massage them."

The Magus took some sandal oil that the yogi loved and the polished granite stone to massage his feet. He was beginning to think that the yogi would never teach him the chants that could control nature. When he had finished nearly all the sandal oil from the bowl, the Yogi said, "So. You want to control Mother Nature?"

"Yes Master. That is my humblest wish."

"Why do you want to control nature? You do realise, it needs a lot of hard work, concentration, sacrifice and penitence?"

"I will work hard, Master. I will do as you bid," the Magus said as he massaged his feet even harder.

"But, why do you wish to control mother nature?" the Yogi repeated.

"It was because of the vagaries of the land and the rivers and the rain that I lost my parents. I saw my homeland destroyed for no fault of their own. I saw my father trying to eke out a living from a dried up land, unyielding and unrewarding. It was heart wrenching to watch my dear mother deteriorate and die a wizened old woman all because the rains failed and the rivers dried up in Ariana. I saw my village wither away into nothing in front of my eyes all because mother nature was angry." Matriya's hands and teeth were clenched as he spoke. His eyes welled up as he continued, "I don't want this to happen to anyone else. I have not harmed nature in any way. Why should I be punished?"

“I can understand your anger, son. But you must expunge your heart of anger. Or else, the hymns will not succeed.” The Yogi could see the hatred in the Magus’s eyes through the tears. “The sages of Bharata use it for the goodwill of the people and help the nation. You seem intent on revenge.”

“No Master, it is not revenge I want. How can I, a mere mortal, take revenge on the Gods?”

“No, you cannot take revenge on the Gods. But you are going at this in the wrong way. Your heart is full of hatred and anger against the Gods because of the loss of your parents. You come into this world by the grace of God and you leave this world at His wish. You have to follow the laws of nature. I can teach you the hymns and the technique, but it won’t work if you use it for your own good.”

“I understand, Master. I will control my emotions and cap my anger within me. Please be reassured that I will only use it for the benefit of my people in Ariana. I want to see happiness and smile on our people, just like those here in Meluhha.”

“No, Matriya. That won’t do.” The Yogi was firm this time. “You have to get rid of your anger and hatred from your heart. You cannot keep it bottled in your heart. Only then it will work.”

The Yogi was asking Matriya to discard something that was ingrained into him over the years watching his parents grind to death. He bit his tongue when he replied, “I will, Master. I promise that I will get rid of the hatred I feel.”

The Magus did sound sincere, the Yogi thought.

“Once the process has started it cannot be stopped. If you give up your training midway, you will never be able to start again. Are you sure you are ready?”

“Yes Master. I am ready. I have been ready ever since I came here and I have been preparing for this day all my life.”

“Then let it be on your head. If it is written that you can achieve this, you will complete the training or forever live with utter failure.

Do you also realise that if you use the powers inappropriately, they can act against you? And your powers can kill you in the process of changing nature?" he asked.

"Yes, Master. I will guard the power with all my heart and will use it only for the good of my fellow beings," the Magus replied.

"We will start tonight after the sun sets," the Yogi said.

The training was hard and long. The Magus nearly died in the process. On several occasions he nearly gave up. But the strength of his desire and the hatred he had for the "rest of the world" kept him going. Whenever he felt he could not go on any longer, he recalled his struggling mother and his ailing, helpless father. He remembered his humiliation and banishment from the court and it strengthened his resolve to continue. It was a long, hard, agonising slog over three years before he mastered the powerful chants and learnt all the yajnas needed to control Mother Nature. There was little time for food or sleep during that long training. He had to learn to control his mind at will. The hardest part was to learn to control his senses. After several months of penitence, during which his body was punished to the limt, he thought he was ready for his final chants.

He turned to the yogi and said, "I am ready for the final chants. If you can teach them to me, I can fulfil my desire to help my people."

"I do not think you are ready yet," the yogi said.

"I can control my mind and all my senses are under my control. What else do I need to do?" the Magus asked.

"So. You think you have the powers?" the yogi asked. "Lift that stone and place it in the stream so that I can go across without getting my feet wet."

"Child's play," thought the Magus dismissively.

He closed his eyes and concentrated on the large granite stone until he could sense it rising. Suddenly, a loud rumble startled him and his eyes snapped open. The rock fell down with a loud thud. A small avalanche of loose rocks from the side of the hill had caused the rumble. Matriya swore under his breath, "For Mithra's sake!"

"Ha! You can control your mind and you can control your senses. But not together. You must have them under control at the same time. You still have not purged your anger and extreme desire fully yet. You also need to overcome your fear before you can control nature," said the Yogi as he walked away.

Matriya looked at the slowly moving back of the Yogi with contempt and swore,

"I will do it if it is going to kill me. I will control my senses." And jumped into the ice cold lake. He spent every waking hour practicing and working. He lost so much weight during the process that he looked like a walking skeleton. He still remembered the day when he could not only lift a stone off the floor, but move it wherever he wanted to. He thought he was ready and went back to the Yogi. However, the Yogi was not convinced and would make him do a different task and fail everytime he tried.

It was another year before he rather reluctantly let an impatient Matriya go.

"You do realise that it will not only fail, but even kill you if used wrongly?" The Yogi had said finally. "If the Meluhhan sages find out what powers you have, they can easily neutralise you. You are no match to them"

'We will see about that' Matriya had said to himself. Finally, he had paid his respects to the Yogi, and took leave of him, promising to return if he was successful.

Now, the opportunity had come and he was ready to put his all into it. If he was successful today, he would do the final sacrifice two week's later in the forest and the river would have to change its course towards his town and bring prosperity to his people. How foolish the Elders would look! The Chief Priest would have to accept him as an equal then, and his name would be immortalised in folklore. They might even compose a hymn in his name!

Matriya knocked a pre-arranged tattoo on Maricha's door. At the third knock, the door opened and he was whisked inside. The room was darker than the street. Someone lit a lamp and he saw two people who immediately prostrated at his feet with folded hands and said in unison, "Namaste and Welcome to our humble abode, O great Magus, our saviour."

"Asmatra Vijayee Bhavathu." (Victory to us.) We have a lot of work to do," he said in chaste Sanskrit with a hint of an Avestan accent and turned to the elder of the two men. "Is everything ready? Have you got everything?"

The men did not raise their heads. They were afraid to look directly at his face, and particularly, at his eyes. They had been told that he was an extremely powerful magician. The elder of the two, Maricha, plucked up courage and said, "Yes, great Magus. We have everything except the Soma plant. That we could not get. The plants are stored in the Temple and the pharmacy and both are strongly protected. We have managed to find the substitute that you had asked for - a somalataa plant." He glanced quickly and fearfully at the Magus afraid that he would lose his temper and turn them into ashes or into some lowly animal. No such thing happened and they were relieved.

The Magus only sighed deeply and said, "Well, that is not as good as Soma. We must have the Soma plant for the final ceremony. Do whatever is necessary to get it, at whatever cost. And remember, I say this again, no one should know what is happening here. If even a hint reaches Sage Shunahotra, all will be lost."

"We will get the plant for next week, Great Magus. And the Sage will not find out; we will ensure that he cannot come here and that he will not hear a word of what is happening here or at our site in the forest," the younger man said.

The Magus smiled derisively. "Shunahotra is so powerful that he does not have to move from where he is to stop our ceremony. I wouldn't be surprised if he knows about it even as we speak here."

The men were shocked. Who they should fear more - Sage Shunahotra or the Magus?

"Do not worry," said the Magus, reading their apprehension. "No harm will befall you when you are under my protection. I have created a shield around this house that will prevent Shunahotra from interfering. He will have no clue what is happening here!"

"Thank you, O great Magus. We pray for your success."

"Pray for our success," he corrected them. "Come. There is much to be done. Have you gathered everyone? Where are they?"

"They are all in the courtyard, Magus. The sacrificial goat has been fed with the Somalataa extract and the altar is ready," Maricha said.

The Magus walked past them towards the inner door, which led into a large courtyard. The courtyard was an open square surrounded by eight houses of the lower town that all opened into it. A brick platform had been built in the centre and the somalataa plant had been tied to a stake in the middle of it. There was an Agni Kunda in the front half of the platform with a small fire blazing in it. Twenty pairs of apprehensive eyes, flickering in the firelight, turned towards him as he walked in. As soon as they saw who it was, they prostrated themselves before him with folded hands. There was a chorus of "Namaste, Oh great Magus, our saviour."

The Magus raised both his hands high in the air, palms facing forward, blessing them all. *"Om Shanno Mithra, shan Varunah, shanno Bhavatvaryama."* (May gods Mithra, Varuna and Aryama bless us). May the Lord Mithra bring what you ask for."

He then went straight to the platform and busied himself with the altar and the materials for a while, grunting 'well done' or snorting with disapproval as he looked at the stuff that had been put together by his followers. He opened his shoulder bag and brought out several mud pots containing potions and powders. He threw a pinch of white powder from one of them into the Kunda. There was bright flash, as if lightning had struck the courtyard, and everyone was momentarily blinded. Then he tipped a drop of green liquid from one of the pots on the fire and there was a bright orange flash and thick smoke. He directed sixteen men to stand on imaginary ends of an eight-pointed star around the altar. He looked around again and rechecked all the ingredients. He chose one of Maricha's neighbours to act as his assistant and spent some time telling him what he wanted done during the ceremony.

Then he checked the two huge kettledrums that stood in the corner of the courtyard. He was concerned that the loud beating of the drums would attract the night patrol. Maricha assured him that the sound of drums and music was common in the lower town and would not attract any attention. So the Magus turned to the drummers and spoke to them in quiet tones for a few minutes. The instructions to the two drummers was explicit it was crucial to keep the beat as per instructions.

Finally, he stood tall and addressed the gathering: "Please listen to me carefully. All of you must follow my instructions diligently. There is no room for errors. No matter what you see or hear, you must focus on my voice alone. The chants must accompany the rhythm of the drums. Even if one of you goes wrong, the whole process will collapse and all your effort will be wasted."

He looked at each one of them as he spoke. They all nodded their heads with apprehension and excitement. Some of them trembled slightly and looked frightened. He could not have anyone fainting in the midst of the chants.

"Remember that I am here and will support you till the end. Success will be ours. All you have to do is to follow me and our future will be bright."

He sat cross-legged at the altar, closed his eyes and with hands together above his head started sonorously reciting the hymns.

He finished the initiation service and turned to the gathering and said, "Repeat after me *Hram, Hreem, Ho hum.*"

They started slowly and haltingly and then with growing confidence as they sipped the somalataa juice that was being passed around in a large gourd. The drummers increased the volume and tempo imperceptibly. Plumes of smoke from the burning incense wafted over the courtyard. The mixture of the somalata juice and the fumes created by the powder that was being offered to the fire was intoxicating. The gathering started to swing to the rhythm of the drums as they chanted. Their eyes were closed and tears rolled down their cheeks whether due to the thick, acrid smoke or with emotion, it was hard to tell. Under the dark, moonless sky, sixteen grown men swayed to the rhythm of the drums as they chanted in one voice, and the intoxicating smoke swirled around them as the fire rose higher and higher. The scene was both surreal and scary.

Maricha, the chief organiser of the event, felt slightly scared and very elated. But when objects on the ground started to move around of their own accord, he became terrified. 'What have I done? Have I unleashed the power of something unholy? Do this Magus know how to control this power?'

He should have asked these questions before inviting the Magus to Harappa, he thought. But, the Magus had come highly recommended by friends from Saraswata and he was weak enough to believe that the Magus' magic would make him more powerful. He had joined hands with some Harappans of a similar bent of mind who wanted power and wanted to control the governing of Harappa. Forty of them had come forward to fund this enterprise and they were willing to take what they had been convinced was a negligible risk of being ostracised and thrown out of Harappa if the plan failed.

A loud bang startled Maricha and he opened his eyes. The Magus was standing up now and was alternately throwing some powder and some leaves onto the fire. The fire roared and the smoke was dense. Everyone appeared to be in a trance, swaying to the rhythm of the drum beats and chanting loudly. He was sure this noise would reach Shunahotra even if he had no supernatural powers of detection. But it was too late to worry about that now.

The Magus asked the assistant to be ready for the sacrifice. The assistant took the long brass sword and with one sweep brought it down on the neck of the goat. The goat had been fed a mixture of drugs in the potion made out of somalataa juice and some liquids that the Magus had brought with him. It made no sound as its head rolled to the floor. The Magus picked up the head and poured the blood into the sacrificial fire. He sprinkled some more of the leaves and the white powder. There was another blinding flash and he threw the head of the goat in the fire. A strong smell of burning flesh mixed with the scent of all the powders he had been feeding into the fire.

The chanting became more intense and the drum beat faster and faster. The drums had reached a crescendo when, the Magus took a small mud pot from his bag and emptied its contents into the sacrificial fire. There was an almighty bang; another bright orange flash and a large cloud of thick orange smoke covered the courtyard. Maricha could not hear Matriya's voice anymore. Within minutes the fire died out and the smoke dispersed. The chanting and the drums slowed and then stopped. Everyone opened their eyes and looked towards the altar. The Magus was not there. His empty shoulder bag and pieces of the broken pot were the only evidence left of his presence. He had disappeared into thin air. It took a few seconds for people to realise what had happened and then there was an audible gasp.

They looked for the Magus within the courtyard and in the houses around it, but there was no sign of him anywhere. They cleared up the altar and all the debris. Maricha was not sure if the procedure had worked or not. For the next few days, he and his friends looked out for any untoward events that might indicate the success or failure of the ceremony. When days went by and all his friends and family remained safe and sound, Maricha breathed a sigh of relief. The experiment had been a success, he was now sure, and he began to look forward to the next stage. He had to somehow acquire the Soma plant -- or at least, Soma juice -- before the full moon.

Maricha knew someone at the hospital who had access to the Soma plants and the juice. He would get a plant or the juice by bribery or by threat.

Chapter 5

A TRIP TO SINDHU

About a week after the earthquake, Father came home late one evening in a very sombre mood. Before any of us could pluck up the courage to ask him what the matter was, Mother called us for dinner.

As soon as we finished dinner he said, "There has been a disturbance in the Prana a few days after the earthquake. Someone in the community has conducted Tantric yajnas. Sage Shunahotra is very worried. I, too, felt the changes that night and it is a matter of serious concern."

"But who could have done such a thing?" Vidhayaka exclaimed.

"The Council of Elders knows who has done it. But we have no proof. We need to catch them red handed. They have only performed the first stage. But that has initiated the forces of the underworld and woken up the forces of evil. We must catch them before they complete the next stage."

I had never seen father so worried.

"I am sure the great Sage Shunahotra can destroy them." Vidhayaka said.

Father was stroking his chin as he replied, "None of us could detect the yajna when it took place. Whoever had done this has built a shield around it. The only thing we know is that it happened within the city."

"Isn't there something that can be done to reverse the process?" I asked.

I had never come across Tantra before. I had heard that Dasyus and Medians used to be active Tantriks and rogue Dasyu tribes along the border had used Tantric magic against the farmers along the border until several years ago - long before I was born - Sage Shunahotra had countered it so effectively that they had given it up completely. There were rumours, however, that there were still some Medians who performed Tantric yajnas.

"They don't realise how difficult it is to control the demons of the underworld once they are released. If we can stop these people from completing the next stage, the process will die a natural death within two weeks of the initiation," Father said.

"But why would anyone want to do such a thing, Father? Harappa is such a beautiful city and hundreds of people come here to settle down every week. They all seem to be happy under Sage Shunahotra's rule," I said, feeling truly perplexed.

"It is not just about Harappa, son. This is an act against all of Bharata. We have known for a while now that there are some disaffected people, mainly foreigners, who cannot bear to see the prosperity of Harappa and want to destroy it," Father said, sadly.

"Why? We offer everyone food, shelter and a comfortable life," I persisted.

"Yes, but evil always finds a place in the human heart, son. And the world has enough people who are never satisfied with what they have and feel that they deserve more without any real effort or hard work. They are ready to support the evil in their bid to get what they want. There are some yogis in the Himalayas who have perfected the art of Tantra and have super-natural powers. Someone must have put in enormous effort and learnt from them. The disturbance felt by all the Elders was quite significant and worrying. We have had minor disturbances in the past, but never anything like this,"

"We have ten more days to stop them," Vidhayaka said.

"Yes. But, there is something else that we need to do now. I have heard from my colleagues at the university in Sindhu (Mohenjo-Daro). Satakratu has been accepted in the architecture course this year. So, one of you has to take him there. I know Vidhayaka is busy with the reconstruction of the collapsed wall. How about you, Upaas?"

"That is great news, Father. The hospital is very quiet at the moment with only one seriously injured patient from the earthquake still there. I will ask Master Ashwin if I can go," I replied.

"I have tentatively told Master Ashwin that you may have to go and he has no objection; but you must speak to him yourself and get official permission. I also want you and Satakratu to practice your archery some more before you go. I know you have been fairly regular, but some extra, intensive practise will be required. There have been attacks by rogue Avestans recently. I will speak to Master Adhvadipa and ask him to give you extra training."

"We will do that, Father. I have to go to the travellers' camp today to get some writing materials, after that I will speak to Master at the hospital. I can leave the day after tomorrow if everything is ready."

I was already looking forward to the trip. It would be nice to see my old masters from the university and visit my Alma Mater again. Sindhu was one of the largest cities of Bharata and the university was well known across the world. People from several countries came to study there. The Masters were among the best in the world. They were in touch with masters in Egypt and Sumeria and thus there was a continuous exchange of thoughts and ideas. Our Masters had visited learning centres abroad and several experts from those countries resided in Sindhu. Sindhu was full of pleasant memories for me.

However, it was thoughts of the beautiful Lopa that kept me awake that night. The earthquake had meant that I had not been able to go to the camp for the writing materials Master Ashwin wanted. The prospect of meeting her the next day was very exciting and when I finally did fall asleep, I dreamt of her jet black eyes and silky, black hair that fell like a curtain down to her waist.

I was out of the city and at the camp quite early in the morning. I walked toward the stationer's caravan, but my eyes were seeking a glimpse of her. There was little activity in the camp. Maybe I was too early, maybe I should walk really slowly and give her time to be walking around, I thought. The stationer was friendly and I quickly bought some steatite pencils and dried and treated palm leaves. I put them all in my shoulder bag and started walking along the longest possible route back through the camp. I did not know which was Lopa's caravan and so I looked searchingly at each one that I passed. I was paying no attention to the path and stepped heavily into a rut full of dead leaves. My foot slipped, I lost balance and landed in a small ditch face down. The bag flew off my shoulder and pencils and palm leaves rolled in the mud.

"If only you would look where you are going..." said that lilting voice with much amusement. "Your palm leaves are ruined. We will have to go back and ask for more. These are quite useless for writing now."

I was acutely embarrassed. I had spent hours dreaming of her and planning all the things I would say to her when I met her again. Lying flat on my face in a ditch was no part of those plans. If I were trying to impress her, this surely would have done the trick. She would never want to speak to me again.

I dusted off the dirt from my clothes and she continued, "Come on. Let us go and speak to the stationer. I am sure he will replace your palm leaves."

Was she now trying to be kind of a fool, I wondered? She had picked up all the leaves and steatite pencils and put them back in my bag.

"Thank you very much. You must think I am very clumsy."

"The carts and caravans have left these deep ruts in the mud after the rains last week. You are not the first one to fall here," she smiled.

My heart began to lift again. Maybe all was not lost. After all, she was going to walk to thc stationcr's with me!

"You are very kind to say that," I said as I walked beside her. I could smell her beautiful fragrance and our hands touched a few times during that short walk on the narrow path. The touch was electric and my heart raced and thumped so hard I was afraid that she might hear it. But she was in a talkative mood and told me all about her family and the families in the caravans we passed, what happened to her dog and why she loved coming to Harappa. This was turning out better than I had expected. I could have walked beside her forever, listening to her melodious voice. I was quite disappointed when we reached the stationer's caravan. I wished there had been a longer route back.

She talked to the stationer as well and he replaced all the damaged palm leaves with a smile on face. Who wouldn't, I thought, when such a charming creature asked!

"You are not the first one to fall, Master Upaas." He said as he handed the palm leaves to me.

We walked back to the edge of the camp towards the city and I said, "I would like to see you again if that is okay." The words rolled easily off my tongue. I felt no apprehension or reticence in asking her. Somehow, without anything significant being said, something between us had changed. But my heart raced at the speed of a galloping horse.

"I would love to see you again. We will be here for at least another month, if not longer," she said with a smile and a warm expression in her eyes.

"I am off to Sindhu tomorrow to drop my younger brother at the university. I will see you on my return."

"How long will you be away?"

"A week, at the most. I will be back as soon as I can," I said and reluctantly walked towards the city gates. At the gate, I looked back and there she was, still standing on the little rise where we had parted. My heart skipped a beat and I waved to her. She waved back and turned and ran towards her caravan. I walked to the hospital with a song in my heart and wings on my feet. I smiled at everyone I met on the road and was still smiling when I walked into Master Ashwin's house.

"You look particularly happy today, Upaas," remarked the Master. "Did you get the writing materials we need?"

"Yes, Master. I have palm leaves and steatite pencils to last for at least a year," I replied, and handed them to him. "My father wants me to take Satakratu to Sindhu to the university. May I take time off to do that?"

"Yes, of course. Your father did mention it to me yesterday. It is quiet at the Hospital at present. Besides, your absence will give Ubhaya an opportunity to shoulder some responsibilities. It is time he learnt that being a physician is not just diagnosing diseases and handing out medicines. It is a whole lot of nitty gritty, hands on work. He still has not learnt to treat a patient as a whole. By the way, there is something that you can do for me since you are going to Sindhu."

"It will be my honour, Master. I am leaving tomorrow morning with Satakratu," I said.

"Please call in on my house on your way and Maa will give you a packet to take with you. It is some work I have been doing for some time on treating infections. I would like to have an opinion of the leading physicians at the University."

"I will certainly do that, Master."

I returned home to pack for the trip the next day. Mother had been busy cooking for our journey. I had to take our horses to the blacksmith to get their hooves freshly shod. My horse, Shankara, was a tall, white steed with a long mane. He was nearly as big as an Elamite horse and very strong. I loved riding Shankara. As soon as he saw me, he reared up and neighed loudly. I stroked his neck and said, "We are going on a long journey, my friend. You will have to look after me and my brother." He nuzzled into my neck. I spent a few minutes talking to him and checking his shoes and saddle. I checked Satakratu's horse and fed him as well. He was dark brown with a white patch on the neck and not as tall as Shankara.

Then, I went to the armoury to pick up bows and quivers for each of us for practice. Father had ensured that all three of us were trained in archery and we were all fairly proficient. But for this trip, we had to be in particularly good form since there was the danger of Avestan attacks. I picked up Satakratu and went to Master Adhvadipa for practice and additional training. We spent most of the afternoon practicing on the shooting range. I was pleased that I could shoot ten arrows in quick succession and hit most of them on target, but Master Adhvadipa was not impressed.

"My soldiers can shoot thirty arrows non-stop and the best ones can shoot up to fifty. If a gang of raiders attacks you, you need to be able to fire at least fifteen to twenty arrows without pause for any chance of success," he said.

It took me hours of practice before I could shoot fifteen non-stop and managed eighteen shots only by the end of the day. Poor Satakratu. I think he was born with two left thumbs. He managed only ten arrows by the end of the day and could not really hit the target more than half the time. Master Adhvadipa was reasonably happy by the time we finished. He checked our bows and gave us several different types of arrows to fill in our quivers. There were the bulky multiple release arrows tied together in copper string and spring loaded, and arrows with magical powers; some of them exploded on impact and there was one that exploded with a bright light to blind the enemy. I particularly liked the one that spewed out a huge cloud of dense acrid smoke on impact.

It was late in the evening by the time I had everything ready. Mother and Nivya had helped pack all the paraphernalia Satakratu would need for his stay at the University and they packed food and spare clothes for me.

The next morning our horses were loaded and we were ready to leave well before sunrise so that we could be in the shade of the forest soon after sunrise. Father, Mother, Nivya and Vidhaayak all came to the door to see us off.

"I do not have to tell you to be careful, Upaashantha. But, please be vigilant on the road and keep a look out for trouble from the rogue Avestans," Father said. He handed me a packet with sage Shunahotra's seal on it. "These are documents from Sage Shunahotra and me. I want you to give them to Sage Vishwamitra Gathinah."

"I will, Father. It will be an honour for me to meet one of the greatest Sages of our time," I replied.

"Did you have a good practice session yesterday with Master Adhvadipa? Are you satisfied with your preparation?" he asked and when I replied in the affirmative he turned to my younger brother. "Satakratu, this is the first time you are going on such a long journey. Please listen to your brother and follow him. I have prayed to Lord Indra to protect both of you. Work hard at the university and serve your Master well. You must remember that your actions must uphold the name of our family. Take care, son. I wish you all the very best," Father said, his voice quivering just a tiny bit.

"Don't worry, Father. I will work very hard and I would rather die than taint the honour of the family. I will try to live up to the standard set by you and my brothers at the university," Satakratu replied.

We both touched the Father's feet and he blessed us, "*Deerghayushman Bhava*."

Mother and Nivya embraced us with tears in their eyes.

We touched the Mother's feet and she put her hands on our heads and said, "*Dheerghayushman Bhava*. May God Indra protect you on your journey. I pray for your safe return."

We stopped at Master Ashwin's house to collect the documents from Maa. She gave us a small parcel as well.

“It is something for your journey, Upaas,” she said.

“Mother has given us plenty of food, Maa. But this is very kind of you,” I replied.

“I know your mother would have given you plenty of food. But, I have packed your favourite sweet. Now, please be careful both of you.”

The soldiers were getting ready to open the gate for the morning traffic when we reached there.

“Good morning Master Upaas,” one of them called out. “You are out early this morning.”

“I am on my way to Sindhu to drop Satakratu at the University,” I replied.

“Be careful. Look out for the Avestans and try to stay off the road at night. You should be able to make the village of Pushkar before nightfall if you keep up a reasonable pace,” he said.

“We will be careful. Thank you,” I replied.

We set off on the road skirting along the eastern bank of the Parushni and were in the forest as the sun was warming up. There were not many people on the road apart from farmers going to their farms nearby. We kept up a decent pace and stopped for a break just after noon, when a patrol of soldiers passed by and the Captain exchanged pleasantries with us. We reached the inn at Pushkar well before sunset.

We crossed the Parushni the following morning and headed in a more westerly direction towards the next halt. We passed several patrols and many travellers, but saw no sign of any trouble. On the third day, we reached the banks of the river Vipas (Beas) at dusk and decided to break journey there. There was a clearing in the forest near the river where some large rocks provided shelter. I chose a spot on a raised knoll with a very large rock on top as our resting place.

We tied our horses to the trees and went into the forest to find some dry wood for a fire when suddenly the chirruping of birds returning to their nests and the gurgling of the river were shattered by a loud scream and then several shouts. We dropped our twigs and branches and ran towards the sounds, which were coming from behind a low rise. I raised my hand to stop Satakratu and knelt down behind a bush to look over the rise at what was happening.

A group of soldiers was attacking a merchants' camp. There were at least six men on very large horses, armed with long swords and spears. One of the tents was on fire and several people, including some women, lay bleeding on the ground, while the men attacked the others and ransacked their goods.

"This is an attack on innocent merchants. Those are no soldiers. We must help. Come on," I said to Satakratu, as I scrambled down and ran towards our horses.

"But remember what the father and the Master told us," Satakratu said as he ran after me.

"I know we have been told to avoid confrontation. But we cannot just abandon these people. By the time we find a patrol of soldiers, they may all be dead. We have the advantage of surprise and plenty of arrows in our quivers. We will attack them from here. These thick trees will give us cover."

By the time we rushed back with the bows and arrows, the situation had not changed much. We took position and strung our arrows in seconds.

"I will take those on the left and you get the ones on the right."

I aimed carefully, knowing that the first shot had to be very good, and fired my first arrow at the nearest attacker. It hit the raider in the chest and with a scream, he fell. The attackers were startled and turned round to see what had happened. I quickly shot ten more arrows and managed to fell one more of them. Satakratu too, fired his arrows rapidly at the raiders on the right, felled one attacker and injured another. By the time they figured out what was happening and started moving towards us, I managed to shoot down another, upon which the sixth man stopped, wheeled round midway and galloped away. The injured man scrambled on to his horse and galloped away, too. There was complete silence for a few minutes as we got up and walked towards the camp. Then, some of the men, women and children slowly came out of hiding and gathered around us.

"We are extremely grateful to you, strangers. We would have all been slaughtered if you had not come to our help," said a tall, rather thin, middle-aged man in Elamite. He had injured his left shoulder.

"I am Upaashantha, a physician from Harappa and this is my brother, Satakratu. We are on our way to Sindhu and heard your screams. I can help you treat the injured," I said and asked Satakratu to fetch my medicine bag.

"You are extremely kind. We do have a supply of medicines and we have a physician with us as well."

Everyone was now gathered around us. There were about fifty of them, including several women and children. There were Dasyus, Elamites and even Sumerians. The raiders had killed three men who had resisted them and six men and two women had sword and spear wounds. The bodies were moved to a spot away from the camp awaiting a funeral.

"Can we move the injured to the shelter please?" I asked.

A bulky Sumerian was the physician with the convoy and he joined me in treating the injured. Several of the women came to assist, and the wounds were soon dressed and broken limbs put into splints.

The Elamite, who appeared to be their leader, said, "Master Upaashantha, thank you so much for your help. Please stay with us in our camp tonight."

"We are grateful for your hospitality sir, but we would not like to impose on you at such a time," I replied politely.

"It is no imposition, Master Upaashantha. Do stay with us."

"Thank you. We will accept your hospitality, sir. But I suggest you send one of your riders to the soldiers' camp. It is half a day's ride to the north. They may be able to offer an escort for the rest of your journey."

"I will immediately despatch our postal riders to the camp and request their help. We are on our way to your great city of Harappa."

We walked down to the banks of the Vipas to wash and refresh ourselves. The wide river flowed leisurely here. I checked our bows and quivers and added the unused arrows from the quivers of the dead raiders. The merchants offered us two large Elamite horses that had belonged to the raiders and we accepted one to carry our supplies and left the other for the merchants.

It was a sombre evening at the camp, with grieving and frightened people. But they cooked a feast for us with Dasyu, Elamite and Sumerian food. As I lay under the stars that night, I mulled over the day's events. I was quite pleased with the way we had managed to overcome the attackers with not a scratch on us. We had acquired a beautiful Elamite horse and won several friends. Satakratu had shown that he could keep his cool and be relied on in a crisis. I turned my head to look at the moon. It was a half moon and I remembered with a shock that it would soon be time for the next stage of the Tantric yajna. I prayed that the Council of Elders could prevent it. The fragrance of some flowers wafted in on the light breeze bringing memories of Lopa and I drifted off to sleep dreaming of her beautiful smile and the electric touch of her hands against mine.

We left early the next morning. The merchants offered us a large basket of gifts, which we politely refused. As we left, we saw their riders return with four Harappan soldiers. The merchants would have a safe journey to our city.

There was a wooden bridge over the Vipas where it was a little narrow. Once we are across the bridge, it was less than a day's journey to Sindhu. Satakratu was really excited about crossing the long bridge. It is an imposing structure, especially thrilling at first sight. There were two tall solid oak columns on the banks on either side of the river. The oak columns were anchored to the ground as well as being tethered by thick hemp ropes. Several thick hemp ropes were strung from the columns across the river from east to west. Thick solid oak planks tied to each other and attached firmly to the trunks on each side formed the road. More large logs were sunk into the riverbed and supported the bridge. Despite that, the bridge swung from side to side in strong winds and when heavy carts rolled over it. We believed that it was the biggest man made structure in the known world until we heard of the large pyramids built by the Egyptians.

Satakratu did not say a word during the crossing. He would hate to admit it, but I knew that he was a little frightened, particularly when the bridge started to swing in the strong wind when we were right in the middle. I smiled, but did not say anything and he relaxed as soon as we reached the other shore. A few more trips and his fear would vanish. Before sunset that evening, we were in the city.

The imposing walls and towering buildings of Sindhu lay before us as we topped the summit of a small hill. The city was much larger than Harappa and like most large cities, it had the upper, middle and lower sections. The Temple was bigger than that of Harappa and was made more imposing by being set on the highest point of the city. Then there were the Great Hall, the Hospital and the University.

We entered through the eastern gate and headed towards the University at the southern end of the city. It was immense, slightly bigger than the Temple, with five floors and over a hundred rooms. The classrooms and offices were on the first four floors, the students' quarters on the top floor. We tethered our horses in the stable just outside the University walls and walked in through the imposing front entrance, which was two floors high. We went straight to the office to register Satakratu and find out where we would be billeted for the night. The familiar corridors brought back memories of the happy times I had spent there and I pointed out all the important places to Satakratu. To my surprise, the officer-in-charge recognised me and the formalities were quickly completed and we were shown to our rooms.

We unpacked and arranged Satakratu's things in the room and then went to meet Master Vishwamitra Gathinah to deliver the documents that the Father and Sage Shunahotra had given me. Master Gathinah lived in one of the largest houses in the city near the Temple. The great sage himself greeted us at the door. He was tall, slightly dark complexioned, had angular features, a long, flowing grey beard and moustache. His hair was rolled up in a bun on the right side at the top of his head and on his forehead were three horizontal grey ash stripes with a central black ash dot. He had an aura of power about him.

We prostrated before him and I said, "Our humblest obeisance, O Great Sage. We bring greetings from Sage Shunahotra and Master Kapila of Harappa."

"Dheerghayushman Bhava," he said. "I was expecting you. You did very well by helping the merchants. How are my dear friends, Sage Shunahotra and Master Kapila?"

Satakratu gasped at the mention of our encounter with the raiders. I will have to tell him a few things about these Sages and their powers before I leave Sindhu, I thought to myself with a smile.

"They send you greetings and these documents. If there is a reply, I will be honoured to take it back," I said.

He unrolled the documents and read them in silence. Meanwhile, the maid brought us a cool buttermilk in small mud pots.

When he had finished reading, the Sage said, "I will have a reply to these letters for Sage Shunahotra and Master Kapila. Will you please collect the letter from the Council of Elders tomorrow?"

"I will certainly do that."

"Please convey my regards to Sage Shunahotra and Master Kapila and thank you for coming to see me."

We were very impressed with Sage Vishwamitra's humility and warmth. His reputation of being extremely short tempered and arrogant seemed to be entirely untrue.

We met many students and some parents in the dining room that night. The initiation was to take place two days later and most of the students had already registered at the University. I wanted to meet the Masters the next morning and finish the errand for Master Ashwin before lunchtime so that I could be at the river crossing before nightfall. Lopa was waiting for me at Harappa and for once, I had no desire to linger in Sindhu.

The next morning, I left Satakratu with his Master in the Architecture Department and went to meet my old Master. He was busy with the new students, so I waited for him to be free. When the last of the students left his office, I knocked on the door.

"Enter."

The Master's voice was as authoritative as ever. He was busy mixing potions and powders and had his back to me. Then he turned round, saw me, quickly put the jars down and rushed up to embrace me with such affection that tears filled my eyes.

"Upaas! This is indeed a pleasant surprise, son."

I was extremely happy to see him and knelt down and touched his feet.

"Dheerghayushman Bhava. What brings you to Sindhu?"

"I have brought my brother, Satakratu, to join the university. He will be studying architecture."

We spent the next hour talking about old times and I told him of all the things that I was now doing. He gave me the news of my classmates and I was surprised to know that one of them had gone to Sumer to learn about their medicines and had not been heard of since. After nearly an hour, I reluctantly left and went to the Great Hall to meet Sage Vishwamitra.

The Great Hall at Sindhu was much bigger than the one at Harappa, soaring ten cubits into the sky. The walls were made of large granite blocks and seemed impregnable. The front door was massive and ornate with carvings that depicted scenes from the story of Sage Manu helping Matsya, the fish. The door frame was clad in brass etched with lotus flowers all around and bronze finials in the middle.

The guard at the front door escorted me inside, bowed low and said, "Master Upaashantha from Harappa is here to meet the Council of Elders."

He withdrew, closing the door behind him.

"Welcome, Master Upaashantha. Our greetings to you and to the city of Harappa. Our deepest condolences to the families who lost their loved ones in the earthquake," Sage Vishwamitra said. "I have discussed with the Council of Elders the contents of the letters you brought from Harappa. There has been a disturbance in the Prana at Harappa. We, too, felt some disturbance here at the time mentioned in the letters. Please tell us about your experience that night when this event occurred."

I had not a clue about the content of the letters I had carried. And though I searched my mind, I could not recall noticing anything unusual that night.

"My humble apologies, Sage Vishwamitra. I did not feel anything unusual that night. The only unusual thing I noticed was the following morning. There was a strong smell of burning flesh in the lower town as I walked towards the hospital."

"That must have been the burnt sacrificial lamb or a goat. Was there anything else? Did you feel any unusual changes around you that day? Any sudden changes in the weather pattern perhaps?"

I racked my brain but could remember nothing unusual about that day a week ago. I was rather flustered. Was there something I should have noticed and had missed? Was I proving to be a fool before the Elders of Sindhu?

"I am sorry. I cannot remember anything unusual that day. We were extremely busy with several trauma cases from the earthquake," I said rather sheepishly. Were they scowling at me for being particularly dense?

"Did you notice anything unusual about the patients coming to you after that day? Were there any patients with burns? Was there any one suffering the after effects of excessive drink or drugs?"

It suddenly occurred to me that there had been more than the usual drink related patients over the past few days.

"Yes," I said eagerly. "Yes, I do remember there were an unusual number of patients with drink related problems. But, no one with burns."

I felt embarrassed and completely inadequate and wondered why they were asking me all these questions. Surely our Elders, particularly Sage Shunahotra, would have communicated with them through telepathy. Suddenly, it struck me that sending a letter with me was very strange indeed. Sage Vishwamitra was smiling at me.

"Relax, Upaashantha. We are not testing you. The disturbance caused was so strong that we are sure the one who performed the yajna can intercept telepathic messages. That is why the written communication. And all this questioning is to try and understand exactly what kind of yajna was performed."

I was amazed at how clearly he had read my mind.

"The Elders of Harappa and Sindhu will take strong action against these people and we will prevent them from performing the next stage of this yajna. They are trying to unleash a power they do not even comprehend and cannot control. They wish to invoke powers to change nature without knowing what powers nature herself can use against them! Please take this letter to Sage Shunahotra and your illustrious father. We have suggested some modifications to the steps they plan take to make sure that we are successful. I know that you will not be tempted to open and read the documents. Remember, you do not have the ability to prevent them from reading your mind. Whoever they are, they will read the document at almost the same time as you do," said Sage Vishwamitra.

He handed me a rolled palm-leaf document closed with his personal seal. For a moment, I stood silently, not knowing what to say.

"I am sure you understand that speed is of the essence. We do not have time to lose. When are you leaving for Harappa?"

"I will leave Sindhu as soon as I have said goodbye to my brother at the university. I should be able to reach Harappa in three days, if I make good time," I replied.

"God speed. Our blessings and prayers go with you. There is no reason to tell your brother about the nature of your business." He said looking at me with unblinking eyes.

"No sir. There is not," I said with alacrity.

"I have thrown a cordon around your prana so no one can trace you as a protection for your journey back home." He replied with his arms raised with palms forward in blessing.

I bowed to the Council of Elders and took my leave. My thoughts were in turmoil. I had to plan the return journey slightly differently now. Luckily, I did not have any heavy luggage with me to slow the travel. I even thought of disposing of the Elamite horse that was presented to me by the merchants we had helped. I went quickly to the University and bid goodbye to Satakratu.

"I will have to leave earlier than I thought, Satakratu. Look after yourself. I know your Master is a very kind person. If you have any problems, discuss them with him. If you want me to come back to see you for any reason, send me a message and I will come immediately."

"I thought we would spend some time together. You said you would show me some interesting places in the city," Satakratu said, disappointed.

"Yes, I know. But something urgent has come up suddenly and I have to go."

Satakratu sighed, but did not say anything. I left soon after lunch through the eastern gate with some trepidation and also sadness at leaving Satakratu. He was the baby of the family and had never been away from home before. But, I had to get back to Harappa as quickly as possible. Time was running out. I spurred Shankara to a canter and the Elamite horse, which I was leading with his rein, easily ran along. We reached the bridge over the Vipas before nightfall. I went to the inn near the bridge where I had often stayed when I was at the University, and I knew the innkeeper well.

"Master Upaas! How nice to see you after so many years! You have not changed a bit. How are you? What brings you here? Are you coming back to work in Sindhu?"

"Bhavadutah, it is nice to see you again. You have not changed either, I see - still talking non-stop! No, I have not come back to work in Sindhu. I came to drop my younger brother, Satakratu, at the University and I am on my way back," I replied. "I hope you have a room for me?"

"You are always welcome here, Master Upaas. You know there is a bed here for you whenever you come," he smiled. "Come, dinner is about to be served. You will like the hot roti. Then, I will show you to your room."

He poured water for me to wash my hands and feet and then led me into the dining room. Two men were sitting at a table across the room in darkness, away from the window, talking in hushed tones. When we walked in, they stopped talking and looked at us. Bhavadutah introduced them to me but I did not catch their names. We smiled politely at each other and they went back to their meal. I sat down at the other end of the room. Bhavadutah was full of questions about Father, Mother, Vidhayaka and Nivya. As usual, he wanted hear all the news and all the gossip. Before we finished our meal, the strangers had left.

"I have an excellent drink to round off the evening," Bhavadutah said and disappeared into the cellar. I sat there looking around the old familiar room where I had spent many a pleasant evening during my days at the University. The room was large with a high ceiling supported by large oak beams and thick wooden columns. There was enough space for six large tables and benches. There were two small windows, which opened out and let in the sunlight. The kitchen was to the left. The walls were painted bright ochre with red skirting all the way round. There were lamps mounted high on the walls. We could hear the fast flowing Vipas and, occasionally, creaks from the bridge whenever a heavy cart passed over it. He still had a large mural on the wall of a human figure with a bird's head and strange hieroglyphics underneath, which a grateful Egyptian had given him. It was a picture of the Egyptian Sun God. There were hangings from several countries on all the walls presents from sailors and merchants on boats going upstream from Saraswata on the Vipas. They often stopped at the bridge for a break and rest and relaxation.

Bhavadutah and his wife came back with the drinks. We sat there for another hour chatting about old times.

"I have to leave before sunrise, Bhavadutah. If I am not up an hour before sunrise, can you wake me up, please?" I asked.

"Of course, Master Upaas. But, what is the hurry?"

"I must be back in Harappa in three days. I have a lot of work to do since the earthquake."

Bhavadutah knew better than to ask more questions. I bid them good night and after my usual Gayatri hymn, fell fast asleep.

It was still dark the next morning when I walked out of the inn. The first thing I noticed was the absence of the strangers' horses. I raised my eyebrows at Bhavadutah who had come out to see me off.

"I heard the horses leave the stable very early. Be careful, Master Upaas. The roads are not as safe as they used to be."

I checked my bow and the quiver of arrows once again to make sure nothing was missing. I waved good-bye and set off across the bridge. For some reason, I kept thinking about the two strangers. They seemed very secretive speaking in hushed tones, casting furtive glances and finally leaving so early without saying good-bye to the inn keeper. Was there something sinister about their behaviour? I wondered. After a while, I decided that I was being paranoid and that they were innocent travellers minding their own business. I needed to concentrate on my riding if I were to reach Harappa on time. I spurred Shankara to a gallop and the Elamite horse easily kept pace with us.

I travelled fast for most of that day, except for an hour's break in the afternoon, and reached the Janshar valley as dusk was setting in. I was headed for the next staging post in the valley when I saw smoke rising from the forest just a little away from the path before me. I stopped, tied the two horses to a tree and went to some large bushes and rocks on the other side of the road, crouched behind them and peeped beyond. There were ten people sitting around a campfire in a little clearing in the forest.

They were dressed as Avestan soldiers, fully armed with swords, bows and spears. Their horses were tethered on the opposite side of the clearing. Two of them looked very familiar and I realised with a shock that they were the strangers from the inn, now dressed in uniform. They must have been in Sindhu and followed me around. They knew then, that I had met Sage Vishwamitra at the Council of Elders. I had not taken any notice of people around me at the time.

I quickly scanned the surroundings for lookouts. There were two of them-one directly above me sitting on the cluster of rocks behind which I was hiding and the other in a tree just above the horses. This is inconvenient, I thought. There were too many of them for me to fight and it would take me at least two extra days if I took a detour to avoid them. I would have to climb up the hill on either side of the valley and down again on the other to reach the staging post. There was no option but to try a diversionary tactic to go past them. The special arrows Master Adhvadipa had provided would probably do the trick.

I crept back to the horses and fed them, in case there was little time to feed them later. While they ate, I formulated and reformulated a plan and chose the arrows I needed, strung the bow to the tension I wanted. The slow walk across the road with the Elamite horse trailing behind was nerve wracking. The clip clop of the hooves, though muffled on the grass, sounded ominously loud in the quiet of the forest. I was sure the Avestan guard would hear us approaching. I had to reach the large oak tree to get a good shot at the guard sitting up on the rocks. I had to take him out without alerting the rest of them, only then would I have a chance of escape. I had to get him in the throat with one shot. The angle of the shot had to be right, so that it entered the neck and went up to the brain, not only to stop him from crying out, but also to kill him instantly. I climbed to a vantage point on the tree and saw the guard looking south over the path I would have to take. I loaded the very fine tipped arrow and took a careful aim at his throat, prayed to God Indra and shot the arrow. The Gods were with me, the arrow found its target and its force made the guard roll sideways and almost fall off the rocks. That would have been disastrous.

I jumped from the tree onto Shankara and walked him down the path. As we approached the bend from where I could see the campsite, I loaded one of the special arrows and shot it straight at the fire, taking care to look away as I released it. The arrow arched high in the sky and came down at an angle, hitting the fire just as I turned the bend and came into direct view of the Avestans. Two of them saw me and jumped up with their arrows, but arrow hit the fire at the same instant and there was a brilliant orange flash, a loud bang and they were all momentarily blinded. I rapidly loaded my next arrow and aimed in the general direction of the flash and shot it before they could recover. There was another loud bang and smoke billowed out as the arrow exploded on contact. It was thick and black and completely covered the clearing. This was my cue and I goaded Shankara to a gallop. My heart thumped furiously as we sped past the camp into the forest. I did not stop until I reached the staging post. It was the most terrifying time of my life. I was sweating profusely and my heart felt as if it might burst. Only when I saw Harappan soldiers at the staging post did I slow down and begin to feel a little safer. When they heard what had happened, the captain sent off a platoon of soldiers to the Avestan camp.

It was not until I had washed and eaten the dinner the soldiers kindly offered, that I calmed down and my heart beat normally again. The captain wanted to know every detail of the altercation. I told him about the two strangers at the inn the previous night and described them as best as I could. I had seen them in poor light and paid them little attention and the captain was disappointed.

"Master Upaahsantha, judging by your description, they do not seem to be professional soldiers of the Avestan army. These are most likely bandits dressed up as soldiers. We will take care of them. If you wish, I can send a guard to accompany you on the rest of your journey."

"That is very kind of you, but now that I am out of the valley, the rest of my journey should be safe. I would not like to take your soldiers away from important duties,"

"With due respect, Master Upaas, protecting you is one of our main duties. Even though you are out of the valley, there are still several ambush points between here and Harappa. I insist that you take one of my soldiers with you as a bodyguard."

The captain would not be dissuaded and a soldier was nominated to accompany me for the rest of my journey. If I had told him the nature of the documents I was carrying, he probably would have insisted on coming himself with a platoon of soldiers! I thought of all that had happened when I lay in bed that night. Though I now knew things I had never suspected before I set out on this journey, there were still gaps in the picture that I could not fill.

There was a connection between the random attacks on outlying farms and merchant camps by men dressed as Avestan soldiers, the disturbance in the Prana at Harappa, the document I was asked to take to Sindhu, the two strangers at Sindhu and now the attack on me. They all appeared to be part of one jigsaw, but I could not piece them together. Finally, I fell into a fitful sleep and felt that I had barely dozed off when a guard woke me up.

"Master Upaas, your horse is very restless and we cannot pacify him. Please come quickly."

Shankara was a very placid horse and would not cause any problems. What had happened to him? I ran to the yard and saw him thrashing and trying to cut loose. Four soldiers were struggling to control him.

I ran and took the reins and called out to him. "Shankara. What is the matter? It is me, your master, what's the matter, boy?"

I tried to stroke his neck and back. He stopped pulling at the reins as soon as he heard my voice. It took me another half an hour to quieten him completely. I fed him the sweets I carried in my bag and gave him some water. He kept snorting all the time. Dawn was peeping over the horizon and the birds had begun chirping. I decided to make an early start, gathered all my belongings and saddled Shankara, who seemed impatient to get going. He turned around and looked at me as if to say, "It's about time."

The sun was high in the sky when I reached the Parushni. It was the final stretch of the journey and I nudged the horse to go faster. But I had just rounded a corner when I saw a dust cloud in the distance and soon heard horse hooves. Oh no, not again! I thought. There were six riders galloping towards me.

The soldier accompanying me said, "We better hide in the forest till the riders pass, Master."

But I had no time to play hide and seek. I had to get back to Harappa quickly.

"No. There are only six riders and we can take them. There is no time to waste. Come with me and don't shoot until I tell you."

The soldier looked surprised and resentful. He did not believe I could do anything, but, he followed me without a word.

We quickly slipped into the trees off the path, tethered the horses and climbed a large banyan tree to take up the position well hidden from the riders, who were dressed as Harappan soldiers and carrying the Harappan standard; but I was not going to take any chances. I shot three arrows across the leading riders' path. The horses stopped suddenly and reared up, the two leaders lost their balance and fell and the others immediately reached for their bows.

"Not so fast, soldiers. I would not do that, if you value your life. I can pick each one of you without moving from here," I said in the most menacing voice I could muster under the circumstances.

There was a gasp and one of the soldiers said, "Master Upaas?"

The voice was familiar, but after what had happened the day before, I did not trust anybody.

"Who wants to know?" I asked.

"We are soldiers from the defence command under Master Adhvadipa. Sage Shunahotra has sent us to look for you."

"Show me some proof."

"We are carrying the standard of Harappa, as you can see and here is the seal of our Command."

He held out his left hand to show the large golden seal of the Captain of the Defence Command of Harappa on his right index finger.

"Lay the seal on the ground. Drop your weapons and step back so that I can check it."

"I am sorry, Master Upaas. I cannot do that. You know very well the only way this seal can be taken off my finger is by killing me."

I heaved a sigh of relief. The royal seals given to Captains and Generals of the army or defence forces once worn, are never removed.

"In that case, get your soldiers to drop the weapons and move well back. And you drop all your weapons and take three steps forward with your hands in front of you all the time."

The soldiers, including the ones who had fallen down, dropped their weapons and stepped well back with their hands held high. The Captain also dropped his weapons – both the sword and the bow and the quiver - on the ground and walked forward.

I jumped down from the tree, and walked forward to inspect the seal, bow and arrow held up, ready to shoot. I recognised the Captain and the seal was genuine. I lowered my bow and returned the arrow to the quiver.

"I am sorry, Captain. I have been under threat twice in the past week and I did not want to take any chances. Now tell me, what is the hurry? I would have reached Harappa tonight anyway."

"I understand, Master Upaas. I do not know why the urgency. We have been sent to escort you back to the city as soon as possible. We can get fresh horses if you like."

"No, no, thank you. My Shankara can outrun any of your horses."

I turned around and whistled and Shankara trotted up with the Elamite horse behind him. The captain was impressed when he saw the two horses, especially the Elamite.

"That is a very nice Elamite horse, Master Upaashantha."

I told him how I had come to own the horse.

"I wish we had accompanied you, Master Upaas. Now we must hurry. Sage Shunahotra wants you back in the city before sunset."

The rest of the journey was uneventful and we reached the southern gate well before sunset. I went straight to the Great Hall where the Council of Elders was waiting for me. They were all very relieved to see me and Sage Shunahotra, my father and Master Ashwin came forward to greet me. I touched their feet.

"Lord Indra's blessings have brought you back home safely. How are you, Upaas? We have been so worried ever since we learnt that the renegade Avestans knew about the letter you were carrying. We did not dare use telepathy to contact you, because it would have given away your location to the rebels," said Sage Shunahotra.

I was amazed that the Council of Elders already knew about the rebels and that the Sage was worried about their powers. I had believed that Sage Shunahotra and our Council of Elders were invincible.

I bowed to all the Elders and said, "I am grateful for your concern. There were some problems on the way, but they were manageable. I met Sage Vishwamitra and he has given this letter for you."

I pulled out the palm-leaf roll that I had tucked under the tunic three days ago. Only three days! So much had happened in between that it felt like three months.

"Thank you, Upaas. The city of Harappa is indebted to you for this. I can see that you are very tired," Sage Shunahotra said, kindly. "But, Master Adhvadipa needs to know everything about the attacks during the journey. It is important that we piece together all the information we can get so that we can capture these people as soon as possible. It is a matter of life and death for Harappa."

Master Adhvadipa led me into one of the numerous side rooms of the Great Hall.

"Come, Upaas. We must talk."

The room was sparsely furnished with a wooden desk and a few chairs on the right side of the door. There were two windows on the far side that overlooked the famous vegetable garden of the Great Hall. The gardener was watering the plants. A guard came in and set a wooden bowl of fruit, freshly picked from the garden, a tray of freshly made roti,a small bowl of honey and a large jug full of refreshing thin buttermilk on the table making me aware of how hungry I was. It was dusk and the light from the windows was fading quickly.

Master Adhvadipa sat behind the desk and said, "Sit, Upaas. Have something to eat. The fruit are fresh from the garden and Ma Ashwin made the roti for you. I know you are tired and just want to get home rather than sit here talking to me," he smiled. "But this is important and urgent."

I helped myself to some grapes and picked up the jug of buttermilk.

"I understand, Master Adhvadipa. It is my duty to help in whatever way I can. I have many questions to ask as well, if you don't mind?" I said, sitting down.

"I am not surprised. So much has happened in the last few days. I think I know what your questions are. Let me try to explain…"

He took a deep breath and leaned forward, looking into my eyes.

"Yes, we have found the persons involved with the yajna which disturbed the Prana. We have known of some dissent among some Harappans for over a year now and we have been keeping a watch over them. The man who performed it is an Avestan Magus who has rebelled against his leaders and has instigated some discontented Harappans to act against us. He has obviously promised them a false Utopia. He is leading a rebel force of Avestans against Bharata.

We have intercepted messages from within the group and we know that they have an informer and spy within Harappa. Unfortunately, we have not been able to find this spy who is helping the Magus. They were aware of your assignment, although we had kept it secret. We discovered their plan to intercept you only last night and we were very afraid that we might be too late to warn you. Despite several attempts by us, and by Sage Shunahotra, we could not find your Prana signal.

"Their next target is to somehow lay their hands on a Soma plant or some Somaras without which they cannot perform the next stage of the yajna. We know who the Harappan rebels are and who the Magus is and where he is right now. Unfortunately, we do not know who the traitor or the helper is. The Magus has thrown such a strong field around him or her that we cannot penetrate it. One way of catching him is to allow the yajna to go ahead and hopefully catch him red handed. There is grave risk in that, because he may be able to complete the yajna before we can capture him. Now that you have brought advice from Sage Vishwamitra, we might be able to stop the yajna and get the spy at the same time."

I was beginning to understand the events of the last few days. It was a far bigger conspiracy than I had imagined.

"Thank you, Master Adhvadipa. Sage Vishwamitra had surrounded my prana with his force before I left Sindhu so that no one can trace me. I now understand what has been happening over the last couple of weeks since the earthquake. I still find it difficult to accept that there are Harappans who are unhappy enough to wish to harm Harappa. I had naively believed that if everyone has jobs, shelter and enough food, they would be happy. Our Council of Elders has kept our society self sufficient for hundreds of years. But I guess the human heart is not easily satisfied."

Master Adhvadipa sighed and said, "The world is full of both good and bad people. There are some who are never content with their lot. Ariana has been plagued with a shortage of water for the past few decades and they have been battling severe drought in the last few years. Their rivers are nearly all dry. There are many discontented people there, who are jealous of the prosperity and bounty of Bharata. We have offered help to them and there are moves to divert some of the waters of our rivers to the west. Sage Shunahotra has met the Avestan King. Unfortunately, the rogue Magus wants to divert the entire river Sindhu to the west. Some fools here in Harappa have decided to help him. Unfortunately for us, there is also someone with access to the information about Somaras, who is acting against Harappa. We have to stop them."

"So does this rogue Magus have the welfare of his people in his heart then? Surely that is not all evil?"

Master Adhvadipa smiled at my naivety and continued.

"If he was only concerned about the welfare of the people he would have supported his King's talks with Sage Shunahotra and accepted our help. No, he wants grandeur for himself. He wants to be a hero at all costs. His own ego is what really drives him."

I had finished the entire bowl of fruit and the jug of buttermilk by then. It was dark and Master Adhvadipa had lit the wall lamps as he was talking and they threw strange, flickering shadows on the walls. I suddenly noticed that it was very quiet. We spent the next hour discussing the events and the people I had met and the attackers

I had encountered on the return journey. It was quite late when I said goodbye and left the Great Hall.

I walked out into the night and stood there for a minute, stretching my arms out and breathing in the fresh, cool night air. The guard had brought Shankara from the stables. The Elamite horse stayed there that night since Master Adhvadipa wanted to check him for any clues of the owner before letting me take him home. I looked up at the starry sky and wondered what Lopa was doing. Was she fast asleep or was she also looking at the same starry sky and thinking of me? Tomorrow I would meet Lopa as soon as I could.

❖

Chapter 6

RENDEZVOUS WITH A DIFFERENCE.

The Magus made his way through the now familiar roads of Harappa towards the eastern gate. He was very pleased with the results of the night's yajna, which had been far more successful than he had expected. Everything had gone according to plan: his subjects as he thought of them, since he was clearly going to be their ruler soon had behaved impeccably and he had impressed them enough to quell any doubts that some of them may have harboured. He had spent months perfecting the potions and powders that the Yogi had taught him to make, with chemicals obtained from Sumerian and Median travellers.

He and his friends have spent the past year scouring the surroundings of Harappa for a suitable site for the eventual Yajns he would have to perform for the attaining power over nature. He now believed that he was more powerful than the Yogi and he could do more than the decrepit old man from the mountains. The disappearing act had been particularly impressive, he thought. His subjects were awestruck and he was sure that they would do his bidding without question.

He was now ready for the next stage, the Gomedha. The Prana field he had generated through that night's yajna would shield his informant in Harappa from even the most powerful Meluhhan sages. It was crucial to keep him on his side not only because he would provide the Somaras, but also because he had promised to bring the full technical details of how to manufacture it. If he would lead him to the source of the Soma plants, the Magus' job was done and nothing and nobody in this world would be able to stop him from reaching his goal. Then it would be up to his allies in the north, particularly those from Sistan and Bactria to do the rest.

He was relying on the vast armies of his allies to do the physical job of capturing Mount Mujavant and the precious fields of Soma. The rebel general, Ardeshir, had promised him the armies and they were waiting to act as soon as he could tell them where Mount Mujavant was located. It had taken all his tact and resourcefulness to convince the general to join him and raise the rebel army. The Magus had called it the "Holy war." Ardeshir was good at his word and there were enough disgruntled and disenfranchised young men in Bactria to follow him. He had soon moved on to other states on a recruitment drive and the last message to the Magus said that he had over fifty thousand young men ready to march on Meluhha.

As soon as Ardeshir gets the signal, it was just a matter of sailing down the river Khuba down to the mighty Sindhu and back up Parushni. The rebel army could be within shouting distance of Harappa in a matter of a couple of weeks. Once he controlled the Soma, he could easily defeat and take over Harappa. Strategically, it was important that he capture Harappa first after Mount Mujavant. First Harappa and then the rest of Bharata. The Magus smiled to himself and quickened his pace.

He had first met "Pakshar" in a wayside inn between Saraswata and Harappa. Maricha had set up the meeting, one more among many such 'important' persons he had brought to him, and they had all been disgruntled people looking for a bit of excitement. None of them had any information about Soma, let alone access to the plant or the Somaras. So, he had gone to the inn with very low expectations. The first impression of the man had been disappointing - he had stood diffidently and uncomfortably in the shadows with a shawl covering his head despite the heat and humidity. He never met the Magus' eyes and seemed tense and on edge. What can such a coward do for me? the Magus had thought derisively. But then, Maricha had told him where the man worked and his interest had been immediately aroused.

"You can call me "Pakshar", the man had mumbled, with a quick furtive look at the Magus. It was obviously not his real name, but the Magus had shown no reaction and continued talking to him. 'Pakshar' had smiled nervously throughout the meeting and said very little. The Magus had to extract information out of him and he had replied in mono syllables and remained non-committal. After about an hour of painstaking conversation, he had gathered that 'Pakshar' worked in a place with access to Soma extract and also that he would be willing to get him the extract for a price. But he had been non-committal about the whereabouts of the Soma fields and Mount Mujavant, though he seemed to imply that he knew exactly where they were. Not as much of a fool as I thought, the Magus had said to himself. A deal had been struck and gold had changed hands. So far, 'Pakshar' had kept his word and they'd had several meetings. Since Maricha and his cronies could not get him Soma, he had to string 'Pakshar' along. Once he had the Soma, there was no way he would fail in his endeavour.

The sun was peeping over the horizon and the Magus' spirits were high as he reached the eastern gate. Not only the Soma fields, but all the Harappan gold would also be under his control. The things I can do with it, he thought. I will become the most powerful Magus in the Universe. He pulled his shawl down over his head to cover his face without making it too obvious. As usual there was a lot of traffic at that time travellers, merchants and farmers waiting to start their day's work within and out of the city. He scanned the crowd to see if he could spot his man. There was no sign of him. Either he was being extra careful or he had forgotten about the rendezvous. He would soon know.

He walked with the crowd for a while waiting for an opportunity to peel off without being noticed. There was a slight commotion ahead of him as some watermelons rolled off the back of an overloaded cart. People rushed to help and he quietly slipped into the trees and hid behind a large bush until the road became empty of workers and farmers. Then he doubled back towards the city and turned off the road again into a path just before he reached the gate. No one had been on the path for a while judging by the overgrowth, he noted with satisfaction. He soon reached the rendezvous point. He had stumbled upon this cave several months ago and had used it a couple of times before to meet his friends. Usually, he never used any site more than twice. Unfortunately, 'Pakshar' refused to travel further out of the city and it was too dangerous to meet within the walls.

He entered the cave and cleared a space to sit. Sun light struggled to filter through the dense bushes and a small waterfall that partially covered the cave entrance, keeping it hidden from the occasional goatherd who ventured there. It was off the beaten track and hardly anyone ever came here, especially since Maricha had successfully spread a rumour about a dangerous wild animal in the area. The Magus sat down and took out the typical Harappan Baati, bread soaked in honey and sun-dried that he had brought with him. There were some dried dates as well in his pouch and he enjoyed his breakfast in the cave. He washed the food down with water from the little pool at the mouth of the cave.

It was the beginning of summer and as the sun rose in the sky, it grew hotter. Where was his man, he wondered? Had he developed cold feet? Had he forgotten about the meeting? Was he lost? Worst of all, had he been caught? No, nobody could break the strong Prana shield he had cast around him. But the Magus was uneasy and decided to look for him from the top of the cave. He peered through the bushes, ensured that there was no one outside and then stepped out, went round the hillock and pulled himself on top of the cave with the help of the branches of an overhanging tree. He managed to scramble up the boulders and worked himself around to the front again to sit just above the cave behind the tree.

It seemed as if he had been sitting there for hours and just as he had decided that the coward had gone back on his word, he heard a sound. It was definitely not the birds, the animals, the rustling of the leaves or other normal forest noises. He scanned the surroundings in the direction of where he thought it had come from nothing. He closed his eyes, concentrated and recited the hymn that would let him see in the dark and into distances. Nothing...? He suddenly remembered that the Pranic field that he had put around 'Pakshar' would not let anyone see him when he was hiding, even with divine vision. So, he focussed on the field he had created and immediately saw an image that was so faint that it had to be his man. The image was still; it had to be that cowardly traitor, who was willing to sell his soul to the highest bidder, crouching there in the forest, too afraid to show himself. The Magus took a deep breath and jumped off the roof of the cave on to the ground beneath.

He landed softly on the balls of his feet in a crouch, stood up and said, "Hello. You can come out now. It is quite safe inside the cave. No one can see us in there."

"Hunh. No. Please stand there where I can see you and turn around slowly. Mmm... Stand facing the cave and can you keep your hands where I can see them, please?" 'Pakshar' mumbled.

There was a slight tremor in his voice and he was obviously afraid, either of the Magus or of being caught by the Harappans or both. The Magus turned around to face the cave and kept his hands at his sides. He heard the spy jump down from the tree he was sitting on and walk forward.

"My apologies. Hunh... But I had to make sure no one was watching us."

The Magus turned round and looked at him. He had his head and face covered with the ever present shawl and looked very tired and apprehensive. His eyes darted around constantly as if looking for something or someone.

"I wondered if you had either forgotten our meeting or forgotten the place."

"Can we go in please? I don't want to be out in the open any longer than necessary."

"Yes. I understand. Please follow me. Be careful, it is very slippery. Just follow my footsteps. The bushes are harmless."

The Magus walked into the cave with sure steps and 'Pakshar' followed gingerly behind. Once inside, he let out a deep sigh. The Magus sat down and put his hands in his bag.

"No. Please don't!"

"I am just taking some bread out for you. You look famished. Have you had anything to eat this morning?"

"Hunh... No. I did not have time. Hunh… I left when it was still dark."

"I looked for you at the gate."

"Hunh.... I did not come through the gate."

So there were ways of leaving the city without going through the gates, the Magus noted. He offered the man Baati and dry dates, which he ate with gusto. That was the first time the Magus had seen him do anything with enthusiasm. He watched him finish the bread and drink the water from his leather pitcher.

Then he asked, "Did you bring it?"

The young man put his hands deep inside the layers of clothes he had covered himself with, pulled out a small leather pouch and held it out rather hesitatingly to the Magus who almost had to prise it out of his fingers. The pouch contained a greenish black powder mixed with dried leaves and some white granules. The Magus had never seen an extract of Somaras before, but he had no intention of letting the informant know that. He assumed this powder was an extract used to transport the precious stuff since the Soma plants could hardly be carried hundreds of yojanas to Harappa from Mount Mujavant in the Himalayas. For the first time, the young man was looking at him intently.

The Magus looked up and said, “This looks good. Approximately how much Somaras can we make out of this?”

“Hunh... One pouch is enough to make one cauldron of Somaras, if you get water from the sacred pool on river Saraswathi. And mmm... I am not sure, how much you will get if you use any other river water. I suspect, mmm... the Somaras will not work if you don’t use Saraswathi water.”

“Then we must ensure that we have water from the Saraswathi,” the Magus replied. ‘You said that you would also give me a list of the ingredients used for the extract?”

The spy looked up at the Magus without meeting his eyes.

“Umm. That was very difficult. Hunh.... I was nearly caught writing things down.”

He pulled out a rolled up palm leaf from another deep pocket and handed it to the Magus.

“Thank you. You will be rewarded many times over when we are in charge of Harappa.”

The Magus unrolled the leaf and began reading. Several lines of text were scribbled in a hurry and there were two diagrams of contraptions that the Magus had never seen before.

“What are these diagrams?”

‘Pakshar’ immediately replied, “Um... The grinder you need to get the correct consistency of the powder from the Soma stalk and the stones for it are from Mount Mujavant.”

“Can you tell me where the mountain is?”

“Hunh... when the time comes.”

The Magus knew that to attack Harappa with any chance of success, he would need more than one cauldron of Somaras. Once the Gomedha was done and he gained control of the rivers and soon, of all of Nature, in fact he would find out the location.

Maybe, he could get Mount Mujavant to come to him, now that was a thought! He took the pouch of gold coins from his bag and handed it to 'Pakshar'.

"Once we have taken over Harappa, you will be richly rewarded," he said again, with a smile.

'Pakshar' turned around to leave. He stood just within the entrance and looked out beyond the bushes and the waterfall to make sure that no one was around, then walked out. He had only taken a couple of quick steps when he slipped and fell down into the pool below. The Magus looked with anger and disdain at the cowardly young man, but he had to humour him until he had the information he needed from him.

He went to the edge of the pool, held out his hand and pulled 'Pakshar' out.

"Join hands with me and you will get everything you ever dreamed of," he said. "Just follow my footsteps as before and you will be safe."

'Pakshar' followed him out of the cave, said, "Thank you. Hunh... I will get in touch when I have some more information," and walked rapidly away.

The Magus sighed deeply and set off towards the place chosen for the final yajna - the *Gomedha*. It was the ultimate sacrifice, which would give him untold powers. He would sacrifice the sacred bull at the end of the yajna. Everything was falling into place. Even the coward 'Pakshar' had come to him at the right time. He had brought him what he needed and he would not need him again till after the yajna, when his powers would be even greater.

"I am destined for greatness and things are conspiring to ensure that," he thought with satisfaction.

He first went to the little temple in the woods where his friends from Saraswata were waiting for him. It was nearly noon and hot. He pulled his shawl over his head and walked faster. He had to get to the ravine before dark. When he reached the little abandoned temple, his friends were sitting down to lunch. They immediately got up and bowed before him. He raised his hands in blessing and noted that they had brought his horse.

"We were getting concerned. It is rather late," Ankasa said.

Ankasa was always in a hurry. He was the Magus's only supporter and follower from his own town and had travelled to Saraswata after the Magus came back from his apprenticeship with the Yogi. The Magus had sent messages to several of his acquaintances to come and join him; Ankasa was the only who had responded. Three other Avestans who had settled down in Saraswata had also joined forces with him.

"I had to wait for my man to turn up from the city. He was late. We may have a slight problem with him he needs a lot of coaxing and cajoling, but won't give anything without being well paid. I still don't have all the information I need. We may have to find some other way of getting it from him." the Magus said, as he helped himself to some hot barley gruel and corn mixed with amlaki (gooseberry) and peppercorn.

"Is there anyone else that we can use?" Ankasa asked.

"Yes. There is potentially someone in the Great Council itself. But I am not sure if that person would go against his chief and country and help us."

"Is it is worth trying to contact him?"

"I don't want to show my hand until we are sure which way he will turn. I know that he is not happy with the way the council is working. But that is all I really know. He has a powerful aura around him and I cannot penetrate it to read his mind."

"Well, maybe we can persuade your man after the Gomedha. He may change his mind once he sees the effect of the yajna. We better hurry now."

They mounted their horses and the five of them set off at a gallop towards the ravine. It had taken the Magus and his friends nearly a year to find this place. Harappa had always been his first choice of attack for several reasons. It was one of the richest in Meluhha and most accessible to the armies of Ardeshir. He could just sail down the river Parushni with his vast army. It was about half a yojana from Harappa and took less than an hour from the eastern gate on horseback. They had come upon it by sheer accident. They were scouting around the countryside for a suitable spot when suddenly Hugav's horse slipped on some loose stones, reared up in fright and Hugav fell down. He had rolled all the way down a steep slope through the bushes to the bottom of what was a hidden ravine, covered with large trees and thick tall bushes. The others had immediately got off their horses and rushed to the edge, fearing the worst.

"Hugav. Are you okay, Hugav?" the Magus had shouted.

Hugav had looked up from where he was lying flat on his back and had slowly got up so that they could all see him. The way he dusted himself told them that all he had hurt was his pride. The Magus had looked around for a path to ride down, since there was no way a horse could go down the slope. They had to go back a fair distance where the slope flattened out and a disused path wound down to the bottom. Half an hour later, they had arrived at the bottom where Hugav was pacing up and down. The memory brought a smile to the Magus's face.

Ankasa, who was riding beside him, said curiously, "Something funny?"

"I just remembered the way we found this place for the *Gomedha*. Hugav was so angry. I had never seen him so vocal before that episode."

Everyone laughed. Soon they were on the path leading down into the ravine, which they had cleverly hidden with boulders and stones. The Magus remembered the Yogi telling him how the Harappans had moved the river Parushni to suit the city of Harappa during a long period of drought hundreds of years ago, and now that he had seen this ravine, he was quite certain that it was the old river bed.

The climb down to the floor of the ravine was slow, for they had to be careful not to trip or slip as that would take the horse and rider to a certain death. The ravine was ideal for their purpose. It had a flat sandy floor with a spattering of red sandstone boulders and a few thorny bushes. The sides rose 25 cubits high, made out of red sandstone cut over thousands of years by the Parushni. They were almost vertical with very few footholds. Only monkeys and there were plenty of those here could climb up or down and that too, only in some places where a few small trees grew out of the cracks in the walls. There were small caves in the walls but most of them were inaccessible. The ravine ran north to south, was long and curved and narrowed sharply at both ends, and once around the corner the walls dropped rapidly and the course was taken over by the jungle. There was a small pool of water right around the corner towards the south with large trees growing at its edges and practically covering it, keeping its waters always cool. A narrow stream, which flowed at the edge of the ravine, fed the pool.

The Magus could hardly believe his eyes when he first saw the ravine. It had everything he wanted plenty of space, complete secrecy from prying eyes and it would be extremely easy to defend in case of an attack and no one would be able to see the smoke from the altar from outside. He had been elated. The Gods had led him here; he was meant to be the saviour of his country and of the world and they wanted him to perform the *Gomedha*.

They set down to work as soon as they reached the floor of the ravine. In a cave just off the pool around the corner, well hidden behind bushes, they had stored bricks and other implements. They had managed to get a cartload of bricks from Saraswata on the pretext of repairing Maricha's house in Harappa and Hugav, who was a blacksmith by profession, had designed a pulley system using large cane baskets and thick hemp ropes to lower the bricks. It had been very hard work. Now they moved the bricks, cowpat powder and powdered sandstone out of the cave and cleared a space near the eastern wall of the ravine for the yajna, which was accessible only through the ravine floor.

The wall at that point was almost vertical and there were large trees at the top overhanging the edge concealing the ravine completely. The Magus marked out the spots for the five altars they would need for the yajna. Then he took out the palm-leaf with the drawings of the altar and directions showing how to build it. The altars would be arranged in a pentagon one at the apex of the pentagon for him and one in each of the other four corners for his friends. The four altars had to be identical and octagonal in shape. His apical one was slightly different it was higher and had sixteen corners. He checked the drawing on the palm-leaf again to confirm the distances between the altars, drew the details in the sand with a stick and called his friends.

"The instructions must be followed exactly and the measurements and directions have to be perfect. We will prepare the floor and the foundations for the altars today and we can finish building the altars tomorrow. Any questions?"

"No Magus. That seems pretty clear to us. We have been through this drill a few times before," Ankasa replied for all of them.

"Yes. I know. But I don't want to any mistakes," the Magus replied.

He looked up at the sky to see the position of the sun. He would have to wait until nightfall to see the position of Arundhati (star Alcor in the Ursa Major) to fix the exact orientation of the altars. They prepared the ground with a solution of cowpat powder, which they dampened down with large wooden stompers to make it flat and even. The area had to be large enough for the five altars with a place for them to sit and perform the yajna and for helpers to move around. His subjects would have to sit on the sandy floor of the ravine, which looked quite comfortable. By the time the ground was prepared for the altars, it was dark.

The Magus looked around with some satisfaction. He had timed this perfectly. He looked up at the cloudless sky and the Arundhati star was just above the northern horizon over the lip of the ravine. He quickly marked its position on the floor and using the evening star, Venus, and Saturn for triangulation, marked out the four altars. With the main altar that he would use at the apex of the pentagon, they formed a perfect arrow pointing directly at the Arundhati.

"Let us get some wood and start a fire. We need light to build the foundation. If we can get the foundation done now, we can spend all of tomorrow building the altars. That will give us two more days for the final preparation plenty of time to make sure everything is perfect."

They gathered some twigs and branches, started a campfire near the building site and went to work. The foundation was soon ready. The Magus checked and rechecked the plans and the designs and nodded with satisfaction at the work they had done.

They all washed at the pond and the twins, who worked as cooks in the Temple of Saraswata, rustled up a delicious meal of rice, long peppers and lotus stem with spices. It was quite late that night when the Magus went to sleep content with the fact that everything was going well beyond his wildest dreams. He banned the use of bhang for everyone that night, which upset Hugav a great deal. Nothing can go wrong now, he thought, and drifted off to sleep just as the moon came up over the rim of the ravine.

The chirping of birds woke him up as the sky was turning pink and orange in the east. Most of the ravine was still in darkness when he went to the pool to wash and offer prayers to the Sun God and Varuna.

He stepped into the pool and poured the cool and fresh water over his head, washed and tied the long greying hair up in a knot. He wrapped his freshly washed loin cloth around while it was still wet. Then he recited the hymns in praise of Mithra and asked him to grant success in his endeavours. He turned east towards the sun and lifted his hands high above his head, read out the hymns in praise of the Sun God. He took the water from the pool in cupped hands, raised them over his head and poured the water back into the pool, reciting the hymns in praise of Varuna.

The others joined him in the pool and together said their prayers to Mithra. The sun was peeping over the eastern rim of the ravine when they started to build the altars and by the time it had reached the zenith they had finished. All that the Magus now needed was his subjects and the right confluence of stars, which was to be two days later. It was time to get back to the inn where he and his friends had been staying that week.

"Ankasa, you must go to Harappa and make sure Maricha and his friends get here on time without arousing suspicion. It is not a good idea for me to show my face there too often."

"I understand. I will leave in the morning for Harappa. I feel the best option is to move them in batches of about 20 people at a time to the campsite in the forest," Ankasa replied.

"I agree. Do we have enough facilities at the campsite for 100 people?"

"I expect about 50 people to attend, but we have facilities for over a 100 people."

They spent the rest of the day at the inn discussing the details of the yajna. The group's knowledge of scriptures was good, but they needed coaching in the intricacies and the different steps involved. He knew that even a single mistake in the performance of the yajna would lead to unimaginable disaster. He shivered at the thought and then brushed it aside. Nothing could go wrong now. The sacred bull was in the cow-shed at the half-way inn along with three other cows, ostensibly on their way to Harappa. Bringing just one bull from Saraswata to Harappa would have roused suspicion. It was now the responsibility of the twins to bring the cows and the bull to the ravine on the day of the yajna.

Twenty soldiers of the elite Avestan forces had been hired to guard the ravine, since he did not wish to trust the Harappans with the security, in case they switched allegiance at the last moment. Only the captain of the platoon knew where they were going and why. He was head of General Ardeshir's personal body guards and worked very closely with the General. The captain had chosen the best of his company for the job, but had not told them what the job was. The soldiers in turn had complete faith in their captain and would follow him anywhere.

Other generals he had approached were very skeptical and did not have any faith in his plans. One of them even tried to dissuade him with,

"The Meluhhan sages are very powerful. The only way to take Harappa is through force and one day we will have the force required to do that. Your way is doomed to failure. You should know that they can read your mind and they have powerful magic on their side," the General had said.

He will sing a different tune when I welcome them into Harappa – the Magus had thought to himself.

It was quite late when the Magus finally fell asleep, content that he had done everything right.

❖

Chapter 7

THE AVESTAN DILEMMA

King Vishtaspa had called for an extraordinary meeting of the leaders of the Council of Elders of all seven districts of Ariana. There were infighting and discontent among the people of the districts, mainly because of water. The land of nine rivers was rapidly drying up and a series of earthquakes had changed the courses of some of the rivers. The districts of Bactria and Gava were particularly badly affected as their rivers had changed direction and were now flowing mainly into Sogdiana. All the leaders had brought their advisers and ministers, as well as their senior Magi, with them and they all eyed each other with anger and distrust.

They were gathered in different corners of the vast hall of the King's court, whispering animatedly and throwing furtive glances at each other. The hall itself had lost its grandeur, though its lofty architecture still gave it an air of majesty. It was large, nearly thirty cubits in length. There was a podium at the far end supported by four exquisitely carved pillars; three steps in the centre led up to the King's throne. There were two smaller chairs, slightly set back, on either side of the throne.

The gold ornamentation that had adorned the walls, the brass plates and shields over the door panels and the silver lamps had been stripped off over time. The walls were now merely painted with gilt to mimic the original. Only the huge, solid wooden doors at the entrance of the hall still had brass trimmings and locks. Even the throne was now an elaborately carved wooden chair, which replaced the one embellished with gold plates and studded with precious and semi-precious stones. A row of chairs, slightly set off the walls on either side, was for the ministers and the Elders of the seven districts and a cluster of benches near the main door was for visitors and celebrities.

There was a small narrow door in the corner to the right side of the main door for the general public to enter to seek audition with the king, which they could freely do when the court was in session. There were guards near the main door and inside the hall, standing rather discretely along the side walls and behind the throne. The walls had brass lamps mounted at a height with oil-fired wicks burning brightly. Plaster peeled off the walls in places and the columns showed signs of decay. For the Elders who had seen the place in its former glory, the decline of the country, so vividly mirrored in the hall, was deeply distressing.

Today, the hall hummed with voices, some frequently raised. The leaders of Areia were particularly vociferous. No one knew why this meeting had been called and everyone was uncertain and afraid. The leaders of Areia believed that they had been called to be punished for the change in the courses of the rivers, while others were afraid that the King had called them to ask for resources to fund his next expedition, wherever it may be. The leader of Carmania was sure that they had been summoned because the King wished to announce the arrival of the long awaited Messiah. There was a long held belief that a Messiah would come to lead the Avestans out of misery into the heavenly kingdom. The Messiah would solve all problems and the country would be rich and prosperous again.

Only the group from Sistan stood quietly in a corner. Isvant, the leader of the Council of Elders, was very worried.

"I hope the King has not heard of Matriya's exploits," he whispered to no one in particular.

"The Energy generated by the ritual was powerful enough to be felt by the weakest Magus. I cannot see how the Master Magus could have missed it. He is one of the most powerful Magi in the country and he is bound to have told the King," his senior Magus, Hutana, whispered back.

"The King will not be happy, Hutana. We will have to face humiliation when all these people find out why Matriya has performed that ritual. We will be the laughing stock of the country!"

"I am not sure you can dismiss what he has done so far. If he succeeds in the next step, we will be laughing at everyone else. If he succeeds, he will be able to control the Energy and he will become the most powerful Magus in the world. Even more powerful than the Sages of Meluhha," Hutana said.

"Unfortunately, I don't have the same faith in the strength of the Energy as you do. If we are humiliated today, we will lose the support of the King and that will be the death knell for Sistan," Isvant replied. "Have you heard anything from our spies in Harappa?"

"No. I am expecting a messenger to come with some news any day now. He has been asked to come directly to Mundigak," said Hutana.

"I hope, for all our sakes, he brings some good news," Isvant said with a deep sigh, his forehead furrowed with worry.

There appeared to be heated argument among the groups from Bactria and Gava. "If your people had not resorted to unholy practices, we would not be in this state right now. The Magi from Areia would not have been able to create those Earthquakes and move our rivers. There was heresy, blasphemy and sinful acts in your district, which reduced the strength of the Energy. It was anarchy in your district which has lead to our downfall," said the leader of the council of Bactria angrily to the leader of the council of Gava, pointing an accusing finger at him.

"That is not true. Our people are pious and have always followed the laws laid down by Ahura Mazda. It must be the occult practices in your district which upset the Gods."

Just then, there was a drum roll and the trumpeters announced the arrival of the King. Everyone in the Hall moved to the side walls and bowed their heads. No one was allowed to look at the King until he was seated. The doors of the hall were thrown open by two soldiers and the King walked in wearing majestic purple robes embroidered with golden threads. On his head was a tall gold crown encrusted with semi-precious stones, and his long blonde hair curled from under the crown to his shoulders. A short beard gave him an air of distinction. But his handsome face was wrinkled with worry. The heavy velvet robes swished on the floor as he walked down the aisle towards the throne to the beat of a large drum. There was a reverent silence as he walked, accompanied by his courtiers, guards and standard bearers.

The royal Magus walked to his left and slightly behind the King and the Generals walked behind him. The portly ministers shuffled ungainly behind the generals. The captains, who were behind the ministers, dispersed sideways as the procession marched towards the throne to line up on either side of the aisle and the guards and standard bearers stood in a line behind the throne. It was an impressive sight.

Once the King reached the throne, the Generals moved to their seats on either side of the long podium at the far end of the hall. The Ministers huddled together near the steps of the podium on the right. The Royal Magus stood on the left of the throne just behind the King. The drum stopped as the King sat down and the Herald stepped up to proclaim the feats and awards of the King; but Vishtaspa raised his hand and stopped him in mid-sentence. There was pin-drop silence as the he stood up to speak.

“This is not the time for self congratulations, when the people of my country are suffering. I am sure the respected leaders of the Council of Elders of our districts are wondering why they have been summoned here. Please be seated. I see that all the Elders have brought their Magi along. It is as well, considering what has happened.”

The Elders bowed their heads again and sat down in their chairs with their Magi standing on one side and their entourage standing behind the chair in a group.

"These are extraordinary times. I will not hide the fact that the country is in deep trouble. Our Gods seem to have abandoned us. It is for the first time, since the great flood several hundreds of years ago, that we have faced such a series of natural calamities. The earthquakes have damaged our rivers and changed some of their courses and our land of nine rivers is drying up. Crops have failed repeatedly and several of our mines have collapsed during the earthquakes. Our Magi say that the Gods are displeased with us and we have to perform several Yasna's. Unfortunately, we cannot do that as the two holy lakes, Kasaoya and Frazdanu in Sistan, have nearly dried up and the fields of Haoma have been destroyed. Without the Haoma plant the Yasna cannot be performed. We face a disaster and we have to find a solution and find it fast. Now, I ask our learned Elders of the seven councils for advice."

There was complete silence for a few minutes: no one wanted to be the first to make a suggestion. Finally, the leader of Areia broke the silence. "Beg your pardon, your Highness. The Medians are going through trouble themselves with strife and internal conflict. We would be successful in any campaign against them."

"I thank the respected Elder from Areia," said the King solemnly. "The Medians may be an easy target for military action since there are no mountains to cross. But our spies tell me that the economic situation in Media is bad and the spoils will not pay for a campaign against them. We are still faced with the problem of obtaining Haoma for our Yasna. So, with deepest respect, I do not think that is a very good option."

"We have had a very good relationship with Elam. Why don't we ask King Awan of Elam to help?' the Elder from Carmania said.

The King turned towards him. Their land bordered Elam and the King suspected that they had an unhealthy friendship with the Elamites.

"King Awan is unlikely to help us since we sided with Media during their war against Elam. Before anyone makes a suggestion of taking armed action against Elam, let me remind you that Elam has become very powerful since the victory over Sumeria."

"We should be looking east towards Meluhha," the leader of the Bactrian Council said. "It is a land of plenty. Their rivers are fed by the melting snows of the Himalayas and they are rich in minerals. And, they have a bountiful supply of Haoma. Their leaders have always been friendly to Avestans in the past. The only hurdle is the mountains. If we can find ways of going over the mountains, that is our best option."

The King smiled and looked at the group from Sistan, which was very quiet.

"I think we should ask the Council from Sistan for their opinion on this. I have heard some intriguing rumours," he said. Everyone in the hall turned to look at the Sistanian group, making them squirm.

"We have had very good relations with the Meluhhans. I am sure they will help," Isvant said, without looking directly at the King.

"That is not what my spies tell me Master Isvant, with due respect to our Elders from Sistan. I am sure you will tell us that our spies were wrong," the King said.

"I don't know what they have been telling you, your Highness. But we have always been very friendly with our neighbours," said Isvant, looking distinctly nervous and starting to sweat. He could feel all eyes on him. Hutana, who was standing next to him, was trying to make himself smaller and smaller and wished he knew how to disappear.

"We are told that some Sistanian soldiers have been attacking merchants from Meluhha and stealing their merchandise. I hope they are not doing that with the Council's approval?" asked the King coldly.

"My humble apologies, your Highness. We have heard that some rogue soldiers have been up to some mischief within Meluhha. Unfortunately, we have not been able to find out who they are or apprehend them. But we are trying to find out and stop them," said Isvant, desperately trying to defend himself and his district.

"We have the greatest respect for our Elders from Sistan. But, we have also heard from Meluhha that one of your Magi has conducted a Yasna inside Meluhha causing a disturbance near Harappa. Is there any truth in that?" the King asked Isvant, but looked at Hutana.

"We are waiting for our messenger to bring some news, your Majesty. He has been asked to bring the message to the court directly," Hutana replied.

"That is the kind of activity which would upset the Meluhhans. They have powerful sages who can control anything. It is not a good idea to upset them," said the leader of Areia angrily.

The King's Magus turned to look disapprovingly at him he had spoken in the King's court without permission.

"Our sincere apologies, your Majesty. We will try and stop Matriya from doing anything more. We are trying to find him," Isvant replied.

"You should stop him. We have sent a delegation to Harappa to ask for a supply of Haoma. The Meluhhans would love a few cartloads of precious stones from our hills in Sogdiana. I am sure our Magi can get as powerful as the Meluhhan sages if we have enough Haoma to perform the great Yasna," the King said, and addressing Hutana he continued, "Please ensure that nothing untoward happens while we are negotiating with the Meluhhans."

"I certainly will do my best to stop him and bring him to his senses, your Majesty," said Hutana, only too relieved to be let off so lightly.

They had expected to be severely reprimanded and even removed from their posts for what had happened. Just as they were breathing a sigh of relief, there was a commotion outside the court and one of the guards came in, and kneeling before the King said, "My sincere apologies, your Highness, but there is a messenger outside who insists on coming into the court. He does not understand that the court cannot be disturbed today. I have taken him into custody."

"Did he say who he was?" the King asked.

"No your majesty. He is not an Avestan, he is a Meluhhan. Unfortunately, none of us can understand his language. He knew only one Avestan word, 'messenger', and he keeps repeating it."

There was a sudden hush.

"Is this your messenger Master Isvant?" the King asked.

"I suspect so, Your Majesty. We have a few Meluhhans working for us and they keep us informed of the news from Meluhha."

"I hope you are not making a mistake, Master Isvant. We have only recently mended our strained relations with the Meluhhans.We do not wish to jeopardise them. Find out what the messenger has to say and let us know."

"We will, your Majesty. If the court excuses us for a few minutes, we will find out what has happened and return quickly," Isvant said, bowed down to the King and the court and walked out rapidly with Hutana through the side door.

The bright sunshine outside momentarily blinded them. The soldier led them to the messenger, who was sitting on a bench looking flustered and angry, with two guards standing over him. As soon as he saw Hutana, he stood up and started to flail his arms about, shouting in Sanskrit, "Let me go, you oafs. I have an important message for the Magus." The soldiers immediately caught him by the arms. "Please tell these brutes to let me go," he said when they came closer. "I am hungry and thirsty. Is this the way you treat guests in your country?"

The soldier with Isvant signalled to the two guards to release him and Hutana said in heavily accented Sanskrit, "Calm down. The guards did not understand your language. You were trying to enter the King's court without permission and they rightly stopped you." He asked the soldier to bring some refreshments. Hutana introduced

Isvant to the messenger while they waited. Once he was fed and watered with honey roasted bread and fresh grape juice, he soon calmed down.

"Now. Tell us what you have found out," Isvant said.

"Your Magus has been very active. He has found several accomplices in Saraswata and some people from Harappa who are willing to help him. He has completed the first stage of the great Yasna, which caused much disturbance in the Energy, or Prana as we call it in Harappa. A messenger was sent to Sindhu for help. The Magus sent spies and soldiers to try to intercept him, but without success. He had planned the next stage of the great Yasna, the Gomedha. I left Harappa over two weeks ago, so I guess he has already completed it."

Both Isvant and Hutana were speechless. They could hardly believe what the messenger was saying. They had dismissed the rumours about the Magus's activities as mere talk without substance and it was shocking to find that they were all true. It was unbelievable that the Magus had completed the Gomedha. The messenger went off to the inn where he would put up for the night before returning to Harappa and the two of them walked back in silence, immersed in deep thought. Suddenly, Isvant pulled Hutana into a dark alcove in the outer wall of the court.

"Now. Tell me. You are a Magus and you should have felt the vibrations if the Gomedha had been performed?" Isvant hissed.

"I have not felt any change in the Energy, Master Isvant. I have been told that the force generated by the Great Yasna is widespread and even the weakest of Magi would have felt it. Either he has not done it yet or he has not been able to complete it," he replied.

"Either way, it does not look good for us at the Royal Court. What are we going to tell the King and the Court?"

"Can you ask for a private audience with the King and explain things to him?" Hutana asked.

"That will agitate all the others. We are in deep enough trouble with them as it is. All of them think that we are the cause of the disasters in this country. No, we will have to tell the truth and hope to be pardoned by the King and the Court. You never know, we might even win some sympathy from them," Isvant said, optimistically. "We better go back before they send out the guards."

They hurried back in through the side door and bowed to the King and the Court.

"Yes, Master Isvant. What's the news?" the King asked.

"I apologise sincerely on behalf of the people of Sistan and myself, both to the King and to the Court. It is as your Highness has heard. The Magus has completed the first stage of the Great Yasna, which produced changes in the Energy around Harappa. We are fairly certain that he has not completed the final stage, your Highness. We will make every effort to stop him from performing the final stage of the Great Yasna."

Furious whispering broke out among the audience. The King raised his hand.

"I am sure the whole congregation is interested in the news that the respected elders of Sistan have brought," he said. "Let us hear what Master Isvant has to say."

There was immediate silence and everyone stared as the royal Magus said something in his ear.

"My learned friend, the royal Magus, tells me that the final stage should have been performed two weeks after the first stage to be effective. He also tells me that he, like all the other Magi in the kingdom, would have felt the changes in the Energy if the final Yasna had been performed. There have been no such reports so far. That leads us to the conclusion that the final stage has been prevented or interrupted by the Meluhhans. Unfortunately, this will have a bad effect on our negotiations with them. It is unlikely that the Meluhhans will now wish to exchange Haoma for our precious stones. We will have to think of other ways of obtaining Haoma for our Yasna."

"The Sistan council should be punished for what has happened and we should make sure that the Meluhhans are made aware of this. Only then will they be convinced there is no official Avestan hand in this Yasna. I have always said that Sistans are not true Avestans. I propose that the Sistan council be disbanded and the King appoint a new Council," said the leader of Areia.

"I suppose Areians will then rule Sistan," Isvant said angrily, outraged at the suggestion that he was not a true Avestan. "Let me tell you that we are more loyal to Ariana than Areains. Our Magi and priests perform the Yasnas and all the Yashts are recited every day in our temples."

The King stood up angrily and thumped his staff hard on the floor. The sound of the brass end of the oak staff hitting the granite floor was like a thunderbolt and everyone was instantly silenced.

"I would remind you that you are still in the King's court, not in a market place. This is not the time for dissent and for blaming each other. The only way forward is to unite and think of an alternate strategy. I suggest we wait for our negotiator to return before making any more plans. I will send word to him regarding the developments and we will request the Meluhhans to consider our situation before deciding on any course of action. I have met Sage Shunahotra as well as the Sage Vishwamitra; they are reasonable people."

The assembly was discharged with the promise that the next assembly would be convened as soon as the negotiator returned.

Everyone stood with their heads bowed for the King and his entourage to depart through the main doors. As soon as the main doors were closed behind him, there was a mad rush towards the side doors to get out. There were likely to be spies in the hall and no one wanted to make any remark that would get them into trouble.

Isvant and Hutana walked briskly and quietly on the way out of the King's court and towards the inn they were staying in.

"I think we should visit the temple before we return to the inn," Isvant said suddenly. Hutana was surprised, since Isvant never visited the temple in the evening. But, no one said anything and they followed him towards the temple of Mundigak. Before they reached the temple, Isvant took a detour into the woodland around the temple. He walked rapidly and they were soon deep into the woods. He stopped behind a large rock outcrop and turned round.

"I suspect that we will be punished despite what the King said in court. So, I don't think it is safe to go back to the inn. Hutana, send two of our men to get our horses from there and if we start to walk now, we should be outside the city before nightfall. I want your men to take the horses towards the western road and work their way around the city to meet us outside. They must be careful not to be recognised or caught. Ask them to remove all the insignia and markings of our district from the horses. The innkeeper is from Sistan and he will help them. We will meet up on the eastern banks of the river Khuba (River Kabul) near the base of the hill where the river curves around."

Hutana despatched two of his most able men with instructions to be careful and to avoid any soldiers and the rest of the party walked along the overgrown path in the rocky landscape interspersed with small, square mud houses and reached the outskirts of the city before sunset. They waited in the shadow of a derelict house - there were several in the district - till it was dark enough for them to go across the clear fields to reach their rendezvous point.

Their men arrived there with the horses well past midnight by which time both Isvant and Hutana had nearly lost hope of seeing them and had begun to think of walking all the way back to Sistan, which would have taken at least three weeks.

Isvant's suspicion had proved to be right. The King's soldiers were waiting for them at the inn. The innkeeper, realising that something was wrong, had moved the horses to a safe place and when Hutana's men came to the inn, he had packed some food for them to take as well. The men had to wait until dark and then dodge all the patrols to get out of the city.

Once they had the horses, the Sistanis rushed homewards. It was a very tired group that trotted into Sistan after several days of almost non-stop riding.

❖

Chapter 8

THE GREAT YAJNA

Everything has worked out perfectly according to my plans, the Magus thought with satisfaction. He wanted to start the proceedings exactly at moonrise. His 'subjects' were assembled in the ravine. They had all followed his instructions bathed in the pool and covered themselves in the holy ash Maricha had brought from Harappa. The ash was from the goat sacrifice two weeks ago. Maricha had distributed the goat's meat among his friends and burnt the skin and the bones on the altar, as instructed by the Magus, then carefully collected the ashes from the altar and stored them in a large brass Urn covered with a hemp cloth dipped in turmeric and sealed with tar. It had been brought to the ravine with utmost care, Maricha and his friends having been warned of dire consequences if the container was opened or even a grain of the ash spilled.

The twins had brought the sacred bull into the ravine the night before and it was tied to a post at the back of the altars. It had been fed with sweets and a whole pot of somaras and it now sat chewing cud and dozing. It had a garland of flowers around its neck, its horns were painted red and their tips covered with bronze caps. A purple and gold cloth with brocade tassels was draped on its back and the hump was painted yellow ochre and red. The brass bells round its neck and anklets on the all four legs jingled whenever it moved. Eight pointed stars were painted on each side of its neck and shanks. The bull looked grand and quite peaceful.

The ravine was guarded by a platoon of soldiers of the Avestan elite forces. The Magus had promised the Captain the post of a general in the Harappan army when he took over the city and had convinced him that the Yajna was being performed on the orders of the Elders of the Great Council of Ariana and had the personal blessing of King Vishtaspa himself. The captain had express instructions from his general, Ardeshir anyway and he knew better than to cross the general.

The Captain had deployed the black clad soldiers along the rim of the ravine at strategic points well hidden from the outside, but with a good view of the ravine and the approaches to it from all directions. The Captain himself took up a position near the northern mouth, considered the most vulnerable to attack.The ravine was narrower there and the walls were low so that horses could easily gallop down if ridden by expert riders.

"Are your arrangements in place, Captain?" the Magus asked.

"I did not realise how large and complex this place is or I would have brought twenty more soldiers. But what kind of attack are you expecting?" the Captain asked. "It is not a place for large armies."

"The Meluhhans don't have a large army in this area. I have spies in their camp who tell me that they don't know about this place or about the yajna tonight. But, one must always assume that the enemy is well prepared. That way, one can be a step ahead of them," the Magus replied.

"Don't worry, sir. We have the place well surrounded and I have spotters on the neighbouring hills as well, who will signal to us if there is any unusual activity," said the Captain confidently.

"May God Mithra protect you and your men."

A few days ago, the Magus had collected two large brass vessels full of water from a pool that connected to the Saraswathi through an underground channel in the Shivalik hills in the north. To his surprise, only a couple of Gandhari soldiers casually guarded the pool and he and his friends simply walked into it at night and collected the water in large leather pouches and poured it into two large brass vessels on their boat. The Magus had marvelled at the mighty Saraswathi on the journey up north into the foothills looking for the sacred pool fed by the waters of the mighty river. The directions given by 'Pakshar' was sketchy, but enough to find with his enhanced powers.

He had been warned of the Gandhari's who guarded the river and the sacred pool. They had parked the boat on the eastern bank of the river in one of the numerous caved along the valley and trekked a short distance to the sacred pool. They were well on their way down the Saraswathi by daybreak. Something about the ease with which all this had been achieved bothered the Magus, but he dismissed the thought. Everything was going smoothly and easily because the Gods want me to succeed, he kept reminding himself.

The water from the Saraswathi, along with all the other ingredients, was in the cave at the northern end of the ravine and after talking to the captain, the Magus quietly went in and performed the sacred Honover (a ritual performed by avestans similar to saying "Om" in Sanskrit) which had to be done secretly before the Yajna.

He remembered his Magus guru's words at his Gurukul, "The pure, the holy, the prompt Honover, I tell you plainly. It existed before the sky, before the sea, before the earth, before the animals, before the trees, before fire, son of Ormuzd, before the pure man, before the Deous, before the whole world; it existed before there was any substance. It should be explained, in its essence, to the magi alone. The common people cannot even know of the existence of this venerated name under penalty of death or madness."

Before anyone noticed his absence, he was out of the cave again and strode towards the altars. Right in the middle of the formation of altars was an eight pointed star painted with yellow ochre. Three more stars were drawn within the larger one, with apices abutting the sides of the large star. In the centre of the drawing was a large red dot, which was slightly raised with dried cow dung cakes. A collection of eight mud pots was placed on top of this. Each mud pot had a circle of five palm leaves at its mouth with a coconut placed in the centre. Stuck to the tip of each coconut was a bunch of incense sticks already lit.

Beside each altar was a container of ghee and small brass and mud pots of the powders and potions that he had made according to the Yogi's instructions. Near the large altar at the apex was also a leather pouch containing a paste. Small brass bowls filled with somaras were placed to the left of the four small altars, while the large vessel was kept at the back, to be brought to the main altar when needed.

That morning had been spent in preparing the somaras. The Soma extract was ground some more and mixed with some of the Saraswathi water. The rest of the water was then poured into a large brass cauldron placed over a fire. When the Magus poured the powder extract into the cauldron, an acrid white smoke arose from it and spread through the ravine. They stirred the cauldron for nearly an hour, eyes watering and the smoke clogging up their chests making them cough and splutter.

Once the cauldron was off the fire, the smoke settled to a faint purple haze over its mouth and the liquid looked greenish with a purple tinge. This somaras was then filtered into two large brass vessels using scraped and thinned sheepskin as a filter as per the instructions given by 'Pakshar' and the filtered juice was mixed with the correct portion of fresh cow's milk. The intoxicating smell of the somaras mixed with the fragrance of the incense sticks filled the whole ravine.

Nearly a hundred people had arrived to witness and participate in the Yajna. They were made to stand in three rows on either side of the altars with the apex of the arrow formation open and the twins distributed small mud pots of somaras to each one. The fumes from the somaras containers, the incense and the drink had had their effect and some of them were already beginning to sway on their feet. Two drummers from Saraswata stood at two opposite corners waiting for the Magus's signal.

The entire ravine was eerily quiet. Even the twittering of birds, the chirping of crickets and the croaking of the frogs by the pool had stopped. Only a lone eagle hovered over the ravine and unnerved the Magus a little. The soldiers tried to shoot it down and chase it away with some arrows, but it would not go away. The Magus was not sure why it was there but there was no time to worry about it now.

He looked up at the sky and saw the moon lining up with the star, Arundhati (star Alcor), and Saturn aligning with Mars. I needed one of them to be aligned, but I have two alignments, the Gods are truly with me, he thought with a surge of joy. Damn that eagle casting its shadow over the moon, he thought, but then pushed it out of his mind and began the ritual.

The five of them took their places at the altars and the Magus said, "*Om Shanno Mithrah Shanno Varunah, Shanno Bhavataryama*. May God Mithra help us succeed."

He then looked up at the people standing before him, lifted his arms into the air and said, "*Asmatra Vijayee Bhavatu*. Friends, this is the day we have all been waiting for. God Mithra will help us and we will rule this land in a just and honourable manner. You will all be rich beyond your wildest dreams. Join me today and pray and make this sacrifice successful."

There was a loud chorus of "Hail great Magus, hail our saviour" with arms raised, palms forwards.

He took a deep breath and closed his eyes.

"This is it. This is what I have been waiting for, all my life. I cannot fail now. God Mithra, please don't fail me," he said softly to himself, as a sudden panic filled his heart.

He took another deep breath and scanned the ravine through his inner eye. Unfortunately, the deep red stone walls contained an element that did not let him see beyond it. It meant that the 'divine vision' of the Meluhhan sages would be useless as well, he thought with relief. The lone eagle in the sky still troubled him.

He picked up the flint stones and set the altar alight, as did the others and started reciting hymns to the God of Fire and pouring ghee into the fire. The prayer went on for a while and when they finished they sprinkled a white powder from one of the containers on the fire. There was loud bang and five huge balls of bright red fire went up in the air. The audience gasped and the drummers began with a roll and fell into a slow beat.

The Magis then poured the contents of one of the brass pots onto the fire and produced a thick, yellow, sweet smelling smoke, which appeared to calm the audience. They stopped swaying and Maricha signalled to them to sit down. A liquid was poured onto the fire, which sizzled and lit up the whole ravine.

The Magus raised his hands and started the chant, "*Hram, hreem, hom, hum*."

The congregation picked it up and chanted to the beat of the drums. As the Magus continued with his hymns praising one God after another, the chanting became louder and louder. The drummers increased the speed ever so slightly at the start of every new hymn. All the five altars were now blazing and cast flickering shadows on the steep walls. Moonlight filtered through the smoke and the ravine was bathed in its eerie glow. The congregation started to sway again. As the moon came up to the zenith, the Magus was ready for the crucial part of the yajna, the soma sacrifice.

Maricha and two others had just lifted the vessel filled with somaras when they heard a swishing noise and looked up to see the eagle, which had been hovering high over the ravine, swooping down on them. They panicked and dropped the vessel near the altar. Luckily, the somaras did not spill. The Magus was deep in his hymns and did not notice. He took a large ladle filled with somaras from the vessel and was about to pour it over the fire chanting the soma sacrifice hymn when three arrows shot into the altar before him, there was a huge explosion and all hell broke loose.

Arrows flew all over the place and exploded over all the altars. Embers from the altars flew out and fell among the people before the fires went out. The congregation panicked and ran to the northern end of the ravine where they had kept their carts and horses. An arrow hit the vessel containing the Somrasa and tipped it over spilling it all over the ground. The Magus stared in disbelief as it flowed down the platform along with his ambitions of power and glory.

He looked around to see where the arrows were coming from and saw his friends all standing still as if mesmerised by what was happening. Only Hugav was running towards the southern end. He wondered why he was running. Then he heard the thunder of horses bearing down on the congregation from the southern end of the ravine.

"Hugav," he shouted, "Don't go there. Come back, come back." But Hugav did not hear him and the next moment an arrow pierced his chest and he fell to the ground.

'Ankasa, Katav, Kurav. Come to me now,' he shouted, as he picked up his leather pouch. They ran to him and he took the powder from the pouch and threw it up in the air over their heads. There was an explosion and a thick cloud of black smoke. Maricha, who was running towards them, stopped suddenly in his tracks. The four had disappeared into the black smoke.

Harappan soldiers rushed up to Maricha, their bows and arrows at the ready, pointed at his chest. The people who were running towards the northern end were confronted by a group of Harappan soldiers and turned around and started to run towards the south, only to be stopped by more soldiers. Some of them tried to climb out of the ravine, clawing their way up the red rocks. As Maricha watched, they all came tumbling down. One of them had nearly made it to the top when his hand slipped and he fell backwards all the way down to the valley floor with a thump.

When Master Ashwin called me to his room, I was a bit nervous. I had not had a proper debriefing since my return from Sindhu and I was afraid that either I had done something wrong or I had forgotten to do something in Sindhu.

"Come in, Upaas. Have you recovered from the trip yet? You do look refreshed."

"Yes, Master. I am fine. The trip was easy, though there was some excitement en route. Our soldiers helped me on my way back."

Master Ashwin smiled at me and said, "Oh yes. I heard about your exploits and I am very proud of you. All that training and time spent in the army school practicing your archery paid off. And now, you may have a chance to use your skills again soon."

"Thank you, Master. I was quite pleased at the way I could handle that situation. And I am always keen to try out my martial skills. It is a change from our daily routine," I said. It must be something to do with the message I had brought back from Sage Vishwamitra, I thought to myself.

"Yes. You are right. It is the message that you brought back from Sindhu." I was shocked at how easily and quickly he could read my thoughts. I had still not mastered the art of hiding them.

"We have identified the culprits who interfered with the Prana and they are getting ready for the next stage of the yajna. Sage Shunahotra says it will be a Gomedha, because these people want supernatural powers to control nature. You know what that means. It will mean the end of our way of life and our country, if they succeed. We have identified where the Yajna is going to be held and when. They have managed to steal some Soma extract from our pharmacy for the Yajna, which means they have had help from one or more individuals amongst us, but we have not been able to identify this person or persons.

A rogue Avestan Magus is leading this Yajna. He may have more Magi helping him. He has thrown such a powerful shield around the traitor that even Shunahotra has not been able to penetrate it. Master Adhvadipa himself is leading a contingent to capture the culprits and stop the Yajna. We have to accompany them with medical aid."

"I am ready, Master. Tell me what you want me to do."

"The Magus has magical powers, so the injuries may not be just physical. There are likely to be chemical injuries, poisoning, as well as burns. So we will need antidotes and burns dressings. We will take two more physicians with us and a cart to carry the supplies. And remember, no one else must know about this. The others will be told that we are going on an exercise with the soldiers and the soldiers have been told the same story."

"When do we have to leave, Master?"

"The Yajna is scheduled for three days later and we will leave in two days. It does not give you much time to prepare the medical supplies. Get Ubhaya to help you."

"Who do you think are the traitors? I find it hard to believe that one of our own can betray us."

"It has to be someone with access to the pharmacy. It could be someone working with us or it could even be someone from the Council of Elders."

"Why would they betray their own people, Master?"

"There can be lots of reasons: they may not be content with their lot; they may have been offered a bribe or there may even be blackmail," Master replied, sadly. "But, no doubt we will find him or them. You better get going, Upaas. You do understand that your father knows about this, but you cannot discuss it with him at home."

"Please don't worry, Master, I won't."

I took the list and left straight for the pharmacy and sent word to Ubhaya asking him to come and help. We spent the whole night getting everything ready and loaded the cart the next day. Ubhaya was unusually curious at the start but had given up questioning after a while.

The next evening, we went to the barracks to join the soldiers who were going on the 'exercise'. The guards of the Temple had been chosen for the job as they were trained for secret missions. We left the city that evening through the northern gate, going towards the mountains. Once we were well out of the city, the General Adhvadipa raised his hand and stopped the column.

"We are going to take a detour here through the forest," he said and pointed to the small path that lead off on the right into the forest.

Quite a few eyebrows were raised at this, but no one dared question him. It soon became apparent to me that we had completely changed direction from going up north to actually going down southeast. By daybreak we had travelled all the way around Harappa and were moving parallel to the road to Saraswata. The convoy stopped around lunchtime for a well-deserved break and at dusk we set off again, but this time we headed directly east through the jungle through very difficult terrain. Within an hour, we stopped again.

The General Adhvadipa came to us and said, "Master Ashwin, this is where we part company. We will scout ahead."

He turned abruptly and galloped off followed by his soldiers.

Master Ashwin said, "Let us keep going now."

It was quite dark despite a full moon and a full starlit sky. That was the first time I saw the lone eagle silhouetted against the bright full moon. The night was deathly quiet and some instinct had made me look up at the sky.

"Sage Shunahotra's eyes," said Master Ashwin quietly under his breath. I looked at him in surprise, but he said no more.

It was not long before we saw the first casualty, an Avestan soldier dressed in black and fully armed. He had been shot between the eyes and had obviously died instantly. Soon we stumbled upon several more dead Avestan soldiers. They had all been killed either with a neck or head wound. Whoever had killed them had made sure that they could not utter a sound before they died. Everyone in our group now knew that this was no 'exercise'; this was a battle of a kind they had never seen before a secret war where the enemies didn't see each other. I saw a cloud of smoke rising above the jungle in the distance. An easterly breeze had picked the smell of incense and something else I could not identify. We saw a couple of flashes of fire coming out of the depth in the distance. Just as we reached the rim of the ravine, I heard the first of several explosions. We all wanted to run ahead and see if we could help anyone, but our Master held us back.

"Only fools rush into the unknown. You don't know what to expect on the battlefield. If there were an emergency, Master Adhvadipa would have sent word for us. Be patient and follow the tracks."

It was all over by the time we reached the lip of the ravine at the northern end. Nearly a hundred people had been rounded up and brought to the platform with the altars. The full extent of the battle became apparent as we looked over the rim. There was thick pungent and acrid smoke billowing out of the floor near the western wall in the middle. It made our eyes water. There were a few bodies on the floor of the ravine. We ran down to see if we could help. The man in the middle was beyond help as he had been shot right through the heart. The body near the wall was lying with its head at an awkward angle, his neck broken.

None of our soldiers had any significant injuries though some of them were coughing and spluttering because of the smoke. I had brought a cream just for this problem and one of our helpers started a fire and boiled some water. I added the cream into the boiling water and had the soldiers inhale the medicated steam. Ubhaya and one of the other helpers were doing the same. There was only one physical injury – a soldier who had lost his footing while coming down the ravine and fallen down badly breaking his arm.

The sun was coming up over the eastern rim of the ravine by the time we finished tending to all the soldiers and the people of Harappa who had come to take part in the Yajna. Master Ashwin and I went to the stream and washed ourselves and sat under a tree for a bit of rest. I looked round at the ravine for the first time. It was beautiful and overwhelming. The walls were steep and the size of the rocks was immense. The floor of the ravine was flat and sandy, strewn with several large boulders of similar colour. I had never seen stones of that colour before.

"They are unusual not only for their colour, but also for their content," Master Aswin explained to me. "There is an element which makes the rocks very strong and also blocks magical powers. These walls protected the Magus and his people, because we could not penetrate their minds to find out what was happening once they entered the ravine. That is why Sage Shunahotra had to send his 'eye' to watch over the ravine."

"The Yajna looks very elaborate and complex," I said. "The five altars are set in an unusual pattern and what do the drawings of the stars and the pots and coconuts signify?"

"The Magus was mixing Tantric with Avestan scriptures. If he had succeeded in completing the Yajna, he would have possessed more powers than even the great sage Shunahotra. God knows what he would have done then. We stopped him just in time."

"And we did it without much loss of life," the General Adhvadipa, who had joined us, added with a note of satisfaction. "It is a pity so many of the Avestan soldiers had to be killed."

Just then, some of our soldiers, who had gone looking for the Magus, came back.

"Hail, General. There is no sign of the Magus or his collaborators. We found this bag and several charms on the floor near the southern end of the ravine. Judging from the amount of horse dung at the site, it looks like they had tied five horses to a tree there for a while. The hoof prints suggest that they must have left in a hurry. Do you want us to pursue them, General?"

"There is no point now. They have had a good start. The way he stage managed his disappearance suggests that he may have more tricks up his sleeve to avoid capture," the General replied. "I will arrange for the wounded to be taken back to the hospital if you wish," he said, turning to my Master.

"That would be extremely helpful. We can treat them better in hospital"

Just then, the second group of soldiers, who had turned up at the southern end of the ravine, joined us with their Captain.

"Our salutations to the General. We have rounded up ninety-five of the collaborators. Most of them appear to be peasants and workmen and they are very frightened. I am afraid we may not get much information from them. There is one Harappan called Maricha, who is a supervisor in the works gang in Harappa. He may be able to give us some useful information," the Captain said.

"Thank you, Captain. You and your platoon did a wonderful job. We will question the prisoners once we get to Harappa. Most of them must be misguided people unlikely to be involved in any conspiracy. Did you have any problem travelling from Saraswata?"

"No sir. We did not have any trouble at all. If the General will excuse us, we will set off for Saraswata tonight."

The Captain and his platoon left with their horses through the southern end of the ravine. It would be a three-day march to Saraswata.

"I think we should make a move as well. We have a lot to do once we get back to the hospital," said Master Ashwin, getting up.

"Thank you, Master Ashwin. I am grateful to you and your team for the wonderful job done today. How many wounded are there?" the General asked.

The master turned to me.

"There are five of our soldiers with chemical inhalation and there are twenty one of the congregation with inhalation and burn injuries, sir. Three of the burns are quite serious and we have to get them to the hospital as quickly as possible," I said.

"How many casualties altogether?" the General asked.

"There are twelve dead. Ten Avestan soldiers, including their Captain, one Avestan dressed as a Magus and one Harappan who fell off the wall of the ravine," I replied.

"That is a pity. We might have got some information from the Captain. It is unlikely that we will get any information from the soldiers," the General said.

We bid goodbye to the General and left the way we came, on our horses. It took us less than half a day to get back to Harappa.

❖

Chapter 9

THE BEAUTIFUL LAKE

It was organised chaos at the hospital. The convoy had returned in the early hours of that morning. Of the three seriously wounded, one had died on the journey and the other two were critical. Master Ashwin had worked all morning to stabilise them. We breathed a sigh of relief when they regained consciousness that afternoon, though they were still struggling to breathe and we could only feed them liquids through bamboo straws. Obviously they were in no condition to give us any information about the yajna. Our scientists had collected samples from the altars and the pouch the soldiers had found at the end of the ravine and were trying to analyse them.

"I have never seen such injuries and I cannot identify what has caused them. It must be something the Magus used during the yajna that has caused the burn injuries to their lungs," said Master Ashwin.

"I wonder if the Elamite who helped us during the earthquake knows something about this. They do have Magi in Elam and he appeared to have some medical knowledge," I suggested.

"Yes, you are right, Upaas. Why don't you go to the travellers' camp as soon as you have finished here and talk to the Elamite?"

My heart immediately turned a cartwheel and my eyes lit up. Master smiled.

"The girl is from a good family, Upaas, and I am sure your parents will approve," he said. I blushed furiously. I must learn how to mask my thoughts; I can't have him reading every thought I have not about Lopa, at any rate, I thought.

"I am sorry, Upaas," Master laughed. "It is difficult not to read your thoughts. It is an old habit which helps diagnose and treat patients. I hope you will learn the art before long; it will help in your profession. Now go and see your girl in the camp, but don't forget to talk to the Elamite."

I went home to wash up and change into fresh clothes before going to the travellers' camp. Nivya was surprised to see me home in the afternoon.

"What are you doing here at this time, Upaas?" she asked.

"I have to go to the Traveller's camp to speak with Shushun, the Elamite."

"And you have to dress up to visit a merchant?"

"Don't you have something to do all afternoon? And it is good to be clean and fresh when one visits anybody," I replied.

"Come on then. What is her name and where is she from?" she asked with a twinkle in her eyes.

"Who? What? I don't know anything about any girl."

"It is not just your Master who can read your mind," she said pertly, and I blushed.

"There you are. I was right. Now tell me everything about her," Nivya laughed.

I sat her down on the chair and went down on my knees holding her hands.

"She is Lopa, daughter of Master Avisthu from the city of Saraswatha. I met her when I stopped at the camp on the way back from the forest a few weeks ago. She is beautiful and she speaks many languages. Her father teaches languages," I said.

"I am glad you have found someone you like, Upaas. Does she love you as well?"

"I don't know yet. She seems happy to meet me."

"You should ask her. You know the travellers won't be here forever and Saraswatha is at least a week away from here."

"I know. I only have a couple of weeks before she goes. Wish me luck."

"I will do better than that. I will pray to Lord Indra to grant you your wishes."

I left home with a song on my lips and a little tension in my heart. At the western gate I told the Captain that I might be late in the evening and would need his permission to enter the gates.

"That is fine, Master Upaas. Remember this code and tap on the panel for the guards to open the door for you," and he whispered the code in my ears and showed me the wooden panel by the side of the door.

The site to house the travellers within the city walls was not yet ready and they still camped outside the walls, protected round the clock by guards. I went to the Elamite's wagon first and knocked on the door. It was an imposing wagon pulled by six bullocks. It had a separate accommodation section at the front and a cargo section at the back and was decorated on the outside with brass finials and carvings depicting the Elamite God, Varuna. There was a gold flag with red Elamite markings flying on a mast in the front.

Shushun himself opened the door.

"What a nice surprise, Master Upaashantha! Come into my humble abode, my friend. Please make yourself comfortable."

He drew a folding chair from under his bed and unfolded it for me. I had never seen such a thing before.

"Thank you and namaste, Shushun. Please call me Upaas. It is very nice to see you too," I said as I sat on the chair, which had a citrus smell.

"It is made of cedar wood which is native to our country," he said, when he saw me examining the chair. "Our carpenters are skilled in making furniture. You should visit our country. There is a lot you can learn from our physicians and you can see our beautiful country."

"I would love to visit your country and learn from your physicians. In fact, I have come to you today to ask for your help. We were involved in a small skirmish with a Magus from Ariana and I have some patients with unusual chemical injuries. Even Master Ashwin has been unable to identify the chemical that caused them. I have heard that there are Magi in Elam, so I wondered if you would know anything about their potions and powders?" I asked.

"Yes. I have heard about your skirmish. Unfortunately, we do have Magi in our country. I say 'unfortunately' because though the Magi traditionally used their powers to help people and nature, many have started using them for their own selfish purposes. They even use occult and tantric arts. I have some knowledge of their potions and have seen some of the injuries caused by them. I will certainly help you," he said earnestly.

"I am so grateful, Shushun. I will come and pick you up on the way to the hospital in the morning."

"Can I offer you some beverage or some sweets from Elam?"

"Thank you, no. I have to meet someone else in the camp and it is getting late."

"I understand. May be next time..." he said with a smile.

I walked quickly to the other side of the camp where Lopa's wagon was parked and knocked briskly on the door. It was a mid sized wagon pulled by four bullocks. It had only one large section for both accommodation and cargo. It was made of solid oak and unusual carvings on the walls that I did not understand. Master Avisthu opened the door.

"Namaste, Master Avisthu. I am Upaas, son of Master Kapila."

"Namaste, Upaashantha. I know who you are, son. Lopa talks about you all the time and now I finally get to meet you. Lopa has gone to the well to draw water. Come, we will just sit outside here; she won't be long."

"Thank you very much, sir. I had come to see Shushun, the Elamite, and thought I would drop by and say hello to Lopa."

"Please sit down. Will you have something to drink?" he asked.

"No. Thank you, sir."

"Tell me, Upaas, what are you doing now and what are your plans for the future?"

"I am a trainee physician, sir, under Master Ashwin. I will be ready to start my own practice in less than a year from now. I spent four years learning medicine at Sindhu. I hope to set up my own practice in Harappa," I replied.

"That is good. I met your father when I visited your Great Hall. He is a good man, and a man of distinction."

"Thank you, sir. What are the figures carved on the walls of the cart? I have never seen anything like that before."

"Those reliefs are Egyptian Hieroglyphs and they are the names of all my family members. One day I will describe them to you."

We sat there talking about Harappa and how it had developed and how it needed a teacher of languages now.

"I see that you two have met. What are you talking about?" said a sweet voice and my heart started hammering as I turned to look at Lopa standing at the corner of the wagon.

"Lopa, your father has kindly agreed to teach me the languages of our neighbours," I said with a smile.

She smiled back and her father stood up saying, "I will leave you youngsters alone. Lopa, give him some of your delicious buttermilk."

Lopa nodded and turned back to me. "I am really happy to see you again. I will get you some butter milk in a minute."

She disappeared into the wagon only to reappear a couple of minutes later with two mud pots. Her father was right and it was the most delicious buttermilk I had ever tasted in my life.

"Shall we go for a walk? I can show you my favourite place where I go for wood. The sunsets there are fabulous," I asked.

We set off together up the hill.

"I was afraid that you might have left Harappa. I have been busy the last couple of weeks and could not come here," I said as we walked towards the hill. I told her about the trip to Sindhu and the skirmish with the Magus and his cronies. She was amazed and shocked at my adventures. She told me that she had two sisters and a brother, all younger than her. She always accompanied her father on his trips and had visited several cities and countries with him. However, this would probably be her last trip with him since her younger brother was now old enough to accompany him in the future.

All too soon we reached the top of the hill and sat on the banks of the stream with our feet in the cool water. I held her hand and when she didn't pull it away, I caressed her foot with mine in the flowing water, half afraid that she would move away. But she didn't and we watched the spectacular show of light and colour that the setting sun displayed for us in a warm and close silence.

"Now I know why you keep coming back to this place," she said when the sun had turned a mellow orange and slipped out of sight behind the hills. "But we better go back. It will soon be dark."

I sighed and got up reluctantly. I wanted to be with her forever, listening to her voice, looking at her face, felling her warmth close by my side. Well, it was not to be, not yet. We soon reached the bottom of the hill and the camp. The campfire had already been lit and we heard the music before we saw the dancers and the musicians. We stopped under some trees in the dark and sat watching the dances and letting the music flow over us. I turned to Lopa and held both her hands close to my heart, looked into her beautiful black eyes and said, " I love you, Lopa. I cannot think of anything but you."

"I love you too, Upaas. I have done so ever since I first met you that day when you were watching the Dasyu dance," she said and I gathered her in my arms and kissed her. "You must come and speak to father before we leave in a few weeks," she said, when we finally moved apart. "Yes, of course," I said, as I walked with her to her wagon. "I will come and speak to your father very soon. I want you to come home and meet my sister and mother. My sister will love you." I kissed her goodbye and reluctantly walked back towards the city.

Nivya opened the door and immediately wanted to know everything that had happened. "Come on tell me what happened. Did you see her? Did you speak to her? What did she say? When are you bringing her home?"

"Calm down, Nivya. One question at a time. Yes, I did speak to her and she turned me down," I said.

"What? Why did she turn you down? You must have said something stupid. You men just don't know what to say! I will go and speak to her," she said.

I started laughing. "No, no, you don't have to speak to her. I will bring her home soon to meet you. My only worry is that after she meets you, she may not want to speak to me again!"

"Oh, stop teasing me! I can't wait to meet her," Nivya exclaimed.

"Don't you want to know about my meeting with Shushun?"

"Oh yes, how did that go?"

"He has agreed to help us. And he has invited me to visit Elam! I am really excited at the prospect. The Elamites have knowledge of both Sumerian and Egyptian medicine. I will be able to learn from Elamite physicians and might even have a chance to visit Sumer, as it is quite close to Elam. I will have to ask the Father and my Master for permission. Anyway, I have lots of things to do tomorrow and I better go to sleep now," I said.

Next morning, I was at Shushun's wagon at the crack of dawn with two horses, one of them the Elamite horse.

"Namaste, Upaas" he said in his best Sanskrit. "I see that you have acquired an Elamite horse?"

"Namaste Shushun," I said and went on to explain the circumstances under which the horse came into my possession.

"Do you know that most of the Avestan cavalry consists of Elamite horses? That is how much the Avestans love our horses. However, that also means that they can fall into the wrong hands."

"I know a lot of Avestans and generally they are very nice people. But, their country is going through difficult times because of drought and other disasters," I replied. "Shall we go to the hospital now?"

"Yes. Certainly. I will see if I can be of help. Do remember that I am not a practicing physician," Shushun said. He mounted the yet unnamed Elamite horse with the ease of one who had spent a lot of time on horseback.

"What is he called?" he asked.

"He still does not have a name. The soldiers wanted to give him an Avestan name, but could not think of any."

"In that case, we shall call him Sampa, which means 'the wind' in Avestan, if that is all right with you. He moves like the wind," Shushun said.

"That sounds nice. He does ride well and is well behaved. I see you have a good knowledge of Avestan."

"I have travelled to many countries since I left home two years ago and I spent nearly six months in Ariana. I picked up their language while I was there. It is similar to Sanskrit. I noticed a lot of unrest among the Avestan population what with the drought and other disasters. In fact, I missed a very large earthquake in Haozdar by just a few days. I believe it left thousands of people dead and destroyed most of the city."

When we reached the hospital, Shveti, a young assistant, was already there checking up on the two patients who were still serious.

She was extremely conscientious and took her job seriously, and I had more faith in her than in the far more senior Ubhaya.

"Namaste, Upaas. Both these patients are stable, but there is no progress. They are still struggling to breathe. If we don't find a cure soon, I am afraid we will lose them," she said.

"Shveti, this is Shushun from Elam. He is a friend of mine and he has seen injuries caused by Magi in his country. He has come to help us."

She looked at Shushun suspiciously and said, "Welcome to Harappa, Shushun. Any help in saving these men would be appreciated."

"I will do my best. I must emphasise that I am not a physician, but I have seen how our physicians treated our soldiers after similar attacks. May I examine the patients please?" he asked. Shushun looked closely at the patients and said to the nurse, "Can you lift the sheets off, please?" When the nurse lifted the sheets off the patient, he saw the burns and the yellow discolouration of the skin. "It looks like gandhaka (sulphur) burns and poisoning to me. I remember a ceremony where the Magi had produced thick yellow smoke and the smell was awful and there were people with similar symptoms," he said.

"We have also heard of lots of thick yellow smoke being produced when the Magus threw a powder on the fire. When we reached the ravine, most of the smoke was gone, but there was an acrid smell that irritated our nose," I said.

"These must be burns caused by gandhaka poisoning. Our physician covered the wounds with a honey and seaweed paste and fed the patients an extract of Neem to get rid of the sulphur from the system," Shushun said.

Master Ashwin walked in just then and I told him the treatment Shushun had suggested for what he believed was gandhak poisoning.

"Namaste, Shushun. I suspected as much. However, I have never seen such burns before. Thank you. I think we will try your remedy and see what happens. Shveti, will you arrange for this quickly, please? But tell me, Shushun. The Magus and his colleagues sit close to the altar while this chemical is released and yet nothing happens to them?"

"I am not sure, sir. Our physicians think that the Magi use the extract of the same plant for some time before the Yajna to protect their body against the chemical. But that is only conjecture; the Magi are very secretive and they perform a Honover which no one knows anything about."

"We will have to try and find out somehow. It will be extremely useful information for our soldiers in the future."

The nurse applied the honey and seaweed dressings that Shevti brought and we all left the room.

"This is the second time you have come to our help, Shushun. We are very grateful to you. You should let us repay you in some way," Master Ashwin said.

"No sir. Your city has been extremely kind to me. I have been well looked after and have learnt so much from your community. I am very impressed with your city's engineering. I have never seen a city so well planned, especially in civic amenities such as water supply, roads, drainage, food storage and cultivation techniques. Even the Egyptians, who are known to be great builders, don't have such well-planned cities. I would be grateful if your Great Council would allow our engineers to come and learn the techniques. And I would like to learn at least some of your Vedas," Shushun replied.

"That is no problem at all. Upaas's father is our chief engineer. I will speak to him and we will arrange a visit for your engineers. As for the Vedas, our Sage Shunahotra's son, Grtsamada, is an expert on them and I am sure he will be delighted to help you. It takes a lifetime of dedication to learn the whole works. I don't think anyone other than the great sages, has mastered them all. Upaas tells me that you have invited him to visit Elam. That will do him good and it will further strengthen the bond between our countries."

Shushun was pleased. I was pleasantly surprised at his tentative approval for my journey. When I had mentioned the invitation to the Master yesterday, he had not seemed very pleased.

"I have seen the work you do here, Master Ashwin, and I am sure our physicians will learn from Upaas as well," Shushun said. "I will be in Harappa for a few more weeks. I will make arrangements for his visit on my return home. Our King will be pleased at any opportunity for improving the ties between our cities."

Master Ashwin left soon afterwards for the Council of Elders and I dropped Shushun back to the camp. Then I went to Lopa's wagon. She was bubbly as ever and even more beautiful. The Elamite horse fascinated her. We went for a ride in the forest and I discovered to my delight that she was a very confident rider. She handled the horse beautifully and the horse seemed to like her as well.

"Where are you taking me, Upaas?" Lopa asked.

"To an enchanted place," I said, with a smile.

She laughed, "You seem to wander all over the forest. When do you get time to treat patients?"

"I make time. You wait till you see this place," I said.

We rode for an hour deep into the forest, round little hillocks and past enormous black rocks until we turned a corner and before us lay the beautiful lake Nishantha. Legend had it that Swayambhuva Manu himself had camped on its shores. It was a large oval lake with clear, calm water that reflected the green of the wide peepal trees growing along its shores. No wonder it was called the 'lake of tranquility'. The shore was sandy with a few large rocks and deer and other wild animals came there to drink water. Lotuses grew in abundance and often covered half the lake with large green leaves and beautiful white and red flowers. The air was full of bird song and the fragrance of flowers.

Lopa was delighted. "Wow. This is absolutely gorgeous. It is so peaceful and gentle."

"There are more surprises here. Come, we will sit on that rock over there. I will get you some fruit you have never tasted before," I said and alighted from the horse. I helped her down from her horse and led her to a large black rock and she stood in its shade.

"Can you see that tree over there?"

"Yes."

"The bright yellow fruits you see on the branches are amra (Mango), the most delicious fruit in the world. I will get some for you," I said.

I took the slingshot from my pouch and chose few smooth pebbles from the beach. The first stone did not hit anything and flew harmlessly through the tree. Lopa giggled. I took careful aim and a juicy ripe Amra fell to the ground. I quickly picked it up, rinsed it in the lake, peeled it and gave it to Lopa. Then I watched as she delicately and tentatively bit into the juicy flesh.

"Ummm," she said with an ecstatic expression. "This is wonderful." I watched as a few drops of juice ran down her chin and when she raised her hand to wipe them off, I quickly stepped closer and held her hand. She looked at me, startled, and I bent my head and gently kissed the juice off her chin. She moved a step back, looked at me mischievously and took another bite of the Amra. Of course, I had to hold her close to me and kiss her face and taste the sweet Amra on her lips and mouth. It took a long time to finish the Amra and then we had to have another and another, until she laughingly broke free of my embrace and ran to the lake.

Soon we were both swimming in the cool water. Suddenly, she turned around, put her arms round my neck and hugged me tight. The bird song faded, the trees disappeared and there was only the warmth of her supple body pressed against mine and the pounding of our hearts. I don't know when we moved to the sandy shore.

We left for the camp at dusk.

"Lopa," I said, as we neared the camp. "Sampa seems to like you very much and you look beautiful on the horse. I want you to have him. I am sure he would rather have you ride him than me."

"Can I, really?" said Lopa with delight.

It was with great reluctance that I said goodbye promising to speak to her father the next day and take her home to meet Mother and Nivya.

The next few days went past in a blur. When I called on Lopa's father and asked for Lopa's hand, he was most generous and said he was thrilled to have me join his family. Nivya and Mother liked Lopa very much and when Father saw her, he approved of her immediately.

My cup of joy was full and all was well with my world.

❖

Chapter 10

THE TRIP TO MOUNT MUJAVANT

"Upaas, we are running short of medicines, what with the injuries we have had to treat over the last few weeks. Our stock of soma is also running low. You will have to go to the Shivaliks and to Mount Mujavant and replenish our stocks. Take Ubhaya with you. It is time he learnt how to identify the roots and flowers we need," Master Ashwin said to me.

"Yes, Master. The last time I had to go further up the mountains for some of the roots and we need to go higher still for the Kantalika (belladonna) plants. So it will have to be a long trip. Besides, the rishi and the Gandharis who guard the Soma are not easy to find. I will take permission from my father and mother and set off tomorrow," I replied.

"I will speak to Ubhaya and also his parents," Master said. "And do not worry about finding the rishi, he will find you. The Gandhari guards are supposed to stay invisible, that is part of their security measures. You will have to be extra careful and keep a lookout for the rogue Avestans as well as wild animals." Master Ashwin cautioned.

"I will be careful, Master. The Avestans have not been seen in the Shivalik hills. It is too far for them and we have too many patrols there. I thought that they do not know of the existence of Mount Mujavant or Lake Sharyanavat?"

"Judging from what happened at the ravine, we have to assume that they know that we will be running short of Soma extracts and will have to go to get fresh stocks. We still do not know who the mole is who is giving them information. He is sure to tell them about your trip and they will come after you. You must be vigilant. As usual, two of our master marksmen will accompany you and Pindaara will look after the cart, but you need to be very alert and extra careful. I have to tell you something else. A negotiator arrived from King Vishtaspa yesterday asking for help. Some of the soma that you will bring back is for them. Now go and fetch Ubhaya. I want to speak with him."

"Yes, Master. I think he is in the pharmacy."

Ubhaya was busy grinding something in the pharmacy and did not hear me come in. He was darker skinned than I and appeared to have a permanent smile on his face. I still remember the first time I had seen him. He was about ten or twelve years old then. He is the son of Krishivala Kutchasa from a village near Saraswatha. He was brought to our house with his parents by the supervisor, Dhuramdhara.

Ubhaya's father had come to the gates of Harappa looking for work, having lost everything in the floods in his village. Dhuramdhara had taken pity on the family and brought them to my father. Father had found him employment and a house to live in and Krihivala had been very grateful. The next time I saw Ubhaya was when he was brought to my father on a summer evening. According to Krishivala, Ubhaya had not done very well in anything he tried and now wished to get a job at the hospital with my Master. His father had pushed him forward and Ubhaya touched Father's feet.

"Ayushman Bhava. May God bless you son," Father blessed him. "What would you like to do?"

Ubhaya had just fiddled with his fingers and said nothing. Kirishivala had tried to prompt him but he had refused to say a word.

"That has been the problem with him all along. He has no ambition. If you can get him any job, I'll be grateful." Krishivala was desperate.

"Don't be so harsh on your son, Krishivala. I'll see what I can do."

Krishivala had left with his son looking rather sullen, I had thought. The father spoke to Master Ashwin and Ubhaya became a helper in the pharmacy. After a lot of effort on Master Ashwin's part, he had progressed to he level of an apprentice physician for the past couple of years.

As I walked in, I stubbed my toe on a copper vessel full of dried roots and Ubhaya looked up.

"Master has sent me. He would like to speak to you. He wants me to take you with me to the hills to collect medicinal roots and plants," I said.

He smiled and said, "I better get prepared then."

"You speak to Master before you do anything," I said.

He washed his hands in the corner and walked back to the Master's room with me.

"I want you to go with Upaas to the Shivalik Hills to replenish our stocks. Get ready to leave in two days."

"I will Master. But I must take my father's permission," he said.

"Of course. Remember that you will have to leave early in the morning soon after sunrise. Upaas will tell you what you need to bring for the trip. It will be cold where you are going and you will be away for at least a couple of weeks."

The next day I met the two marksmen who were going to accompany us. I knew one of them, Astravid, the best sharpshooter in our army. We spent some time deciding on the weapons we would take with us. He insisted that we take our bows and arrows and he spent considerable time choosing the type of arrows we had to take. He seemed to have chosen a veritable arsenal for himself and I kept reminding him that we were not going to war!

When I reached the Temple on the morning of our departure, Pindaara was already there with his bullock cart and his favourite bull, and Astravid was there with four horses. Soon Ubhaya arrived accompanied by his father. He was carrying a satchel over his shoulders and a sack on his back. I hoped that he had brought the skins I had advised him to bring; the mountains can be very cold.

The Temple looked majestic in the predawn light. I went through the north gate and the main Temple was on my right and the great Pushkarni on the left. The apprentice priests were already waiting outside the doors with everything needed for the morning prayers. We walked down the steps of the Pushkarni ghat and washed our hands and feet in the cool, refreshing water. As we walked back up, the elephants of the temple, all bedecked for the morning prayers, were ushered in.

Sage Shunahotra and the Master Priest, Khodandaki, arrived and went down to the Pushkarni to wash their hands and feet. Then we all stood at the foot of the steps in front of the great doors of the Temple, waiting. The two doors were made of solid teak wood covered in copper and brass finials and with small built-in alcoves hung with hundreds of tiny brass bells. Whenever the doors moved, the bells jingled melodiously. Every one's attention was on a small opening with a large diamond embedded in the upper half of the great door, bordered with a strip of brass.

The sun rays slowly moved up the door towards the opening as the sun came up over the eastern horizon. The rays touched the brass strip around the diamond and the whole place was lit up, and the moment they reached the opening, the bells within the Temple started to peal, slowly at first and then faster and louder. Two of the priests picked up a large conch each and started to blow them.

Thousands of birds rose up into the sky from the trees at the sound, and the priests began reciting hymns in praise of God Savitr and invited him to open the door of the Temple for us. The great drum in the anteroom came alive and in the background was the very gentle, mechanical noise of the wheels within the doors and the walls of the Temple, and then the great doors started to open with a creaking sound. Now the tinkling of a thousand tiny bells added music to the rhythmic drum beats, the sonorous bells, the conches and baritone chanting of the Vedas. It was a stirring experience and never failed to thrill me every time I witnessed it.

The Temple was so well planned that the first ray of the sun which went through the openings in the two doors to the sanctum Sanctorum touched the feet of Lord Pashupathi and started the mechanism that set the bells ringing. The rays falling through the windows in the antechamber set off the great drums; the sound of the two conches got the mechanism working that opened the doors. It worked on an intricate system of pulleys and wheels that made very little noise and have needed no repair for several hundred years now.

The Temple itself was built on an eight pointed star shaped platform with the great door facing east. We had to climb eight steps before reaching the pedestal of the Great door. The door was flanked by two massive columns covered in brass and made them look like two golden columns. There was a tall alcove on the side of the column where stood the two guardian angels - the two Varutrs. The two statues were full size nearly 6 feet in height and imposing.

The carpenter who had made the idols had an eye for detail. He had captured the serene peacefulness of the Varutr along with the ferocity of strength to protect. One got the impression of being safe in their presence. There was a small, yet fast flowing stream of cold water just in front of the pedestal at the entrance to the door. This cleansed our feet as we entered the Temple. As we entered the doors into the anteroom, it was a different world.

Both the walls were plastered and painted with bass relief. The colours of yellow ochre, red, green, bright blue and red were striking.

The left wall depicted the stories of God Indra's exploits - the war against Viratra and the battle to free the primal Cow, Kamadhenu. The right wall depicted the story of Pralaya (the great deluge) and how Swaymbhuva Manu along with seven Rishi's (Saptharshi) saved the humanity on the boat with the help of the God Vishnu in his Matsya form (the fish).

Colourful images of the various Gods and their exploits embellished the ceiling in all the four corners. In one corner was the Agni, the fire god blazing in bright red and yellow ochre. The opposite corner was Varuna, the God of Sea with a flowing bright blue mane. The other two corners showed off the two great Ashwins who were protecting all of us from above. The ceiling was quite high, but the images looked as if they were next to your nose. The smell inside was of the sandal incense mixed with the burnt ghee that the priests used for their lamps.

There were four huge brass lamps in the four corners with flames blazing to show off the images. The flickering shadows produced by the flames gave an eerie feeling as they made the horses and elephants on the left wall come alive. The ocean flood myth on the right wall looked as if it was still flowing. There were large vents immediately below the ceiling, let just enough light to illuminate the ceiling and with the smoke wafting slowly towards the vents, the whole scene was surreal.

The middle door was slightly smaller than the front great door and with a slightly larger opening just below the middle, again bordered by shining brass. Two large wooden columns covered in bronze flanked the door and in the light of the lamps and the reflected light from the top vents looked bright red and imposing. There were Bass-reliefs on the bronze columns again depicting the exploits of God Indra. There was a large pedestal across the door and one had to step through yet another stream of running water to get into the main hall. Thus cleansed our feet once again before facing the sanctum Sanctorum of the Temple.

The main hall was large and imposing with a ceiling at least ten cubits high. The vents in the walls near the ceiling let in enough light to give the place an ethereal atmosphere. The sun rays had moved up from Pashupathi's feet to the knees by the time we entered and as they travelled higher up, the magnificent statue dominated the hall. Lord Pashupati sat cross legged with a Rudraksha mala in his right hand and a Shalya (Spear) in the left hand. The image was made of pure gold except for the half closed eyes, which were made of ivory and black granite. The eyes conveyed a sense of calm and yet emanated an exuberant energy. One could palpably feel the powerful presence of the Lord.

The young priests anointed the statue and decorated it with flowers - brilliant white Jasmine and bright yellow Champaka flowers from the garden around the Temple. The Vedic chants continued and Sage Shunahotra made the offerings.

Once all the rituals were complete, Sage Shunahotra turned to me and said, "Please come with me, Upaas. You will need directions for Mount Mujavant and Lake Sharynavat."

Master Ashwin came with me into a small and dark chamber behind the sanctum Sanctorum. I could hardly see anything. He signalled to me to kneel at the Sage's feet and close my eyes.

Sage Shunahotra put his hand on my head and said,

"*Ayushman Bhava*. May the Lord of Soma help you in your quest," and recited a Soma hymn I had not heard before. I closed my eyes and as soon as I did so, the temple disappeared and thousands of images flashed before my eyes. There were jungle paths, huge mountains, lakes, rivers and forests. And there was snow and ice, a lot of snow and ice. There were soldiers and a Rishi is talking to me and saying something I could not understand. Then I heard Sage Shunahotra say, "You can open your eyes now, Upaas."

I opened my eyes and found that I was standing outside at the back of the temple. Sage Shunahotra gave me a small leather satchel full of small pouches and one small mud flask, which was closed with a string around the neck.

“Keep this satchel beneath your clothes and use it for emergencies only,” he said, looking into my eyes. I looked completely blank. “You will know what to do with it when the time comes.” He lead me back into the chamber where my Master was still waiting for me.

“Now, there is no time to waste. God speed and May God Indra be with you.”

Pindara was waiting with his cart already loaded and Astravid and the other soldier were at the gate with the horses, including my beloved Shankara. We bid goodbye to everyone and started on the journey. I had a sense of apprehension, which I could not understand. This was not the first time I was going on this trip and we had no problems before. Although this time Master Ashwin was not going with us and I had to negotiate the path and make sure we came back with everything we had set out to bring.

The two marksmen lead the way to the northern gate of the city. We had to go northeast to the western bank of the Saraswathi and then follow the river north. If we made good time, we would reach the travellers’ inn well before nightfall. We fell into a pattern on the road, I in the front with Astravid, followed by Pindara on the cart and Ubhaya and the other marksman at the rear. For the first time since Master Ashwin had asked me to go to the mountains, I had time to think and reflect.

My thoughts obviously went straight to Lopa. I had gone to her to tell her that I would be away for a while. She was very crestfallen and it was painful to say goodbye to her. We held each other for a long time, neither of us wanting to let go. She had stood at the door of her caravan waving to me until I was out of sight. I love adventure and travel, but at the moment all I really want to do is spend time with Lopa, I thought with a sigh.

I followed the well-trodden path leading to the city of Kalibangan. The sun had just passed the zenith when we stopped to rest at the banks of a stream at the bottom of a small hill. Ubhaya was obviously not used to riding for long periods and complained of pain in his thighs and back.

"Why don't you ride on Pindara's cart?" Astravid suggested.

"I have ridden on horses all day before. But this horse is not comfortable. I have been given an old horse which cannot walk properly."

"Master Ubhaya, that is not true. Yours is the youngest of the five horses we have here. Do you want to swap horses with me?" Astravid said.

"No, thank you. I will manage."

He ate his lunch sullenly and did not speak to anyone. I followed him to the stream to wash my hands and as we were coming back said, "I think you should take the cart, Ubhaya. I don't want you to be ill when we reach the mountains. It is hard work there."

"Well. Umm. If you insist," he said.

"I do. It is better that you are fit when we reach the mountains and are able to help me collect the roots and seeds and plants. The final leg of the journey to Lake Sharyanavat is even harder."

It was finally agreed that he would travel in the cart with Pindara for part of the journey and ride the horse for short periods only. We reached the inn well before nightfall and left the next morning before sunrise, reached the Saraswathi by late afternoon and started the arduous trek northwards. We reached the village of Vapri after three days of hard riding. We were half way up the Shivalik hills and we had to collect the roots, plants, fruits and seeds in the adjoining forest.

Vapri simply meant 'ant hill' - the place was littered with numerous ant hills, mainly because of the abundance of plants with juicy roots. There we met Rishi Vatula who helped us identify the plants we needed and also helped us prepare them for storage.

On the second day, Rishi Vatula called me into his hut and said;

"I think you have enough supplies to last six months. Sage Shunahotra tells me that you have to go to Mount Mujavant?"

"Yes sir. We need to replenish the supply of soma."

I was not surprised that Sage Shunahotra had sent him a detailed message of our trip. Their powers of communication over long distances were legendary. My Master had tried to teach me the technique with very little success so far.

"You will have to leave your cart with the supplies here. It cannot go to Lake Sharyanavat. I am sure Sage Shunahotra has given you directions to the Lake?"

"Yes sir. And I remember some of the way from my previous trips with Master," I replied.

"Good. In that case you should rest here tonight and set off early in the morning with your companions. You will need enough food for at least three days of travel two days to go up the mountain and one day to come back down. I will ask the cook to give you enough to last for four days, just in case," the Rishi said.

"Thank you, sir. You are most kind."

It was very cold that night. There was a fire in the middle of our hut which kept going out every time a breeze came in through the large crack in the door. It made no difference to the two soldiers and they slept through the night, snoring away loudly. Ubhaya complained constantly, even though he was the nearest to the fire and the Rishi's wife had given him extra blankets.

A thick fog covered the mountain when we started our journey in the morning. We could barely see the path winding through the thick forest. But Shankara, my horse, was full of beans. He had been tethered for the past three days while we gathered plants in the forest and now he was rather skittish, pulling on the lead, raring to gallop. I had to use all my powers of persuasion and a supply of sweets to calm him down.

Rushing down the path would have been dangerous. The path up the mountain was just a narrow ledge clinging onto the mountainsides. The ground was wet and slippery with well-rounded rocks along the path, which was obviously rarely used. There were little streams flowing across it in many places, which made the rocks even more slippery.

The sun came up and the fog was soon dispelled, but the path became narrower and steeper. It soon deteriorated into a dirt track with lots of loose stones. The horses slipped and knocked off small stones that disappeared off the mountainside into the deep gorge down below. By the time the sun was over our heads, we came upon the first of snow and ice on the ground.

The fog had disappeared and there was bright sunlight. We were climbing one of the taller mountains towards the west of a deep valley. There was thick forest down to the valley below us and bare rock covered in green moss and clumps of purple heather high above with splashes of blueish white snow everywhere. I could not really see the tops of any of the mountains around us. There was a range of mountains on the eastern side of the valley and they looked very steep and rocky. I could not see any paths where we could take the horses. These were the images I had seen in my mind when Sage Shunahotra had put his hands on my head in the temple only last week.

There was a lone eagle flying high up, circling around the eastern side of the valley, looking for its prey. The path wound around the mountain and as we turned the corner, moving northwards, the valley became narrower and the sides steeper. I could see a clearing just ahead. By this time, Ubhaya's protests and complaints were irritating even the patient Astravid. He was hungry, cold and sore all over. So we decided to take a break.

"Master Upaas, I can see a stream and shelter in that clearing. We can rest there." Astravid must have read my mind.

"Yes. We will stop and have our lunch here. There is still a long way to go. We have to cross these three mountains before nightfall," I said pointing to the three mountains with jagged peaks ahead of us. "We have to be at the Alinas' rock before sunrise. If I remember the hymn correctly, Savitr (the Sun god) will show us the way in the morning. If we miss the sunrise, we will have to wait another day," I said.

The clearing was not very big. There was a mountain stream on one side flowing down to the valley. There were some bushes and a twisted pine tree in the corner. We tethered our horses to the tree and unpacked the lunch we had been given to find sour bread, clarified butter in a rolled up green leaf, pickles and ripe Amra. I was surprised to see Amra at this altitude. We had not seen any Amra trees on the way or anywhere near the village. Ubhaya promptly fell asleep in a small crevice in the back, protected from the cold wind. I walked across to the edge of the clearing to enjoy the beautiful vista.

The majestic mountain range on the other side of the valley rose from the darkness of an invisible bottom and seemed to be straining to meet the sun and the sky. The sky was a clear blue and the white peaks were sharply etched against it. The tallest one toward the north zoomed straight up into the air to its first bastion, the pinnacle of the nort-west buttress. Above the buttress there was a small dip, then a second ridge climbing to another pinnacle, twin to the first, then another ridge that led to the summit itself.

The mountain slightly to the north of it was a little smaller and had multiple small peaks, as if a giant had taken a bite out of the top with crooked teeth. The mountain to the south of the tallest one was much smaller and had a smooth rounded peak and with the bulge in the middle that looked like a pot bellied bald man. The most interesting of them was the one to my right which had a wavy top and protruding promontory right at the top. It was called the Asura's nose for obvious reasons.

The river flowing down the side of the Asura's nose made it look like it was suffering from a permanent cold One of those mountains was Mount Mujavant. Until we reached the Alinas' rock, we would not know which one of them was the mountain we were looking for. If only Ubhaya knew this, he would run back home! It was a good thing that we would not be able to see the path to Alinas' rock till the last minute.

Legend has it that Alinas, a Gandhari Yaksha, sat on that huge rock in penance and prayer, without moving, for a whole year. Lord Savitr finally appeared before him and blessed him with divine vision. He showed him the path to Mount Mujavant and Lake Sharyanvat where Soma grew in abundance. Alinas soon became more powerful than the Harappan sages and started to threaten the surrounding cities and towns.

It was Indra who finally pacified him after a duel. Since then, he has been the guardian of these mountains and particularly of Lake Sharyanavat. Without his help it is impossible to reach Mount Mujavant or the lake on top. There was a Gandhari regiment posted in the mountains to help him safeguard the soma. No one ever saw the Gandharis as their movement was shrouded in mystery and they were known to have magical powers.

"It is beautiful here, so tranquil, no wonder the Gods want to live here," said Astravid, who had come up quietly behind me.

"Yes, it is very peaceful. That is why the sages come here to meditate," I replied. "But I think we better start moving again. We have to reach the plateau before nightfall. You better wake up our sleeping baby."

Ubhaya woke up after some protest and we set off again up the mountain. I did not want to be on the mountainside when it got dark. The path nearly disappeared as we climbed up and was more a space between the boulders. Our horses stepped gingerly between the rocks and it was very slow progress. We steadily climbed north and the sun was going down towards the peaks of the mountains; in no time it would drop down behind them plunging the valley into utter darkness.

We had already reached the glacier and there was snow everywhere masking the stones on the path. Just as I was losing hope, the path cleared up a little and the horses could move faster. The altitude was affecting us all, horses and men. On my earlier trip with Master Ashwin, a soldier had been affected by altitude sickness and within minutes of complaining of feeling unwell, he had gone blind and began to rant incoherently in panic. Before anyone could stop him he kneed his horse, which reared up dropping the soldier several hundred cubits down the mountainside. It took a platoon of Gandhari soldiers all day to find his body at the bottom of the gorge.

Our Master had described the symptoms of the sickness, told us the warning signs to look out for and what to do in the event of the sickness striking anyone. The treatment was so simple. All one had to do was go down the mountain as quickly as possible. I kept looking back at others to make sure no one was showing any signs of altitude sickness.

By the time the sun went down, we had reached a wall of rock with a trail scooped out of it by ibex, through which we went easily enough. On the other side, we found ourselves in a vast clearing with three sides shut in under the west wall of the mountain towering above us on the left. It was a dark fearsome place in the dusk, full of swirling mist and black rock underfoot in which were pools of water covered with ice. It was littered with fragments of rock that had fallen only quite recently.

We got off the horses and moved gingerly around; small rocks came whistling down, none of them larger than a marble but heavy and quite lethal. It was dark and we could hardly see much of the place. Everyone was tired and uncertain and no one said a word. I had no way of knowing for sure where we were. If we had reached the Alinas' rock, there should be a cave nearby. I peered around in the dark, and after a while found the cave.

Astravid insisted on going into it first to make sure there were no dangerous animals inside and then we rode into it as it was quite large with enough place for our horses as well inside. The temperature had dropped as soon as the sun set and we all shivered despite the effort of climbing. We had our skins and woollens with leather boots and caps on, but it was still bitterly cold.

Luckily, we had collected dried wood on the way up. There was no way of looking for wood in the dark. Astravid and his companion were very good with their axes and soon a roaring fire was warming us. Pindara set about warming a brass vessel full of water in which he prepared a decoction using some leaves from his satchel and jaggery cubes.

Our packed food tasted delicious with the warm decoction. We settled well at the back of the cave, protected from the chilly winds and warmed by the fire, and took turns in keeping awake to keep the fire going. Astravid had the early morning watch and it was his duty to wake everyone up an hour before sunrise.

We were all ready on our horses when dawn broke over the eastern range of the mountains. I was greatly relieved to see the huge Alinas' rock not very far from the cave opening. From what I could remember, we had to stand to the left of the rock facing the valley when the sun came up and the path would be revealed to us. We could dimly see the valley in front of us and the silhouette of the mountains on the other side. But there was no sign of a path anywhere.

"Don't you remember the path from your last trip? Why don't you just lead us forward?" Ubhaya asked petulantly.

"It doesn't matter how many times I have been here, things look different every time. Remember, this is the magical Gandhari land." I replied.

"That is what worries me." He mumbled, still unhappy.

The sky changed colour from dark blue to deep orange and yellow before the sun came up over the mountain blinding us with its brilliance. In a few minutes we saw a narrow, winding path on the mountainside, which went downwards for a while before climbing back up on the other side of the valley. The north face of the valley was hidden by a trick of light during most of the day and it looked as if the path was cut off half way down the western face of the valley.

Astravid lead the way down the side of the mountain and we were on the other side of the valley by the time the sun came up over our heads.

The images Sage Shunahotra had instilled in my mind took us to a large clearing below the top of the mountain on the western wall of the valley in the early afternoon. We were on a beautiful rocky plateau. Wild bushes had taken over the whole area and we could barely see the ground. There was no lake and there certainly were no fields of soma. I don't remember seeing this place before, though that did not mean anything in Gandhari land. But, I did begin to wonder if we had missed our way and ended up in the wrong place. I stopped at the end of the clearing where the mountain rose steeply up into the sky and I could clearly see the mountain peak now.

An ibex stood near a stunted tree looking lost. I got off the horse and walked towards it. It did not run away and kept staring at me. I stroked its neck wondering at the strange behaviour of the animal.

I pulled some leaves off the tree and offered it to the deer when suddenly, a deep voice said behind me, "Don't do that, Master Upaas. Those leaves are poisonous."

I turned around to see a scraggy looking man of indeterminate age standing behind me with a wooden staff in his hand. He had a great flowing white beard and a thick moustache. The deep lines on his face made him look like a gnarled old tree.

I recognised him immediately, bowed my head with folded hands and said, "Namaste, great Alinas. I bring greetings from Sage Shunahotra and Master Ashwin."

"How is my friend Ashwin and the Sage? Are they well?" Alinas asked.

"Yes sir. Everyone in Harappa is well. We have had some problems and are out of Soma." I told him about the Magus' yajna and described the ravine. He listened intently and nodded his head.

"I gathered something was afoot when there were changes in the Prana. There are forces out there that will want to take advantage of the situation. I have never known Bharata to be as vulnerable as it is now. This acute shortage of soma is not good. We must be extra vigilant and amass large stocks of soma as soon as possible."

Alinas' long white beard bobbed up and down furiously while he talked. The others came up and all of them bowed their heads to the Great Yaksha and greeted him with folded hands.

"I don't think you can afford to waste any time now. The Gandharis will help you collect the soma stalks and there is plenty of prepared Soma extract which you can take with you," he said.

"But great Alinas, the entire soma field appears to be overgrown with weeds now. I cannot see any soma plants. I cannot even see the lake," I said, perplexed.

He smiled and said, "Look behind you, Upaas."

All of us turned around and found to our utter surprise that we were actually standing on the banks of Lake Sharyanavat. The field of what looked like wild bushes had turned into a field of soma surfeit with beautiful yellow flowers at the far end of the lake. The whole plateau was covered with a thick carpet of mauve primulas. There were countless thousands of them, delicate flowers on thick green stems. Before us was the brilliant green lake, several acres wide and in the shallows and along the streams that spilled over from it, the Soma grew in clumps and perfect circles.

The glacier rolled down towards us from the east like a tidal wave, stopping short at the far end of the lake in a confusion of moraine thrown up by its own movement, like gigantic shingle thrown up by the sea. There were a few Gandharis busy plucking well-chosen succulent stalk from the soma plants and dropping them into the baskets on their backs. They were tall and very fair with striking features and no facial hair. They paid no attention to us.

"How did this happen? Is this some kind of magic?" It was the first time Ubhaya had spoken and he was quite shaken. "It was a field of wild shrubs just now and we rode through it. We should have sunk in the lake... It must be a mirage."

"Mirages happen in deserts, Ubhaya. Your eyes see what your brain tells them to see. This is as real as you and I," Alinas replied.

"Where did the Gandharis come from? I don't trust them. They are sorcerers. They were not there before," said Ubhaya, still agitated.

"The Gandharis have been here all the time. It is their duty to remain invisible to strangers. They are the real guardians of the fields of soma. I am only a custodian," Alinas smiled. "Come, I will show you where they prepare the extract."

We followed Alinas to the far end of the lake against the mountain, to what in the distance appeared to be just a large rock covered in ice. He walked into the stone and disappeared. Only when we came closer did we see that the large rock covered an opening behind it. We walked through the opening in the rock and found ourselves in a very large cavern. Many Gandharis were there, working circular stone presses. The leaves were stripped off the stalks of the soma plants before the stalks were fed into the grinding stone presses. A large bull turned each press.

A reddish liquid dripped into the press from a brass container hung above it. Dark green syrup poured out of a spout at the bottom. A Gandhari collected the green syrup and spread it over a very shallow brass cauldron at the far end of the cavern under which a fire burned with very little smoke. The odd thing was that despite all the activity, there was no sound. Even the stone grinders made no noise.

"This is where the soma extract is prepared. It is not practical to carry the soma plant everywhere. To get a spoonful of extract, we have to grind several plants. That would mean carrying several cartloads of soma plants for just one yajna," Alinas explained to Ubhaya and the others. "The stalk of the plant has to be exactly right not too young and not too old. The grinding stones are made from granite rocks of Mount Mujavant. The shape and size of the stones are as stipulated in the scriptures. There are special ingredients added to get that red solution. Those ingredients are secret and known only to a chosen few. The heat to dry the soma extract has to be just right. If it is not dry enough or if it is burnt, the extract is useless."

I had seen it all before but it was still fascinating. The efficiency and the silence were impressive and a little frightening. Ubhaya could not take his eyes off the Gandharis and kept fidgeting all the time.

He finally said to Alinas, "How are we going to carry this to Harappa? There are bandits in the mountains."

"There are no bandits on this mountain, Ubhaya. There are only wild animals and they will not attack you without provocation. Besides, you are well armed and supported by guards," he said, his eyes twinkling with amusement. "Each one of you will get two satchels and one of them will have the soma extract and the other some harmless powder.

Only the sages can make out which one is the true soma. If you are attacked, give them the powder. This mountain is guarded by fiercely loyal Gandharis, Ubhaya. No one will attack you here. They have watched you all the way up the mountain path since you left the village."

We loaded our horses with satchels of soma extract and the dummy powder. Once the loading was done, the Gandharis disappeared as quietly as they had come into the forest.

"It is getting dark now. The cooks have prepared a meal for you and there is a warm shelter at the back of the cavern where you can sleep tonight," Alinas said.

We were grateful for the warm food and the drink made from soma, which put all of us in high spirits. Only Ubhaya could not be brought out of his sullen mood. He still mistrusted the Gandharis and said to no one in particular in a hushed voice,

"It is all very well, this eating and drinking. When darkness falls we will have our throats slit. I know that they are cannibals. When darkness falls, they turn from beautiful people to demons and asuras and eat people."

Charming fellow, I thought. I wonder what makes him fear the Gandharis so much.

"There is nothing to worry about, Ubhaya. Astravid is here with his arms and we have Alinas himself who has promised to protect us. I have been here before and spent the night in the same cavern safely with the Master," I said, hoping to calm him down.

But he was not convinced "Maybe because of our Master they did not eat you."

"Enough of this nonsense.," I said, thoroughly irritated by now. "Be thankful that they have helped us and protected us so far. I don't want to hear anymore of this nonsense about demons and asuras."

That appeared to shut him up. Astravid and Pindara looked at each other and did not say anything. Each of us found a suitable spot at the back of the cavern where it was warm and comfortable and we were soon asleep. Even the frightened Ubhaya was soon snoring away much to Pindara's amusement.

"He snorts like my bull," he whispered, suppressing a laugh.

A thick fog covered the mountains the next morning and we had to wait for a while before the sun cleared the path for us. When we came out of the cavern, there was no sign of the Gandharis in the field.

Alinas called me aside and said, "Upaas, there are people who will try to stop you from reaching Harappa. You need to be extra vigilant once you leave Mujavant. The Gandharis can only protect you while you are on the mountain. I have reason to believe that there are moves, as we speak, of attacking Harappa. These same people will try to stop you to get hold of the soma extract you are carrying. Be on your guard," He bent down and picked up another satchel and said, "This has fresh soma stalks which are more powerful than the extract. Under no circumstance should this fall into the hands of the enemy, whoever they are. And keep the news of the attack to yourself. We don't want to start a panic now."

Ubhaya was looking at us intently and wondering what we were talking about. Fortunately he could not lip read or read anyone's mind. Astravid was busy getting the horses ready for the trip down the mountain and Pindara was making sure we had enough food for the journey.

I turned around to say thank you and goodbye to Alinas, but there was no one there. He had disappeared from the spot where he stood only a moment ago. I turned back and found that the soma fields and Lake Sharyanavat had disappeared as well and we were back in the wild bush covered plain of the day before. Everyone looked startled. Only the satchels on our horses convinced us that it had not been some crazy dream.

"What happened?' Astravid said.

I had seen this happen the last time I had visited Mujavant the Lake disappeared and the scenery changed to a different one each time. I still had not got used to it and I don't think I'll ever will.

"Alinas and his Gandharis do their job of protecting this sacred place best by staying invisible," I said. "Let us get going now. We have to reach the village before nightfall. Rishi Vatula will be waiting for us."

"The sooner we get off this mountain the better. It gives me the creeps," Ubhaya said. The trek down the mountain was much faster but trickier. There were several places where our horses nearly lost their footing over loose rocks on the narrow ledge along the mountainside. We reached the village without any incident well before nightfall. Rishi Vatula was glad to see us return and his men helped us unload our horses. Pindara went to check on his bulls and I went to the Rishi's hut to tell him of the next day's plans.

"We will start early in the morning tomorrow soon after sunrise, Rishi Vatula. I would like to be back in Harappa within the next three days. I have to take a message to Sage Shunahotra as soon as possible," I said.

The Rishi smiled and said, "The great sage already knows, Upaas. Alinas has sent the message to me and to Sage Shunahotra. It is your duty now to make sure the soma reaches Harappa safely and quickly.

You will have to be extra vigilant on your journey. You have to have faith in yourself and your team. I cannot help you once you leave the village."

"Thank you for your help, Rishi Vatula. We will be careful and I will make sure the supplies reach Harappa safely. But, tell me, if you can, what kind of trouble should we expect? Alinas did not elaborate," I asked.

"We don't really know. Since the attempted Gomedha by the Magus, there have been changes in the Prana that cannot be explained. Our Sages are working on it and until stability is attained, we are vulnerable," the Rishi replied. "Now you should rest. You need a good night's sleep if you want to keep your faculties sharp for the journey tomorrow."

I thanked him again and went back to the hut. Ubhaya had been already asleep and the two marksmen were getting ready to sleep. There was no sign of Pindara. I looked questioningly at Astravid.

"You know Pindara. I am sure he is raiding the kitchen to get as much food as possible for the return journey. Don't worry about him," Astravid replied.

It was quite late when Pindara came into the hut and went to sleep.

❖

Chapter 11

THE GLORIOUS SUVASTU VALLEY

"Master Upaas! Master Upaas! Someone has been at the cart!" Pindara ran into the hut in great agitation early in the morning. I sat up in alarm, shook the sleep from my eyes and stared at him.

"There are two baskets missing; someone has taken them!"

"Calm down, Pindara. It is still dark, check the cart properly," I said. But I knew that Pindara was meticulous and he would never make such a mistake.

"I have checked twice. Two baskets are missing, and they were there last night when we came back. Someone has stolen them!"

"Let's go and check what is missing," I said and got up from my bed.

Pindara's loud voice had woken everyone and Astarvid came with us to check the cart and the horses. Two baskets, which had Kantalika and some other herbs, were missing. Luckily the satchels with soma were in the hut. But we could not return to Harappa without Kantalika - it was crucial for many treatments.

"We will have to go back into the forest," I said.

“Master Upaas, can you borrow horses from the Gurukul? Suvikranta will go with you. I have to get our horses ready for the journey,” Astravid said.

“Right. I will ask Rishi Vatula to lend us three horses. We have to hurry.”

Rishi Vatula was shocked that a theft had occurred in the Gurukul.

“It has never happened before. Obviously there is some kind of shield covering whoever has done this, otherwise we would have caught him. It has to be the Magus or his men. This is very disturbing. I will ask Alinas to send some of his Gandharis to accompany you back home. They will be here by the time you come back from the forest,” he said, looking more worried than I had ever seen him before.

I returned to our hut to find that Ubhaya was just waking up. How could he have slept through all that commotion? I told him what had happened and that we had to go back to the forest and he was very indignant.

“Why do I have to go to the forest again? I have done my bit of digging and picking for you. I will wait for you here.” he declared.

“It will take me very long to collect all the herbs by myself. I am sorry, but this is unexpected and it will be quicker if you help.”

“It was your responsibility to keep the supplies safe and you did not do your job properly. I don’t see why I should do all the work,” Ubhaya retorted.

I lost my temper. “Don’t be insolent, Ubhaya. Freshen up and be ready to leave when Suvikranta gets the horses,” I said.

He went off with a sullen expression. I would give him a piece of my mind when we got back to Harappa. If he wants to be a physician, he had to learn to work very hard and to take responsibility seriously.

Suvikranta came with three horses to the hut, saddled and ready to go and Ubhaya was still inside. It was exasperating. He seemed to be doing his best to delay us.

"Ubhaya, it is time to go. Come on," I called out.

Ubhaya came out reluctantly and we set off into the now familiar forest at a gallop. We soon had our satchels full of herbs, but we needed some more Kantalika roots. Ubhaya pointed out a large plant just off the path with plenty of roots exposed.

"Oh yes, that plant can give us all the roots we want," I said and got off my horse letting the reins trail. I took the sickle from the back of the horse and cleared a path to the plant. Ubhaya did not move. I glared at him angrily and decided to dig out some roots on my own. Suvikranta had got off his horse and bent down to pick up the reins of my horse when there was a sound of metal rushing through the air followed by a thud. I was looking down at the root I was trying to cut without damaging the whole plant, and I looked up just in time to see Ubahya galloping away as fast as he could and Suvikranta lying quite still on the ground.

I rushed to my horse and had reached for the bow when a deep resonant voice said in heavily accented Sanskrit, "I would not do that if I were you, Master Upaas. There are twelve arrows aimed straight at your heart."

I turned around: twelve horsemen surrounded me with bows drawn and arrows aimed at me. I looked down at Suvikranta.

"Will you at least let me help him?" I asked.

"There is no need. He is only unconscious and has a small wound on the shoulder. Your friend who ran away will bring help," the tall man with a short-cropped beard and no moustache said. He was obviously the leader of the group. The riders wore thc Avestan army uniform with shields and insignia of an Avestan regiment. They were riding tall powerful Elamite horses with typical Sistani saddles and were armed with bows and arrows and long brass headed spears. The horses also carried saddlebags. It appeared to be an advance scout party of the Avestan army. It suddenly struck me that they had addressed me by name.

"You have me at a disadvantage, sir. You seem to know who I am, but I don't know who you are," I said to their leader. The soldiers still had their arrows pointed at me. I stepped away from my horse as I spoke and they lowered their bows. I did not take my eyes off their leader.

"My apologies. I am Apam Napat of the Sistan Regiment. We know who you are and why you are here. We know you have just come down Mount Mujavant with Haoma or as you call it, soma. We planned to negotiate with Alinas for a supply, but we could not find him nor the sacred lake,' he said. "So, if you hand over the soma extract, we will leave."

"I am afraid I don't have any soma with me. I have come without Master Ashwin for the first time and I could not find Alinas either."

I was trying to buy time, hoping that the Gandhari soldiers had arrived at the Gurukul and Ubhaya would come back with them, assuming he had gone to the Gurukul for some help. Besides, I had to keep the soma out of their hands at all costs.

"Come now, Master Upaas. You don't expect us to believe that. We know that you came down the mountain last night carrying satchels full of soma. Tell us where you have hidden the soma and we will let you go back to Harappa."

"I tell you, we did not bring any soma down the mountain as we could not find Alinas or lake Sharyanavat."

This went on for a while until the leader said, "You leave us no option but to take you with us. Get on your horse."

"At least let me get the arrow out of his shoulder and apply some poultice," I said, pointing at the unconscious Suvikranta.

He nodded in agreement. It did not take me long to get the arrow out of his shoulder, clean the wound and apply a poultice. Suvikranta did not come round through the entire process, but he was breathing normally. They had obviously used a poppy extract tipped arrow without any arsenic. I mounted my horse feeling thankful that our own horses were at the Gurukul and the soma was safe.

Apam Napat took the lead and rode behind two of his soldiers with me beside him; the rest followed.

"Don't even think of escaping, Master Upaas. My soldiers can shoot down a fly at thirty paces while riding a horse," he said to me. They had taken away my bow and arrows and my spear. "It will be cold on the way. I hope you have your skins and woolens."

"I think you are making a mistake by taking me with you. I am only a junior physician in the hospital. I will not be of much use to you," I said. But he merely laughed.

I wondered where they were taking me and why. I was angry that I had allowed myself to be caught. It suddenly occurred to me that I might never see Lopa again and I knew that I had to find some way to escape. I had so much to live for. But I was surrounded by expert marksmen and I did not wish to test their skill without very good reason. I was no good at telepathy and so couldn't contact anyone at Harappa. I so desperately wanted to tell Lopa what had happened and that I missed her. I took a deep breath and recited a hymn Sage Shunahotra had taught me at my initiation. That calmed my mind a bit. The path was getting trickier and I had to concentrate on my riding. I would be of no help to anyone if I had an accident.

We were climbing north on a ledge with snow and ice and loose rocks. On my right was a snow covered mountain and on my left a deep chasm disappearing into darkness beyond the reach of sunlight. They rode in silence, other than occasional swearing by a soldier when a horse stumbled and missed its footing on the icy path.

The sun went down the western mountains quite suddenly and plunged the eastern slopes and our precarious path into darkness. The lead soldier called out and raised his right hand and everyone stopped, got off their horses and took long torches from the saddlebags. The lead soldier took some powder, set it down on a dry rock and struck a flint against it as another soldier held the bitumen and oil soaked end of his torch near the powder. It flared up immediately. The lit torches were passed back and the unlit ones forward until all the torches were flaming. Our path was now brightly lit. I wondered what the powder was and resolved to try and get a sample for our people.

When we reached a plateau on top of the mountain, we headed towards an opening in a cluster of large rocks in a dip away from the lip of the mountain. We dismounted and entered through the opening into a large cave. The torches illuminated a well-used cave with a makeshift fireplace in the centre and skins and woolens neatly folded in a corner. A small alcove at the back was used as a store and had satchels full of bread, fruits, nuts and even a jar of honey. There was a pile of logs in one corner. Soon a roaring fire warmed the cave and a meal of meat, bread and honey was prepared. They even had a jug of wine.

After dinner, Apam looked sternly at me and said, "You may think that you will soon have a chance to escape, but banish the thought. There will be two guards on duty and you are in the middle of nowhere. The guards are there to protect us from wild animals rather than to stop you from escaping. Even if you do manage to get out of the cave, it is unlikely that you will go further than a couple of hundred cubits before you fall off the edge. And if you don't, this mountain has enough snow leopards, jackals and bears to take care of you."

I well knew the risks of a plainsman on foot on his own at night on a Himalayan mountain and I had no intentions of being foolhardy. If they were taking me across to Sistan, we would have to climb down into the Suvastu valley and I would try my luck there. I had been through the valley several times in the past with the Master, collecting herbs that grow only on the lower slopes of the Himalayas.

We did go down to the Suvastu valley, only we went not westwards, but towards the north and west, away from the borders of Bharata.

The landscape was glorious as we climbed down the mountain, and we reached the river Asikni (Chenab) in the evening. The river was still quite narrow there, but filled with molten ice from the Himalayas that flowed with a strong current through the deep gorge that it had cut into the reddish mountain rocks. I wondered how they would cross this fast flowing river with no beaches anywhere, but here I saw a most wonderful contraption.

We reached a platform in the rock downstream with some ropes dangling across the river to the opposite side. A brass mechanism made up of five pulleys had heavy hemp ropes that passed through the pulleys and disappeared into the distance on the opposite side, slightly downstream. One end of the rope was tied to a ring cut out of the rocky side of the gorge. Two men undid the knot from the ring and ten men started to pull the rope. The pulleys moved smoothly with very little noise and soon a huge wooden raft came into view over the river.

When the raft was close to the edge of the gorge, it stopped moving sideways and rose up in the air until it reached the level of the platform. Two men threw hooks across and pulled the raft close to the edge and fastened it to two more rings cut in the rocky walls of the gorge. All the horses were loaded on to the raft and we all climbed on.

Four men took hold of the ropes that were dangling from the far edge of the raft and pulled them taut. As the raft was untied from the rock wall, it started to swing dangerously and it took brute strength to stop it from hitting the rocky sides of the gorge. It was soon steadied and lowered down and pulled across to the other side. We all walked off it and over to the bank and were met by more Avestan soldiers.

The sun was down by this time and we camped for the night.

The next morning we travelled west and slightly north, following what appeared to be a disused path to reach the banks of river Vitasta (Jhelum). We were now in the northern borderlands, sparsely populated mainly by roaming Gandhari groups and nomadic Avestans. We crossed the Vitasta on a similar but simple raft and camped on the other side. It was quite pleasant and not as cold as before. The soldiers knew that this would be my chance of escape and were much more vigilant. My ankles were tied to a large tree and I was guarded through the night.

We headed south and west in the morning through the picturesque Suvastu valley. It was lush green, mainly with grass and shrubs, interspersed with clumps of tall trees. There were rolling hills as far as eye could see. Tall, snow capped Himalayas in the background made it look like a painting come alive. We reached the banks of the Sindhu (Indus) well before nightfall. The river here was in full flow and quite wide and we crossed it using three large, rather flat river barges, which were hidden in the thick undergrowth along the banks.

That night two men visited the camp. They did not look like soldiers and were rather unkempt with long dark beards and moustaches covering their faces. I wondered if they were Avestans. They huddled together with Apam and spoke in hushed voices for a while, but soon there were animated gesticulations and raised voices. We heard them clearly over the roar of the Sindhu, but I could not understand their language. How I wished Lopa were there to translate what they were saying.

The two strangers left and disappeared into the forest and Apam returned looking unhappy. He gathered his soldiers around him at the far side of the camp, leaving just one man to guard me and talked animatedly and pointed his finger at me on several occasions. The men looked at me now and then as well. Whatever news the strangers had brought was not good and they all looked glum afterwards.

The next day I was woken up quite early and we set off before sunrise, riding rather rapidly westwards for most of the day up the Pariyatra mountains (the Hindukush mountains). The change of scenery was gradual from lush green valley to dry, brown, dusty surface to dry, hot, parched, cracked land. There were no trees and, therefore, no shade; the earth was red and burning hot and dust swirled around us. Somewhere along the way we crossed the border into Sistan, going through mountainous areas with large rocky hills and boulders. The paths were familiar to the men and we moved swiftly. The sun beat down on us, the dust that the horses kicked up choked our throats so that we had to cover our faces with cotton wraps.

We turned yet another corner over a large rock formation and there it was before us: the huge mud brick fort of Haozdar, rising like a phoenix out of dry wasteland. The fort walls were huge with massive doors. Guards opened the doors to let us in and I looked around eagerly. I had heard of the great city with a magnificent fort, large market and rich culture.But before me lay a city whose days of glory had long ended. The main street was lined with dilapidated houses, the pale yellow mud bricks crumbling in several places. There were hardly any traders in the market and people walked around with heads bowed in defeat. An air of desolation permeated everywhere.

We went to a large official looking building where I dismounted and a tall, emaciated man took the reins and led the horse away. Suddenly, there was a yell and then more shouting as a little boy came running towards me, chased by two grown men screaming abuse at him. He tripped on a stone slab right in front of me, fell headlong and the bread he was clutching in his hand came flying and landed at my feet. The two men pounced on him and started beating him. The Avestan soldiers accompanying me looked on disinterestedly.

I picked up the bread and shouted in broken Avestan, "Stop beating that boy. It is only a bit of bread."

Apam turned round and shouted at the men but they paid no heed. He went across and kicked one of them hard and two of the soldiers pulled them round to face him.

"You should be ashamed of yourselves beating a little boy. Pick someone your own size. If I see you doing this again, it will be the dungeons for you."

"But he has stolen bread from our stall. It is all very well for you; you don't have to worry about food or water. It is time the King did something for us."

"How dare you question the King? Our King has plans for the whole country. The Gods are displeased because of your behaviour and we are being punished for it. Now be off with you."

The men went off and the little boy grabbed the bread from my hand and ran away, the look of terror still on his face.

"Come on inside," said Apam. "Our officers await you."

It was very dark inside the building, but cool. When my eyes adjusted to the darkness I saw that we were walking down a long corridor to a darker room where two men stood against a small window at the far end. There was no furniture other than a wooden stool in the middle of the room on which I was made to sit.

"This is the Harappan, Upaas, who went to collect soma extract from Mount Mujavant. He has refused to tell us where the soma or the lake is. He is the son of Master Kapila, a member of the Council of Elders in Harappa. I am sure he will be able to give you good information. I will go and report to the King", Apam said and left the room.

The questioning went on for several hours. They were gentle at first and gradually grew more aggressive. There was a constant unspoken threat of physical violence, which was very disconcerting, but never any real violence. They wanted to know where Mount Mujavant and Lake Sharynavat were. They wanted details of our army, our defences and our weapons. I held out through the questioning without giving anything away. In my mind I kept reciting the hymn taught by Sage Shunahotra to give me strength. Finally, the two examiners stopped when they realised that they were not getting anywhere.

"We will come back for you tomorrow and then we will not be so kind. You will be sorry you did not answer our questions," one of them said to me.

A soldier led me along another long corridor to a dingy little room with one barred window overlooking an alley. I heard the padlock turn in the door behind me. The window had brass bars interspersed with leather strips and I immediately tried pulling the strips. But they were very strong, so after several attempts, I gave up. I was tired and hungry and desperate and afraid of what the next day would bring. How would I cope under torture? Would I ever go back to Harappa again? Would I ever see my family and my beloved Lopa again? I prayed that I would have the strength to bear the torture without breaking down. I tried telepathy again without any success. I remembered Master telling me, 'you must clear your mind of all thoughts. Only then can you channel all the force into it and communicate with anyone anywhere.' But however hard I tried I could not empty my mind.

At some point I dozed off on the ground until a sound of falling bricks woke me. I looked at the door and then the window. It was pitch black outside. I realised with a sudden surge of hope that all the leather straps had gone and someone was pulling at the brass bars of the window. One of the bars was already down and as I looked the second one came loose and dislodged some more bricks, which fell outwards into the alley. I hoped the guards had not heard the noise.

The wall was obviously in a poor state and crumbling in the hands of my benefactor. If I had only pushed instead of pulled, I could have removed all the bars! A small head peered at me through the window when all the bars were removed and to my great surprise I saw the big blue eyes of the same little boy who had stolen the bread. He signalled to me to follow him and disappeared. The window was not set very high on the wall and I easily squeezed out. I saw the boy standing with a horse at the end of alley. He ran away as soon as he saw me, leaving the horse with the reins trailing. I covered my head and face, picked up the reins of the horse and followed him. The moon was a small crescent giving very little light.

The boy paused at an intersection to ensure I could see him and then ran off again to the right. I followed him. I could just make out his silhouette moving along the walls of the houses. He suddenly turned left and disappeared into some ruins. I followed suit, gingerly finding my way among the rubble and nudging the horse to follow. Before I knew it, I was on a slope outside the walls.

I turned to thank the boy, but he had disappeared. I looked around for a while and then led the horse down the slope and soon found myself on a path. I knew I had to go east to reach the border town of Roruka (Nausharo) in Bharata, where I could get help and cross the Sindhu. Luckily the sky was clear and I could see the stars. I knew that Venus was on the eastern horizon in the early part of the night and the pole star was clearly visible. However, I was not sure if it was the first half of the night or the latter half. I decided to take a chance and follow Venus, which by then was quite high up in the sky.

I rode very carefully in the dark, unfamiliar territory; it became easier once the sun broke through at dawn. The fact that I was going down the Pariyatra mountains helped. I was tired and extremely hungry I had not eaten anything for nearly two days, except for the loaf of bread the boy had left with the horse. There was no vegetation to forage for food so I pressed on towards Roruka as fast as I could. Roruka was a small town just within the borders of Bharata at the foot of the mountain pass.

Late in the afternoon the gates of the little town lay before me and urged my horse to go faster. But when I got close, I saw an Avestan flag on the walls and immediately veered off the path. I had to find a way into the town that was not manned by soldiers. I came upon a cluster of trees and a pond just outside the town the town where I washed myself and drank the slightly brackish water. The horse nibbled happily on the sparse yellow grass on the ground. There was a tall tree between two very large rocks, and I lay down under it and promptly fell asleep.

The sound of cowbells woke me up. The sun was nearly down on the western horizon and a cowherd was washing his hands and drinking from the pond. His dress proclaimed him to be from Bharata.

I stood up and said, "Namaste, my friend. How are you?"

He was startled and jumped up and stared at me uneasily. I must have looked a frightful sight with dishevelled, dirty, torn clothes and a scraggy unkempt beard.

"Who are you? What do you want?" he said finally, firmly holding on to his wooden staff.

"I am Upaas from Harappa. I need some help to get back to Harappa," I said.

"You are a long way from home, friend. What are you doing here?"

I explained briefly how I came to be so far away from home and asked, "Why is there an Avestan flag at the gates of Roruka?"

"A large army of Avestan soldiers marched into town and just took it over a few days ago."

The town had been taken by surprise without any battle or resistance. We had always lived in peace with our neighbours and there was no need for the army to man this outpost, which had never been attacked in living memory. The only people who used this pass were merchants from Ariana and Elam. A small platoon of border guards was posted in the town, more for technical reasons than for any real protection.

"There are few Avestan soldiers in the town right now. Our soldiers have been locked up in the stockade. We will go in through southern entrance which has no proper gates and is usually unmanned," he said. "I am sure we can get you some help in the town."

We simply walked into town behind his cows and went to his house where he left me with his soft-spoken wife and went off somewhere. She fed me a sumptuous meal and gave me a new set of clothes. The cowherd returned after half an hour with a giant of a man, built like a fighter.

"This is Parthava. He will help you across the Sindhu in the morning," he said and turning to the Parthava added, "And this is Upaas."

I stood up and said, "Thank you so much for agreeing to help me. It is vital that I reach Harappa before the Avestan army does."

Parthava nodded. "There is no need to worry. Their army is large and will take time to cross the river. If we leave before sunrise with fresh horses, we can reach the crossing slightly south of where the army will be trying to cross before sunset. I know a fisherman there who will take us across the river in his boat."

"Thank you, Parthava. I am truly indebted to you."

"I would do anything to help, if it rids us of Avestans from our land," he said with a wide grin, and left, telling me to be ready well before sunrise.

Parthava arrived before dawn with two fresh horses. He had also brought bows and arrows. The cowherd's wife packed bread, honey and nuts for the journey. I thanked my hosts for their generosity and left while it was still dark. We went out the same way that we had come into town and rode south to meet a path going east. The ride was bumpy, and at times treacherous, since it went sharply down the mountain.

Once we were on the path the journey was faster and we reached the western banks of the great river before sunset. The arid and barren mountains gave way to lush green meadows, meandering streams, ponds and lakes, and low rolling hills. We did not come across any soldiers anywhere.

"They will not use this path," Parthava said when I asked him. "They have chariots and large carts full of supplies. They could not have come straight down the mountain the way we did. They would have to follow the regular path that winds down the mountain for at least two days just to reach the plains. I don't think they will have reached the Sindhu yet."

"How big is their army?"

"I did not count, but it took a whole morning for the army to pass through our town. They have these two-wheeled chariots pulled by two horses that can go really fast. There were several large carts filled with supplies, including large amounts of wood. It is a slow moving army. It will take them at least two more weeks to get anywhere near Harappa. They have to cross both the Sindhu and the Vitasta. If they miss the right fork after the Sindhu, they will have to cross the Asikni as well. For an army this size, it will be hard in the north where it flows through deep gorges.'

Parthava had not seen the contraption they used for crossing the Asikni in the mountains and I told him about it. He was not very impressed.

"Well, if they had sense, they would use the southern route and not cross the Asikni in the high mountains at all. Crossing the Vitasta is not hard even for an army of this size."

The fisherman at the banks of the Sindhu was mooring his boat after the day's fishing when we found him. Parhava introduced me to him and asked to be taken across the river. The fisherman smiled at me and said with a twinkle in his eyes, "Sure. I hope your horses are good swimmers. The current here is strong. If the horses are not used to some chopping and turning, they can easily topple the boat."

"I would not worry about that. Both the horses have been on boats several times and they are used to it," Parthava replied.

"Why did you not use the ferry up north?" he asked Parthava.

Parthava and I exchanged looks and I nodded. He told him that the Avestans had taken over Roruka and then explained who I was.

"But the Avestans have always been friendly in the past. They have never ever attacked. Why would they do so now?"

"I don't know. But, even as we speak, a large army is marching towards Harappa. Upaas has to reach Harappa to warn them," Parthava replied.

The fisherman finally agreed to take us across the river. We climbed aboard the large flat-bottomed fishing boat with the horses, soon reached the other bank and went straight to the inn nearby. Parthava decided to accompany me all the way to Harappa on the pre-text that 'someone has to mind your back and stop you being captured by Avestans again.' It would be the beginning of a long lasting friendship. The innkeeper was friendly and had not heard anything about an Avestan attack.

"I have heard of Avestans attacking travellers and stealing their goods. But, I have never heard of an army attacking our country," he said anxiously.

"Do not worry, they will not attack civilians. That would be against the rules of warfare," I reassured him.

That night I slept peacefully for the first time in many days. Less than two days of riding later, we had reached the banks of the Vitasta. The ferry took us across and then Harappa was only a day's ride away. I would soon meet Lopa again, I thought, and nudged my horse to go faster. I could not stop talking about Harappa.

"You love your city dearly, don't you?" remarked Parthava with a smile.

I laughed, realising I had been talking continuously about Harappa since we had left the inn two days ago.

"I am sorry. I must have really bored you."

"No, no, I don't mind. I feel as if I know your city almost as well as you do. I had heard of the City of Gold from travellers, but this is the first time I have heard a resident of the city talk about it," he replied.

"Thank you, Parthava. I love my city and I miss my family and my people."

"And your love, Lopa," he said, chuckling.

"I knew I should not have told you about Lopa…" I retorted as I playfully tried to push him.

We were half a day's ride from Harappa, when we met a platoon of Harapan soldiers sent by Sage Shunahotra to escort us to the city.

The dust they raised had been visible from a distance and we had come off the path and waited until, with great relief, we saw the insignia and the standard of the Harappan regiment. Both of us stepped out from our hiding place behind the trees onto the path.

The Captain of the platoon raised his right arm high over the head and said, "Hail, Master Upaas. Sage Shunahotra sends his compliments and he has sent us to escort you back to Harappa safely."

"Hail, Captain. We are grateful for your escort," I replied.

"Can I speak to you privately, Master Upaas?" he said.

I looked at him quickly, apprehensive, wondering what bad news he had to impart. We walked a few metres away from the path and he turned around to face me.

"Master Upaas, I have bad news. A large Avestan army is headed this way and we expect them to reach Harappa in less than four weeks. Your services are urgently required."

To his surprise, I let out a big sigh of relief.

"Did Ubhaya make it back? What happened to Suvikranta and Pindara and Astravid?" I asked.

"They all returned safely. Suvikranta is recovering well. Now, if you will excuse me, we must hurry back to Harappa," he replied.

"I have Parthava from Roruka with me. He helped me escape and accompanied me on my journey back. I have promised him passage into Harappa and lodgings there," I said.

He nodded his head and said, "No problem, Master Upaas. That will be done."

Both Parthava and I were given fresh horses and the rest of the journey to Harappa was swift and uneventful. I introduced Parthava to the captain. It turned out that Parthava was a soldier for a while in the Bharata army and had left to look after an ailing father; so they got along very well together. I wanted to know what had been happening in Harappa in my absence, but the captain was not much of a talker and I did not get much information. We reached the outskirts of Harappa well before nightfall. The west gate came into view as we climbed over the last hill. I stopped for a moment to savour the sight and took immense pleasure in showing Parthava the city glowing in the light of the setting sun.

"It really is a city of gold!" he exclaimed.

❖

Chapter 12

THE PUZZLE OF THE MISSING SOMA

There was unusual activity in the field where the travellers' camp used to be. A large number of soldiers were camped there, war elephants were being put through their paces and I could see our own two wheeled chariots doing laps around the field.

"What happened to the travellers?" I asked the captain anxiously.

"They are now inside the city walls for their own safety and security. Their camp is in the east just beyond the lower town."

"Oh," I said, relieved, and wondered if I should ask him about Lopa. I was desperate to see her.

"I would have asked him about her if I were you," Parthava whispered to me. I was taken aback. Now, everyone had become a mind reader except me!

The captain led us directly to the Great Hall. The news of my return had reached the city well before me and people had come out of their houses and lined the streets and were waving at me. Several wanted to touch my hand and pat my back and many called out 'Hail Upaas', 'Dheergayushman Bhava' and 'well done'. There was much waving of clenched fists in the air. It was an unexpected welcome and I was deeply moved. Parthava enjoyed it as if it was his own victory celebration.

How different was my beloved city from Haozdar, I thought as I walked down the streets. There was life here, vibrant and thriving; there was the solidity of the Temple and the security of the Sages; several races of people lived here and everyone flourished.

At the Great Hall, I took a deep breath, said goodbye and thanks to the Captain and urged him to look after Parthava. Sage Shunahotra, Father, Master Ashwin and all the Elders were there. I bowed my head to the deities on the platform, without whose blessing I would never have made it back, before turning to them.

Sage Shunahotra raised his hands in blessing and said, "Welcome home, son. By God's grace you have come back to us safe and sound." I touched his feet and he raised me up saying, "*Dheergayushman Bhava*. We know you have been trying to contact us through telepathy."

I touched my Master's feet and when I bent down to touch the Father's feet, he took me in his arms and said in a slightly shaky voice, "*Dheergayushman Bhava*. May God Indra bless you throughout your life. We have been so worried, though we knew you were alive by your attempts at telepathy. Lopa comes home almost every day to ask about you."

I hugged him back wordlessly.

"Welcome home, Upaas. There will have to be a debriefing like last time before you go home, I am afraid. There is no time to waste and we need as much information as possible from you," said Master Adhvadipa, the commander whose responsibility it was to safeguard Harappa and Bharata.

"Yes, of course, Master Adhvadipa."

We went into the side room and I described the events of the previous two weeks in as much detail as I could. He was very interested in the town of Haozdar and there were many searching questions about the Avestan army. He also wanted to know everything about Parthava and was particularly interested in knowing who had introduced him to me and how he had behaved during the travel back to

Harappa. He was keen to interview Parthava as soon as he learnt that he had seen the Avestan army march through Roruka.

"The period of tranquillity is now at an end, Upaas. The Council of Elders have decided to consecrate Sage Shunahotra in preparation for the impending war. We will have to perform the Rajsuya Yajna, which we have not done in a long time. He will be the King for the duration of the war. The rituals will start in a couple of days when Sage Vishwamitra arrives to officiate at the ceremony."

I had nearly finished the huge bowl of fruit that was on the table just as I had after the trip to Sindhu. Was that only a few weeks ago? It felt like years ago.

"It is a pity that we have to fight a war with the Avestans when we have always had friendly relations with them. They treated me very well while I was their captive, you know. Except for the threat of torture, of course," I remarked.

"That is good, Upaas. King Vishtaspa had dispatched an emissary to Harappa, who appears to have gone missing on his way here. There will be a council of war between Sage Shunahotra and King Vishtaspa along with their generals and ours before the war begins, to lay down the rules of the war. Judging by your experience, they are likely to abide by the rules."

"Did Ubhaya and the others come back safely?"

"Yes. They did. Thanks to your efforts, all the herbs, and more importantly, the soma extract were saved. The satchel full of fresh soma plants that you had tied to Shankara's neck will be used for the Rajasuya Yajna. Alinas and Rishi Vatula are in constant touch with us. The only odd thing is that Ubhaya got lost when he escaped from the forest and did not return till a few days after the others. He also had some minor injuries to his shoulder where he said an Avestan arrow had grazed it. At his debriefing, he described the attack by the Avestan soldiers and how he fought with them before escaping. Thanks to his efforts, Suvikranta is alive."

I stared at Master Adhvadipa dumb founded. Ubhaya had run off as soon as the first arrow was shot at Suvikranta. But I said nothing. It would get Ubhaya into trouble. I wondered why he had lied to Master Adhvadipa and would certainly ask him. But right now, there were more important things to do.

"What happened to the Magus who tried to do the Gomedha Yajna? Has he been caught?" I asked.

He hadn't, but one of the men who had helped the Magus was found dying of burns he had sustained during the Yajna. He revealed a lot of information to our officers. All the Harappans who were caught had been questioned and punished. Except for three of the collaborators, everyone else had been released back into the community.

Harappan spies had infiltrated the King's court and gathered vital information about the impending war. The Avestans too had a contact within Harappa who was feeding them information, probably the same person who had given the Magus the soma extract. Unfortunately, the Magus' spell was still shielding him.

"It is very important that we catch him before the war begins. With the combined powers of Sages Vishwamitra and Shunahotra, we may be able to break the protective barrier the Magus has built around him. We have even moved the merchants and travellers inside the city walls to keep an eye on them and for their own protection. I am sure we will be able to catch the traitor soon."

He had a few more questions about the size of the Avestan army and any unusual weapons I may have seen. When all his queries had been answered, he led me back into the Great Hall where Father and Vidhayaka were waiting for me.

Vidhayaka immediately came and hugged me saying, "Welcome home, Upaas. Good to see you back, brother. Let's go home, Mother is waiting to see you. She has been praying to all the Gods she knows for your well-being. And Nivya and Lopa visited the army officers so often to ask for news of you that they must be heartily sick of them! Come, I have brought Shankara round for you."

I touched father's feet and stood up,

"*Dheergayushman Bhava*, son. It is good to see you."

"Thank you father. It is really great to be back home in one piece. There were times, when I thought I would never see Harappa again!"

As we walked out of the Great Hall, Father said, "Would you like to visit Lopa before you come home? She has been very worried about you. She is a wonderful girl, Upaas."

"Thank you, Father," I said, with a grateful smile. "I won't be long."

I quickly rode off towards the lower town. I had only gone a few cubits when a rider came galloping furiously towards me on a beautiful Elamite horse. The horse was expertly reined in and Lopa jumped off him just as I dismounted, came running and flung her arms around me. We hugged and kissed and she laughed and cried. Then we sat on a little platform by the side of the road and I told her everything that had happened to me in the last two weeks. I also told her how frightened I had been when threatened with torture. It was something I would not readily admit to anyone else.

After a while, I walked her back to her caravan and went home. I was very tired and at peace after a long time and that night I slept like a log.

The next day I went to the hospital a little late in the morning. Shveti, was tending to the patients in the ward and greeted me with a big smile.

"How is everyone here?" I asked.

"Quite well, although we lost one of the injured patients from the ravine. The other one is recovering. Otherwise things have been quiet," she replied.

"What about Ubhaya? I heard he was injured? And did Pindara bring all the supplies safely? Was Master happy with the quantities of herbs and soma?"

"Oh yes. Pindara brought everything back and he carried Suvikranta in the cart as well. Ubhaya came back a couple of days after Pindara with a wound on the back of his shoulder. An unusual wound. It looked rather like a cut. Master had a look at it and dressed it himself.

Ubhaya came to work for only one day and then sent a message through his father saying that he needed some time to recover from the inujuries. Master agreed and so he has not come back to work after that. Master is happy with the supplies, Upaas. And by the way, your friend Shushun has been asking about you."

"Thank you, Shveti. I will go and check the supplies now. May be in the evening I will visit Shushun."

I walked across to the pharmacy and pulled out my list of roots, flowers, stalks, fruits and seeds to tally what I had picked with the herbs that had been stored there. The only thing I had not recorded were the herbs we collected the day I was kidnapped. The soma plants had been sent to the Temple as they were of no use in the hospital. Everything else tallied until I came to the satchels of soma extract, which were kept in a separate alcove in the pharmacy.

I was shocked to see that all five satchels were only three quarters full. I distinctly remembered filling all of them to the brim and we even had difficulty closing them. They were stitched with hemp rope and sealed with my seal. None of the seals were broken. I could not understand it. There would be some reduction in volume when the powder settled, but not nearly a quarter of the bag. I called Shveti. There was a sharp intake of breath as soon as she saw the satchels.

"No. That is not how they were last week when Pindara brought them inside. They were full. Someone has stolen the soma extract, Upaas. But no one has access to the pharmacy other than us physicians and the nurses. I have been here every day and anyone going into the pharmacy would have to pass me or one of the other physicians."

"Who else has been working here in the last two weeks since the supplies came?"

"Let me see. Ubhaya was here on the day he came back to work and the Master gave me leave to visit my dentist. Apart from that, no one else."

"I will have to tell Master and may be ask Ubhaya if he saw anything suspicious while he was working in the ward," I said and went to Master, who was busy with a new recruit, Vyadi, form Sindhu.

He dismissed the young man and asked me, "What is wrong, Upaas?"

"There is a problem, Master. I have just checked the supplies Pindara brought."

"What has happened?"

"I think we have a thief. Someone has pilfered the soma extract."

Master stood up, shocked. "Are you sure? That can mean only one thing the Avestans have got hold of the soma. And someone has found an access to the pharmacy."

We rushed to the pharmacy where Shveti was examining the satchels from all angles.

"I don't understand, Master. I had checked the bags myself when Pindara brought them in. They were filled to the brim and closed with Upaas' seal on them. Now, they are only three quarter full. All the seals are intact, I have examined them from all angles and there is no sign of any damage anywhere."

"Are you absolutely certain?" Master knelt down to check the seals and the bags himself and examined every bag minutely. "Hmm. Let us take this one out and examine it in the day light," he said, picking one bag.

We took the satchel into the courtyard and Master examined it carefully again. He ran his fingers along the seal and his hand over it inch by inch, watching the hemp cloth all the time. Then he smiled. "I know how they have done it. They have used the funnel technique."

Both of us looked at one another. We had never heard of this "funnel technique".

"It is an old Egyptian tool used to check the contents of a sack without damaging it. It is just a funnel with a bevelled end at the spout. The sharp spout is pushed into the sack to drain some material from inside. The spout pushes the fibres of the sack aside without damaging them and if you look carefully, half way down the side of the satchel, you will see the line of fibres is slightly wavy compared to the rest of the satchel. This is where the soma extract has been drained out." He took the satchel back inside.

"We must find out who has done it. My suspicion is that it is the same person who has been giving information to the Avestans all along and who has been protected by the Magus' spell. There are very few people who have access to the pharmacy. Since the arrival of the supplies nearly two weeks ago, one of us has been in the ward all day –Shveti, Ubhaya or me. We would have noticed anyone going to the pharmacy. Or they may have broken into the hospital at night. But there is no sign of that. I suggest you speak to Ubhaya in case he saw something suspicious."

I rushed to Ubhaya's home at the edge of the lower town. It was odd that he had not come to meet me since my return. When I got off the horse outside his house, I noticed that the front door was ajar and I felt uneasy. Had something happened? I went up to the door quickly and knocked.

"Ubhaya, it is me, Upaas."

There was no response so I pushed at the door. It opened with a slight creak. It was quiet and dark inside.

"Hello. Anybody there?"

There was not a sound.

"Come on Ubhaya, stop playing. Where are you?" I said raising my voice.

I walked through all the rooms in the house. Nothing. The house was empty, completely empty. They seemed to have left in a hurry. There was still some food in the kitchen and the stove had half burnt wood in it. There were a couple of vessels lying on the floor and the wood in the store was only half used. The vessel and the stove were cold. They had left at least a day ago. There was no sign of struggle, so they had left of their own free will.

But why? Ubhaya had an excellent job and could become a Master in the next three to four years. His family were well settled in Harappa and had made it their home since leaving Saraswata so many years ago, as destitutes. There was something not right here and I galloped off towards the hospital to inform Master Ashwin.

"We may have a problem on our hands, Master," I blurted as soon as I entered his room. "I cannot find Ubhaya. The whole family seems to have abandoned their house and left in a hurry."

"Are you sure? They may have gone to visit someone else?"

"The house is empty, Master. All their belongings are gone. There is half eaten food on the table, the kitchen and the store have been emptied. As far as I could make out, there was no sign of any struggle. I spoke to the neighbours and they told me that the family left quietly without telling anyone where they were going."

"That is odd. I will have to speak to Sage Shunahotra. Keep this to yourself for now, Upaas. We do not have much time. Our information is that the Avestan army will reach Harappa within next two weeks. There is a lot to do and this is something we did not anticipate."

I took that as a dismissal and made my way towards Lopa's caravan.

"I thought you would never come!' Lopa exclaimed as she ran down the steps. "Let us go to our favourite place. I have been there several times, but it is not the same without you. I have brought some food," she said indicating the basket she had tied to her saddle. "We can have dinner under the stars tonight if you like."

"That will be wonderful," I said.

The sun was a large orange ball on the horizon when we reached the lake and the trees cast their shadows halfway across the water. The birds chattered loudly as they returned to their nests and a gentle breeze produced small ripples on the surface of the lake. I spread a sheet over a rocky platform.

"Lopa, sit here, I'll get some water."

She opened the basket and an appetising fragrance greeted me when I came back with a pitcher of water. It was the best dinner I had had in a long time.

After dinner had been cleared away, Lopa held out something to me and said, "Take this amulet, Upaas, and keep it with you all the time. It is made of Balasurya (lapis lazuli). It will protect you from evil."

I held the amulet up to the sun. It was made of a brilliant blue stone speckled with gold. There was something inscribed on the back in a script I had not seen before. A hole bored through the top of the stone was strung with a cotton thread so that I could wear it round my neck.

"Thank you. It is gorgeous. What does it say?"

"It has your name written in Dasyu language. Our friend, Battora, gave me the amulet and I had the jeweller carve out your name on it. It has magical properties and will protect you from all evil."

"I will have your name inscribed on the other side. Thank you, Lopa." And I kissed her as she put the amulet around my neck. We both lay back on the rock and looked at the star spangled sky.

"Make a wish," Lopa said, when a shooting star sped across.

"Why?"

"If you make a wish when you see a shooting star, it will come true."

I closed my eyes for a minute and smiled.

"Why are you smiling?"

"I just wished that this moment should go on forever," I said. "Now your turn."

When another shooting star disappeared into the distance, she closed her eyes.

"Yes. What did you wish for?"

"I am not going to tell you. Mother says the wish will not come true if it is spoken."

I smiled and pulled her into my arms.

It was quite dark when we decided to go home. The evening had gone by very quickly, too quickly.

As I was saying goodbye at the door of her caravan, she took my hand, looked into my eyes and said, "Upaas. I want you to promise me that you will not take any risks during the war."

"I promise. I have everything to live for now and I have no intention of spoiling it," I said smiling.

"I was not joking," she said, seriously.

"No. I did not mean it as a joke. I may not be in the battlefield at all. As physicians most of our time will be spent at the medical site. We only have to go onto the battlefield at the end of the day to pick up the injured soldiers. The rules of battle are very strict. No soldier will attack a doctor. Don't worry."

I kissed her goodbye and left.

Chapter 13

THE WAR COUNCIL

It was a very quiet gathering at the King's court in Mundigak, Arachosia. King Vishtaspa had convened an emergency meeting again. Two in two months was unprecedented, a sign of the difficult and extraordinary times. Normally there were two meetings a year, once before the harvest and one soon after. The council leaders of all the seven districts were there with their ministers, their senior Magi as well as their generals, who had been specifically asked to attend the meeting. Unlike the last meeting only a month ago, there was complete silence today.

Isvant and Hutana had waited in the dark alley next to the hall until the last minute. The King's messenger had told them that it was imperative for them to attend and the King's soldiers would protect them in Mundigak. But Isvant refused to take any chances. He had brought not only his general, but also a platoon of hand picked guards with him. Not that they would make much difference against the might of the Avestan Elite Guards; but if he had to die, he wanted to die fighting.

His worry was that he would have no protection once inside the hall, since no soldiers other than the royal guards were allowed to enter the King's court. Isvant and Hutana slipped in through the side door and sat in one corner of the great hall, trying to blend into the shadows. But their presence did not go unnoticed. The group from Bactria spotted them first.

"You have the temerity to show your faces in this court after bringing us to the brink of war!" the Magus of Bactria shouted. "You ran away the last time like thieves. How dare you come back?"

Everyone else picked this up and a chorus of accusations was aimed at the Sistans. Hutana, who dreaded fights, was terrified. "Where are the soldiers who are supposed to protect us here?" he wondered, looking around desperately for a friendly soldier.

The hall reverberated with anger. Everyone had heard of Matriya's attempt to perform the Gomedha Yajna and its utter failure. They had heard the rumours that the Meluhhans were gathering a massive army and marching towards Mundigak in retaliation. And all because of a minor, renegade, Sistani Magus.

The beleaguered Sistani group wondered if they should leave the hall before they were physically attacked when the bugle sounded the arrival of King Vishtaspa. Isvant and Hutana immediately stood up, took their headgear off and bowed their bare heads to the king as he walked down the central aisle of the hall.

The rest of the gathering gasped. This was an act of complete submission to the king. Both Isvant and Hutana had decided that the only way, not only to save their skins but also their state, was to surrender to the King; which meant that the state was now ruled by the King and he could do whatever he pleased with it. It also meant that the King was duty bound to protect the state and its citizens.

The King stopped and looked at the Sistani group without a word. There was complete silence in the hall. The King's temper was well known and no one knew how he would react. After a minute, he took a deep breath and started to walk again, then stopped and went back. The Sistanis who had just begun to raise their heads quickly bowed low again and Hutana could feel his knees wobble.

"Oh please don't let me collapse in the front of the King," he prayed. If he did, he would be taken out and beheaded like a common criminal.

The King again stood in front of the group for what seemed to be a very long time and then put his hands on Isvant's shoulders and said, "Rise, Master Isvant. It is not your fault that your renegade Magus has caused us so much trouble. The desperation of the situation must have driven him to it. You have done the right thing by submitting yourselves to Royal custody. It is now our duty to make sure we get out of this situation and protect our civilians, our country and our way of life."

"Thank you, your Majesty. We tried our best to stop him. But Matriya was deep inside Meluhha and we were helpless against his powers," Isvant said in a trembling voice.

Hutana and the rest of the group still had their heads bowed down to the floor. "Our Magus, Hutana, tried to nullify Matriya's powers, without success. The renegade has spent a lot of time in the Himalayas with a Yogi and has become very powerful."

"But not powerful enough to succeed in the Yajna! Right, Hutana?"

Hutana slowly lifted his head and body up and looked at the King before speaking. "Yes, Your Majesty. Matriya has become very powerful. The only reason he failed was because he did not have enough Soma plants to complete the Yajna. Otherwise, he could have built a powerful barricade around the site and completed the Yajna without any interruption."

"And why did he not have enough Soma? It is foolish to start something of that magnitude without full preparation."

The King turned around and walked quickly to the throne. As soon as he sat down, everyone in the hall raised their hands and said, "Hail our Saviour. Hail Ariana, Hail King Vishtaspa."

Once everyone was seated, the King stood up and said, "We are in a situation where our hands are tied and we are being pushed into war. The action of the renegade Magus has upset the Meluhhans. Our emissary to Harappa has disappeared, probably a victim of mountain bandits. There are rumours that the Meluhhans are already marching towards Mundigak with a large army. However, we have not had confirmation of any such activities from our messengers so far.

I say no news is good news. One thing is certain: Matriya has shown that Meluhha is not invincible. There are ways to enter the country and there are disaffected people in Meluhha who may be of use to us. I ask the elders of our districts: what should we do next? Since the problem has started with the Sistanis, I invite their leaders to put forward their suggestion first."

Isvant was very surprised. Once he had submitted Sistan to the King's rule, he had expected to be completely ignored. All eyes were on him as he got up to speak.

"It is very kind of your Majesty to ask for our humble opinion. We feel that we should pre-empt any action from Meluhhans and march on Meluhha immediately."

The men from Carmania, who have been always averse towards violence, gasped. But several other heads nodded in agreement.

"Why does Master Isvant think that is such a good idea? Are our armies prepared for such a war? Remember we have to travel a long distance and cross mountains and rivers," the king said.

Isvant felt slightly bolder now. He had been thinking of war for a long time and the Sistani council had discussed several strategies at length. He also knew that most of the other districts had been preparing for war for several months now. They had discussed the crossing of the mountains and the rivers and also the target. Harappa was the most likely target as it had the largest stock of Soma in Meluhha.

"Begging your pardon your Majesty, but all the districts of Ariana have been preparing for war for some time now. We will never be prepared enough for any war, as Your Majesty well knows. And as you so rightly said, Matriya has shown that Meluhha is not impregnable. He has managed to get help from Meluhhans themselves. We believe that he has a spy within Harappa who was close to their Council of Elders."

Isvant felt the congregation mellow slightly towards him at this information.

"Thank you, Master Isvant. This information will help in our planning. Now, what do the others think we should be doing?"

No one wanted to give his opinion first until the leader of Carmania stood up; then everyone spoke at the same time.

The King raised his hands for silence and the leader of Carmania said, "Thank you, your Majesty. We think it would be a mistake to march on Meluhha. Meluhhans are not warlike people and they will understand that it was a renegade Magus who has done the dastardly deed. We face a very depressing economic situation and our population is suffering due to the prolonged drought over the years.

We cannot afford a war. Are we strong enough to face the powerful sages of Meluhha? They have magical powers. Our s criptures tell us that our Messiah will come and save us from death and destruction. Our council thinks that we should wait for this messiah to deliver us from disaster."

There was a chorus of dissent at this suggestion and everyone started to talk together again. The King signalled to his Herald and he lifted his bugle and gave one short burst. Everyone fell silent and the King said, "I think we have heard enough and I can see which way this congregation is going. We have waited for this messiah for hundreds of years and there is no sign of him. There is no reason to believe that he will come now.

Our destiny is in our own hands. We have decided to form a Council of War, which will include representatives and generals from each district. This council will decide what we must do. My minister has the list of members with him and I invite the council to meet immediately in our council chambers to discuss our course of action."

With that, the King walked off towards the council chamber in the back of the hall, accompanied by his ministers and the senior Magus. One minister waited on the platform till the entourage had gone and read out fourteen names - two members from each of the districts. The members, with their generals and Magi, headed towards the council chamber.

The council chamber was much smaller than the great hall. It was square with high walls and small windows nearly at the height of the ceiling. The windows let in very little light. As the sun was setting, multiple little shafts of light shone on the wall to the left of the door forming a square pattern which clashed with the woven pattern of ochre and red on the wall. There was a musty smell from the dried out walls and the floor that had been cleaned with soapy water just before the meeting.

A long table in the centre of the room was surrounded by twenty chairs, the one at the top being a little taller than the others. The king was seated on this chair and the members were ushered to the chairs around him. They were all served a locally grown pomegranate drink and then the King rose to address them.

"We have to make important and urgent decisions and the squabbling between districts has to stop immediately. If we don't cooperate among ourselves now, we cannot succeed. Do not underestimate the power of the Sages or the strength of the Meluhhans. Our forward scouts had been searching for the sacred mountain and the lake for some time now to get hold of Soma plants or even some Soma extract. The good news is that they have captured a Harappan physician. He is the son of one of the senior members of the Council of Elders of Harappa. He will be a very useful bargaining tool, if necessary. He is being brought to Haozdar where we can pick him up on our way to Harappa."

There was a murmur of excitement at this news. The King raised his hands again to quieten them down before continuing, "We have to decide right away what the strength and content of our army will be and the route we must take. I will need help from all the generals in planning the battle itself. I have decided that we will need at least ten thousand soldiers for this campaign. What do the generals suggest?"

He looked at the general from Areia, who was the senior most general. He had been in several successful campaigns in the past with King Vishtaspa's father and was highly respected for his knowledge and skill.

General Parviz stood up slowly and cleared his throat. "I thank Your Highness for giving me this opportunity to serve you. I agree with Master Isvant from Sistan all the districts have their armies ready now. We have been preparing for something like this for several months. Our armies are as ready as they can be. As you have rightly pointed out, our only hope for the future of our homeland is to look towards Meluhha. The renegade Magus has ruined our chances of negotiation with them and we have lost our emissary.

The Meluhhans are known to be peace-loving people. But, they also have a powerful army and even more powerful sages. It does not behoove our King to go to the Meluhhans with a begging bowl for the sacred Soma. Without the Soma, our future is bleak. Hence, I support the idea that we should march on Meluhha."

The General bowed his head to the King and sat down. It was finally agreed that the only way forward was to march on Meluhha as soon as possible. The armies of Arachosia would set out the next day and join the Sistani army at Haozdar on the way to Roruka. The Areians, who were already on their way, would reach Haozdar in couple of weeks. The Carmanians were camped outside Zabol in Sistan and would join the Sistanis on their way to Haozdar. All the four regiments would camp at Haozdar before marching together to cross Sindhu.

The Sogdianians and Bactrians would reach the head of River Parushni and sail down to meet the rest of the army north of Harappa. The Gedrosians would follow the western bank of the Sindhu and join the main army south of Harappa. The leaders were all reminded not to engage in any action against any Meluhhans on the way and wherever possible, to avoid all contact. There was discussion about the size of the regiments from each district.

The Carmanians wanted to send a smaller regiment than the others on the grounds that the war did not really affect them as much. When it was pointed out that Carmania was the biggest district and had the largest army and also that without Ariana, Carmania would struggle to exist, they changed their mind. After much discussion it was decided that the battlefield should be on the western banks of river Parushni, though it would have to be discussed with the Meluhhans at the pre-war council.

The meeting went on into the night and it was early hours of the morning before the King finally said, "I bid you farewell now till we meet again on the road to Roruka. May God Vratra bless you all and grant us victory in our battle. We march at daylight day after tomorrow."

Master Isvant and Hutana were the most relieved of all the people coming out of the war council. No one spoke until they were well on their way out of the city towards Zabol. Then Hutana said, "What does it mean for us in Sistan?"

"One thing is for certain. The troubles of our state are now the King's troubles. The war has come at the right time. It will be a distraction and as part of the army has to pass through Sistan, it may even generate some income for our people. We may have lost control of Sistan for now, but it will improve the lot of our people," Isvant replied with a mixture of sadness and relief.

Two days later the Arachosian regiment had assembled on the outskirts of Mundigak and awaited their King. There were nearly two thousand soldiers and with porters, engineers, cooks, physicians and nurses, the number had swelled to nearly three thousand. They had the largest number of chariots among the districts both two wheeled and four wheeled, and were harnessed to fast and powerful Elamite horses. As the sun peeped over the eastern horizon, the bugle sounded the arrival of the King. The King rode a majestic white Elamite horse adorned with a leather saddle, silk tassels, gold braids and dark brown leather blinkers.

He sat bolt upright and the regal appearance was enhanced by a silk and gold brocade coat and bright white headgear slightly slanted to the right and peaked with a clutch of eagle feathers. The Avestan standard of a winged disc was behind him, while the ever-present Herald rode behind and to the right of him. The elite bodyguards, all dressed in black with their faces covered except for the eyes, rode at a discrete distance on either side of him. When he reached the end of the field, he stopped and turned around to face the gathered army.

As soon as the King turned around to face the soldiers, raised fists, waving flags and a roar of "Hail King Vishtaspa, Hail Ariana, Hail our Saviour" filled the air. The King made a rousing speech to encourage the soldiers and Magi prayed for their safe return. Then the army was on the march towards Haozdar, watched by friends and family who silently waved their goodbyes as the soldiers marched to the slow rhythmic beating of kettle drums. The King lead the army followed by the cavalry. The foot soldiers were behind the cavalry and the chariots brought up the rear. The supply wagons had already left the city the day before.

They soon caught up with the regiment from Areia and their numbers swelled to over four thousand. In just over three weeks they reached the northern gate of Haozdar. The Sistani and the Carmanian regiments were camped outside the Haozdar fortress on the road to Roruka, the windy city. The commander of the garrison was waiting outside the gates of the huge mud brick fortress to welcome the army. There was a guard of honour from the garrison with the usual band and flag waving with "Hail King Vishtaspa" and "Hail our Saviour."

The King got off his horse and the commander knelt before him, bowed his head and offered the ceremonial sword as a mark of respect. The King accepted the sword, pulled it out of the scabbard and put it back after a brief inspection in the sun.

"Thank you for your welcome commander," he said. "We are very anxious to see your Harappan prisoner. I would also like to meet the brave soldiers who captured him."

The commander stood up slowly and looked extremely uncomfortable. "Thank you, Your Highness. You are very kind. Let me introduce you to the captain who brought the prisoner to Haozdar, your Highness." He turned around and signalled Apam to step forward. "This is Captain Apam, your highness. He will tell you about the prisoner."

"Why are you being so modest, Commander? I commend you on your bravery and success. Tell me how you captured him."

Beads of sweat appeared on Captain Apam's forehead and he stuttered as he spoke. "Your Highness, it is a great honour to meet you at last. We did capture the physician while searching for Mount Mujavant and brought him safely to Haozdar. We did our best your Majesty. But ..." His voice trailed off into a mumble and he bent his head.

"Speak up man. What is the matter with you? You are an Avestan soldier, not a weak farmer. Stop grovelling," the King's said. He was losing his temper rapidly.

"Unfortunately Your Highness, someone helped the physician escape from the stockade," the garrison commander said.

The King stared at him and did not say anything for a minute. Then he took a deep breath and looked around at the army that was patiently waiting behind him before turning back to the captain and the commander.

"And you expect a messiah to come and deliver you from strife and sorrow? I am surrounded by useless and incompetent people who cannot even guard an unarmed physician for a day and we have begun a march over mountains and rivers to challenge a powerful kingdom! A kingdom supported by a powerful army and even more powerful sages with magic and sorcery at their fingertips... You might as well pack up and go back home to your wives and children.

This is a futile attempt. Do our scriptures not tell us that God will only help those who help themselves? I have an army of over ten thousand soldiers marching towards the greatest battle we have ever fought. How will they feel confident to fight if we cannot hold one unarmed physician? I want the Avestans to show what they are made of – their strength and their power! We are the most powerful people in the world."

He tuned to the commander and said more quietly, "You have to find who was responsible for this Harappan's security and make an example of what happens to those who fail. You must punish him for treason."

He turned quickly around and went towards the royal tent that was set up just outside the walls of the fort. The commander looked stunned. He followed the King and asked for an audience with him. The King was pacing up and down restlessly and did not stop at the sight of the Commander.

"I beg your pardon for this intrusion, Your Majesty. I have a problem."

"What? More problems? What is it now, commander?" the King asked.

"The man you have ordered to be punished is the brother of Master Isvant, the leader of Sistani council. He is very popular in Sistan and considered next in line after Master Isvant to lead the district of Sistan. I am not sure how the Sistani army will react to the execution of their favourite son.'

The commander looked extremely uncomfortable. What he was doing now, could be considered treason as well and his head could be on the block.

"I respect your judgement, Commander. But we have to make an example and make sure the soldiers know the command structure.

We cannot let failure go unpunished. Please carry out my orders. If you cannot, my soldiers will. I want the Sistani Regiment to witness the execution as well, to reinforce the effect."

The commander looked visibly sick. He had made the situation worse. Executing Apam in front of the Sistani soldiers would enrage them. Thank God he was not going with them on this nightmarish campaign.

The execution of Apam and two of his soldiers, who were responsible for the security of Upaas, was swift and orderly without any melodrama. All the soldiers of the three regiments were assembled at the fortress wall to witness it. The commander had deployed enough soldiers to cope with a minor battle as a safety precaution. But, all the soldiers watched the execution in silence, including the Sistani soldiers. The reputation of the King as a fair but ruthless leader had something to do with the lack of resistance or protest.

When the Avestan army sets off again east from Haozdar, on the road to Roruka, it was without any pomp and fanfare. They now numbered over ten thousand including the support wagons and workers, engineers, carpenters and cooks. They reached Roruka within a couple of days and took the unsuspecting town without any resistance. The town was too small to hold the army and they camped outside the walls for a few days until the regiment from Gedrosia arrived. The captains had been instructed to use the time for more training. General Parviz had posted guards not only at the periphery of the camp, but also lookouts in strategic positions outside the camp to alert him to any unusual activity.

On the third day, a lookout on the south side of the camp spotted four riders on tall Elamite horses in the distance. All of them were covered from head to toe except for their eyes. They only carried bows and arrows. They were immediately surrounded and asked to surrender. They dismounted and the guards lead the horses away and took their arms.

The tallest man in the group, who was their leader said, "We come as friends and mean no harm to the magnificent Avestan army from Ariana. We would like an audience with the great King Vishtaspa."

There were at least a dozen arrows pointed at his heart when he spoke.

"Who are you to seek an audience with our King? I cannot disturb the King for any stranger," the captain of the guards replied.

The man thought for a minute and said, "Then may I speak to General Parviz?"

The captain was surprised. Was this man a Meluhhan spy, he wondered? But he spoke perfect Avestan. Before he could decide what to do, General Parviz, who was doing his rounds of the camp, came there with his aides.

"Is there a problem here, captain?"

It was the tall man who replied. "Greetings to the famous General Parviz. You do not know me, but your fame precedes you, sir. I am Magus Matriya from Sistan. I would like an audience with the King as I have some very important information which will be useful in his campaign."

He took the cloth off to reveal a scraggy weathered face with a long greying beard and a sharp nose. As soon as he mentioned his name there was a sharp intake of breath from the two aides who accompanied the General. There was no sign of recognition or any emotion on the General's face.

"I cannot promise you anything, but let me hear what you have to say and I will see what I can do."

The General was a seasoned campaigner and he knew exactly who Matriya was; but he had no intention of presenting him before the King unless he knew exactly why he was here. The four of them were taken to the General's tent inside the camp under guard. Two others of the group had uncovered their faces, but the fourth one kept his mask on. The General insisted the stranger remove his mask.

"I am sorry, General," Matriya explained. "It is important that he keeps his face covered for now. He is here to help us in the campaign and that is all we need to know at present. All I can tell you is that he is a highly placed official in Meluhha and he will be extremely useful to you. But he wishes to remain anonymous until the campaign is complete and Ariana is victorious."

"I will have to speak to the King and see if he will grant an audience. This is highly irregular," said General Parviz, unhappily. Taking a stranger with his face covered into the presence of the King was definitely not in any rule book. He was away for a long time while the four waited under the watchful eyes of heavily armed guards much to Matriya's amusement.

As if these puny soldiers could stop the great Magus from escaping if he wished, he thought with a smile. Eventually, a couple of soldiers came back and searched them again. This time they took away the little sachets of powders Matriya had hidden in the folds of his clothes before taking him into the royal tent. The King had agreed to see the Magus alone.

"Rise, Magus," said the king, when Matriya knelt down and bowed his head in front of one of most powerful kings of the known world. "We have heard a lot about you and your exploits. We did not expect to see you after what happened at your Meluhhan Yajna."

"I am extremely grateful to the great King Vishtaspa for granting me this audience. It was unfortunate that I did not have enough Soma to complete the Yajna. We have been hiding in the ruined city of Sudra (Mehragrah) since our escape. I have with me a gentleman, who is highly placed in Harappa. He has information which will be invaluable for your campaign. But, he would like to remain anonymous for the time being."

The King listened intently to Matriya and then he and the General asked numerous questions about the mysterious masked man. A scribe took copious notes. It was late at night before Matriya and his group were sent back to a well-guarded tent. Both the General and the King agreed that Matriya and his men would accompany the army to the battle.

"If the masked man is truly who Matriya says he is, he would be extremely useful throughout the war." General Parviz has said.

The regiment from Gedrosia arrived and the regiments from Bactria and Sogdiana were making good progress on the river. All appeared to be going according to plan. They would be near Harappa within the next four weeks. The road from Roruka down to the great river Sindhu was cool and green and there was plenty of fresh water, fruits and game.

The army camped on the west bank of the Sindhu exactly six weeks after they had set off from Mundigak. The presence of the Magus Matriya, and the masked man was resented by some of the soldiers. The story of the Magus and his failed Yajna was widely known and they held him responsible for starting this war. So, Matriya and his men were kept separate from the soldiers and travelled close to the Royal caravan, well protected. The King and the Generals decided that the quickest way towards Harappa would be partly by river and partly by land. It meant building boats and carrying them on carts to avoid cities and villages and kept the engineers and carpenters busy for the next few weeks.

❖

Chapter 14

THE RAJASUYA YAJNA

Harappa rapidly began to transform from a prosperous trading centre to a city at war. The Rajasuya Yajna to anoint sage Shunahotra King for the duration of the war with the Avestans was the first step and elaborate preparations for it were well under way. I was busy making the hospital ready to handle casualties from the battlefield. Master Ashwin had brought out some old contingency plans used a long time ago during a battle with Dasyu rebels. We had to update them to cope with a far bigger war. The information we had received was that the Avestans had gathered regiments from all the seven districts of Ariana and had nearly fifteen thousand soldiers, including four hundred cavalry and two hundred chariots. No one had ever seen such a large army.

Father came home late every night with worry writ large on his face. One night he called all of us together and said, "Vidhayaka and Upaas, this battle is going to be fierce and there will be a lot of casualties. We must plan for all eventualities. I should have sent your mother and sister off to Sindhu some time ago; now there is a block on all travel.

The messenger who had gone to King Sudas for help has just returned with bad news-King Sudas will not be able to help us. He is sending his minister to discuss something with the

Elders. We have to face the fact that we may lose the battle if we don't get enough support. If that happens, you must go to my brother, Gopayana in Udaypuri. You will be safe there. It is unlikely that the Avestans will wish to expand their territory and go down south. They only want Soma since the drought has dried up their sacred lakes Kasaoya and Frazdanu and their Soma has died out."

We were silent. Then Mother said, "Please don't worry. Lord Indra will protect us. Nothing will happen to us and our Harappa."

"Father, our armies are no pushover," said Vidhayaka. "Sage Shunahotra is powerful and some of our Masters also have command of powerful magic. We have the famed Gandhari regiment and our elephants can put the fear of God into any soldier in a battle. And most important, we are morally right."

"Yes, Father. We are well prepared for this battle. The Avestans will be sorry they attacked us," I added.

Father smiled. "I hope you are right. Anyway, the preparations for the Rajasuya are going well. Sage Vishwamitra has agreed to come from Sindhu to officiate at the ceremony. We hope Sage Vasishta from Ila will attend as well. By the way, Upaas, we have learnt that your friend, Shushun, is the second son of King Awan of Elam. He is travelling incognito to study the cultures of the world. He has a lot of experience of battles with the Sumerians. Sage Shunahotra has asked him to attend the meeting next week as well."

I was astonished. However, I recalled that Shushun did have a royal bearing and a phenomenal amount of knowledge. He was too sophisticated to be a simple merchant from Elam selling oil.

"The rituals for the Rajasuya will begin two days later on the day of the full moon. The army has been put on extra alert," Father continued.

In the past such ceremonies were attacked by rebel Dasyus who believed that their power increased every time they destroyed a Vedic altar. Since Sage Shunahotra defeated them so many years ago, these attacks had ceased. But, to stop a Rajasuya would be a feather in the cap of any Dasyu rebel. A Rjasuya Yajna is second only to an Ashwamedha Yajna as far as spiritual power is concerned.

The place chosen for the Yajna was a beautiful valley not far from Harappa. A small stream flowed at its edge and it was full of Neem, Ashoka, Kavudi (Cork tree), Arjun, Vata (Banyan) Deodar, Sal and several Ashwattha (peepal) trees. Monkeys feasted on the figs of the Udumbura (Cluster Fig or Gular) trees and created a racket. The shrubs of Ashwagandha and numerous Tulsi plants made the air fragrant.

A large area was cleared for the altars and for the congregation to sit. The ground was watered and pounded to even it out, cow dung solution was sprinkled to waterproof and sterilise it and then the juice of Tulsi leaves was sprinkled on it to mask the odour. Grtsamada supervised the positioning and building of the altars to the exact specifications given in Vedic scriptures. Master Medhatithi (Rigvedic mathematician), Master of Mathematics in Sindhu had come to assist him.

They marked out the crucial Prushtya line (East-West axis) using new bricks covered in lime. Once the stars were visible at night, they aligned the centre point of the Mahavedi (the stage for the Yajna) where they would build the fire altar for the ritual. Once the centre point was decided and marked, they measured the eastern and western boundary of the Mahavedi as well as the northern and southern boundaries based on the height of the Yajamana or the performer of the Yajna in this case, Sage Shunahotra. The fire place for cooking was built in the southern half of the quadrangle. The ritual would take five days to complete and culminate in a sacrifice on the final day.

The shapes of the altars were crucial. The first layer was in the shape of a falcon about to spread its wings and the central altar was a perfect rhomboid and rose up to five layers of bricks. There were four altars around the central one. Each layer had to have the exact numbers of bricks and the pattern was also according to established rules.

Instruments and articles required for the Rajasuya were being prepared: five large ladles were made from the wood of the Ramontchi tree (Indian plum) to pour the oblations into the fire, several aranis (flints) were made ready and two kept near each of the altars. The fresh Soma that I had brought was used to prepare fresh extracts and juice for the occasion and the sheep skin for filtering the Soma juice was thinned out repeatedly between polished wooden rolls. Ten cows were kept at the site for fresh milk for the Soma extract.

Some of the Soma plants had been left to dry for the Soma ritual, which was one of the important parts of the Yajna. Sandal wood sticks had been brought in for the altars and several large bronze cauldrons of ghee (clarified butter) were prepared. Vessels were specially made with Ashwattha wood to serve the offerings after the ritual every day. Large pestles were made using strong Kadira wood to pound grain for the rice cakes, which would be both offerings and oblations during the ritual.

The Elders of the Councils of all the cities of Bharata were expected to attend. They would be housed in the rooms within the Temple and in some guest houses within the city. Engineers were busy ensuring the water supply and drainage worked well. Father checked the water level in the tank every day. The kitchens of the temple were busier than ever. There was an air of celebration and apprehension everywhere. Everyone was excited about the Rajasuya, but no one spoke of the war.

Sage Vishwamitra arrived a couple of days before the Yajna and inspected the preparation in the valley. Both he and Sage Shunahotra were very impressed with Grtsamada and Medatithi's work.

"You have excelled yourself Grtsamada. This looks to be perfect. I am particularly impressed with the central altar in the Mahavedi. It matches the measurements in the Vedic scriptures perfectly," Sage Vishwamitra said with a smile.

"Thank you, great Sage. I had the help of our excellent Master Medatithi from Sindhu."

Sage Vishwamitra inspected the security of the valley with Sage Shunahotra. Master Adhvadipa had personally led the platoon that searched the valley and its surroundings for hiding places. He had positioned his best soldiers within the valley dressed as ordinary devotees in case there was a breach in external security. Master Kodhandaki was in charge of the security at the periphery of the valley and he had positioned the elite Black Platoon of the Gandhari regiment all round the borders of the valley.

"We have the situation well under control," he said when the sages came to inspect the security arrangements. "Not an ant can enter or leave the valley without being seen by one of our soldiers."

Finally, when they were fully satisfied, Sage Vishwamitra turned to Sage Shunahotra and said, "I think we better get back to the city to welcome Sage Vasishta. He will be arriving soon. We don't want to keep him waiting."

The regiment from Sindhu had arrived with sage Vishwamitra and was stationed on the western side of the valley along with the Harappan regiment. The Gandhara regiment would have arrived before the Yajna started, but were held up because of landslides in the Suvastu valley. The Bharata regiment from Ila and a regiment from Manusa (Kalibhangan) were expected to arrive any day now.

Mother, Nivya, Satakratu and Lopa were at the valley long before sunrise on the first day of the Yajna to help in the preparations. Father, Vidhayaka and I had stayed at the valley the night before, as we had to be at the altar in time to start the rituals. It was very sultry summer's day and I went for a swim with Vidhayaka in the middle of night before having a bath in the stream with everyone. It was a sight to see over a hundred men in the stream chatting away under the star lit sky as they poured water over themselves. The valley was lit up with torches and it was an eerie sight with hundreds of people walking around in brilliant white dhotis in the flickering light.

The Yajna started before sunrise with the ritual cleansing of the entire site with the sprinkling of cow's urine before the devotees entered the valley. The Rajasuya, like any other Yajna, needed four priests. Sage Vishwamitra was the Bramhan, Sage Vasishta the initiator of invocations who invites the Gods to the Yajna, Grtsamada the Priest in charge of the physical structures and Master Skanda incharge of the hymns and chants. Sage Shunahotra was the Yajamana at the head of the altar. Deer skin mats were spread around the central altar for the priests to sit on. Sage Shunahotra sat at the south of the altar and the other three priests on the other three sides. Grtsamada was moving around the entire mahavedi like a mother hen making sure everything was just right. The apprentices sat in rows of three on three sides of the main altar shaped like a raising falcon.

Sage Vasishta first invited Lord Agni with the lighting of the sandal wood sticks in the altar with aranis. Sage Vasishta chanted the hymns. The timing was so perfect that the sun came up as he invoked Savitar, the Sun God, as if in answer to his invocation. Then, he propitiated the Soma and other Gods.

The devotees were given some Soma juice to drink and rice cakes to eat in the afternoon as well as in the evening. The ritual continued for five days. All the men stayed in the valley throughout the Yajna while the women went back to the city at night and returned in the mornings. Prince Shushun spent all the five days with me and observed the rites very closely. He was impressed by the similarities between his culture and ours.

When Sage Vasishta invoked Varuna, the God of Wind, he said, "We have a beautiful temple of Lord Varuna in Susa on the banks of river Karun. It has one thousand pillars."

The Gandhari regiment reached Harappa on the third day of the Yajna and camped at the mouth of the valley towards the north. The Yajna site was now surrounded on all four sides by our army of over fifteen thousand soldiers. The elephants from the Manusa regiment were posted on the eastern side of the valley often made a racket with their trumpeting.

On the fifth day of the ritual, Sage Shunahotra was anointed King of Harappa and taken with great pomp into the city in a grand procession. The new King Shunahotra held his first court on the same day. Visiting dignitaries from various cities in Bharata presented gifts to him. Shushun gave him a large gold necklace and a head band and an offer of friendship from King Awan of Elam.

All the Elders of the Council and Sages Vishwamitra and Vasishta attended the meeting in the Great Hall a couple of days later. Prince Shushun was invited as an adviser. King Sudas's minister had arrived the night before with a large retinue of military advisers. I was asked to attend by Master Advadipa to tell the Council of Elders what I had seen of Ariana and its army.

Messengers had returned with the news that the ten thousand strong Avestan army had left the city of Roruka and marching north nearly halfway to Harappa. When the regiments from the northern districts of Bactria and Sogdiana join them, it would have over fifteen thousand soldiers.

The Hall was quiet as Sage Shunahotra made the offerings to the residing deity, Lord Indra.

"I would like to thank everyone for their help during the Rajasuya Yajna," he began. "We now have to decide on our strategy in this war. Our armies are ready and waiting. We are more than a match for the Avestans. But, I would like to invite Prince Shushun to give us his view of the situation."

"I am honoured and extremely grateful for this gesture by the King of Harappa. It is true that Elam has been involved in conflicts with the very large Sumerian army. My father, King Awan, marched with an army of twenty thousand to face a larger army occupying our land.

The battle was fought in a valley and we gained an upper hand despite being outnumbered because we ensured that the battle took place in the location of our choice. My suggestion is that you should march out of Harappa and stage a confrontation in a place of your choosing. I am sure your commanders will be able to identify a such a place."

Several heads nodded at the suggestion.

"I agree entirely with the honoured prince," said Master Advadipa. "We have identified places south of the city where the valley broadens out a little and is shallow enough to give an impression of flat land. If we position our armies on the higher ground, our archers will have an advantage over them. Our elephants will find it easier to charge and the upward slope will be disadvantageous to the Avestans."

"Thank you, Master Adhvadipa. You have thought of everything, a usual," Sage Shunahotra replied. "Yes Master Kodhandaki. You have something to say?"

"My Gandhari regiment in the north has informed me they have spotted the Avestan regiments from Sogdiana and Bactria on the Sindhu and the Parushni in the Suvastu valley. We still have the reserves of the Gandhara regiment along with those guarding Mount Mujavant. They can stop these two regiments from meeting with the main Avestan army."

"That is a very good idea. Tell me Master Kodhandaki, what is the strength of the reserves and the regiment on Mount Mujavant? Are they strong enough for the job?"

"We have just over one full regiment. And we will have the advantage of surprise, as well as the fact that our Gandhari's know the land like the back of their hands. They will be no match. I am quite confident that we can stop them."

There was a lot of discussion among several people in the Great Hall. Some thought the Gandharis were overconfident. I had seen the Gandhari soldiers in action and believed they could do it. They had not only the close knowledge of the land, but also by all accounts, they knew as much sorcery as the Dasyus.

"Master Kodhandaki, if you think there is sufficient number and strength, then we should implement your plan," said Sage Shunahotra and then turned to me. "You have had some first hand experience of their army, Upaas. What can you tell us about them?"

"From what I saw and heard, they appeared to be very disciplined. The command structure was strong in some aspects and casual in others. The security of the place where I was held was weak, luckily for me. The town of Haozdar looks desolate and the people live in very hard conditions. They do not have much love for their soldiers." I described the scene of the little boy stealing a loaf of bread and the reaction of the soldiers, which shocked most people in the hall.

There were more detailed discussions about the size and content of the forces and it was late in the evening when the meeting was adjourned. It was decided that the army would march south to face the Avestans in the valley chosen by Master Advadipa. It would take three days to reach the spot and the commanders wanted at least a few days in the field for training and planning strategies. That meant the army had to set off from Harappa within two days.

I rode straight to meet Lopa from the Great Hall. I wanted to spend as much time with her as possible before setting off with the army. I did not know how long the war would last or what the outcome would be. We went to our favourite spot near the lake and the amra tree. Lopa was disconcertingly quiet.

"You are very quiet, Lopa."

"I am worried about this war. I wish you did not have to go with the army."

"I have to accompany the army, Lopa. I will be leading the medical corps in the war. We will be there only to treat the wounded. No one will hurt a physician. I will be fine."

"I hope so, Upaas. In the last battle my father was involved in, the entire medical camp was wiped out by the Dasyu army."

"Those were Dasyu rebels and they did not follow any protocols of war. I have seen the Avestan soldiers. They are much more disciplined and civilised."

"You have the amulet I gave you?"

"Yes," I said, pulling it up round my neck and showing her. "All the time."

It was with sad hearts that we returned to the city. I kissed her goodbye and wipes the tears that spilled from her eyes. But my eyes were brimming when I turned away. Would we meet again? Or was this to be our last kiss, our last meeting? I wondered what the Gods had in store for us.

❖

Chapter 15

THE GREAT WAR

We spent the next couple of days checking and rechecking our medical stocks - bandages, splints and cast material, powders and potions and herbs. Master Ashwin checked everything twice and made sure that we would lack nothing on the field.

I was at the hospital well before sunrise on the day of departure. The army had assembled outside the southern gates on the field next to the river over the previous weeks and had been training intensified. I had to undergo some training as well.

Vidhayaka had already left the day before with the other engineers and cartloads of materials to prepare for the arrival of the army at the battlefield. Special prayers were conducted at home that morning and the fire in the altar that was built in our courtyard would burn until our return. Vidhayaka had built a roof over it to prevent the rains from dousing the fire. Mother, Nivya, Lopa and Satakratu saw us off tearfully.

At the hospital gates, everyone, including Master Ashwin, was ready for departure. I was really proud to be asked to be the lead of the corps. Pindara was there with the cart. I jumped off Shankara and touched the Master's feet. To my surprise, Shushun and Parthava were also there.

“I could not let you go there with no one to show you how to treat wounded soldiers properly!” said Shushun with a smile.

“And someone has to keep an eye on your back and make sure you don’t get kidnapped again,” said Parthava.

I hugged them both.

The caravan consisted of one big cart, which Pindara drove, and two smaller carts that carried supplies such as splints. We were twelve people including six nurses. The sun was just coming up as we reached the southern gate and the last of the army, mainly the elephants and some cavalry, were leaving. We stayed just behind the last column of soldiers. We crossed the Parushni at its narrowest part where it went through a steep gorge and our engineers had put up a wooden bridge strengthened with new trusses of heavy oak logs. The bridge swayed dangerously when the elephants sauntered across and everyone sighed with relief when the last elephant had crossed.

The Harappan army camped on a small hillock covered with tall trees on the slope away from the direction of the wind, so that smoke from the cooking fires could not be seen from the other side of the hillock. It was dusk when we reached the camp and reported to General Nahusha.

“Welcome to the camp, Upaas,” he said. “The Avestan army is only a few days away from here. I am sure they know by now that we are camped here. Our forward scouts still have not encountered any of their scouts.”

The general was a tall man who walked with long strides and I had to practically run to keep up with him. The whole place was a hive of activity with soldiers practicing with their swords and maces and spears. The cavalry was putting the horses through their paces and practicing firing arrows at targets while on the run. Right at the edge of the tree line, archers were practicing firing at moving targets.

On the right of the path, the Gandhari regiment were firing what looked like normal arrows, but which burst into flames as they hit the target. There were also arrows which broke up into several smaller arrows as they neared the target. At the far end was a group of people mixing powders and potions into several cauldrons over fires. The smell coming from some of them was overpowering, but did not appear to affect them. Some of the cauldrons were bubbling and giving out yellow and purple vapours.

One of the men took a small satchel, opened it and threw it over his shoulder. There was a loud bang and a bright flash, which nearly blinded us. He disappeared and then startled me by tapping on my shoulder from behind.

"How did you get behind me so quickly?"

He just smiled and walked away.

We walked to the end of the treeline where the ground was dry and sandy and trees were sparse. In a clearing in a thicket several tents had been set up. Vidhayaka was bent over a desk in the largest tent and stood up as we entered.

"Sorry. I was using this as our field office. Good evening, General. This is your field hospital, Upaas. We have set up more tents around for you to stay in."

"This area is isolated from the battlefield by the knoll on the west side. There is a passage for the stretcher bearers and the wounded to and from the battlefield. This area will have complete protection," the General said to us. "I will send some soldiers to help you unload your carts and set up your equipment in the morning."

The passage leading to the proposed battlefield was a small gully in the side of the hillock which wound around in a sharp curve westwards opening into a large field. The land sloped so gently down to the river that unless a trained person pointed it out, it looked completely flat. The river was a dark ribbon flowing gently in the distance.

That night I decided to sleep under the stars in front of the tent. As I lay there looking at the sky, I remembered Lopa lying next to me counting and naming the stars in her melodious voice. Her presence was so real that I almost turned my head to look at her. I remembered the way she had galloped towards me on her horse and I smiled. I wonder when I will see her again, I thought with a deep sigh.

"Love is painful," Shushun said out of the darkness. "But it is the best feeling in the world."

"How long have you been here?"

"Long enough to see both the smiles and the tears."

"Well, my friend, I think it is time to sleep now. We have a long day ahead of us now."

"Yes we do. Good night, Upaas."

I soon drifted off to sleep.

On the first day at the battlefield we unloaded the carts and set up our hospital. The beds and the stretchers were made ready. On the

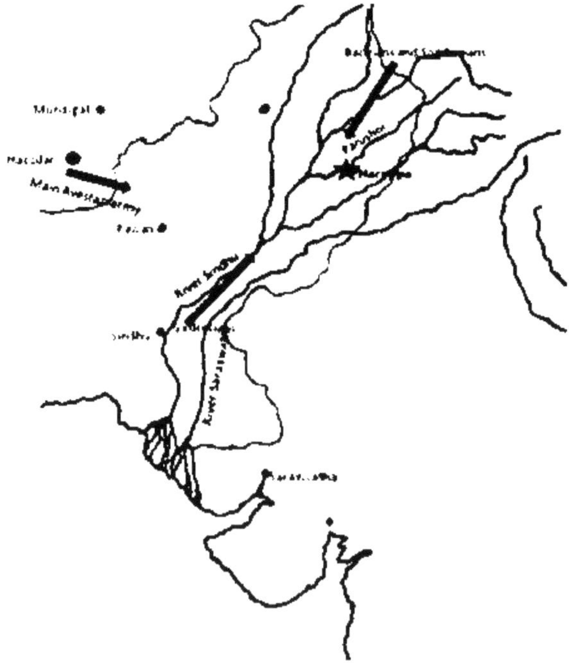

second afternoon, Shushun, Parthava and I went to see the battlefield. It did not look like a battlefield, it was so peaceful and calm. There was a gentle breeze that swayed the trees on the copse behind us and on the far bank of the Parushni. The field was quite large, ran north to south, slightly narrower at the north end than the south.

The Parushni formed the eastern margin and the copse on the little hillock the western margin. On the far side of the river, the banks rose steeply. The river itself did not flow fast here. To the north and east were distant snow capped mountains. Our General had chosen the place extremely wisely. There was a barely noticeable slope down to the river from the north and west to the south and east towards what would be the position of the Avestans.

The river was wide and strewn with large boulders creating eddies and making it hazardous to cross. The western bank was rocky and covered with shale. The enemy would have to land further south and march north into the field.

There was good news next morning. The Gandhari reserves had stopped the Avestan regiments on the Parushni river. The two regiments were attacked with a barrage of fire arrows. Several boats were burnt down and many Avestan soldiers were captured. The rest had retreated back up the river.

The main body of the Avestan army reached the battlefield two days later. The loss of two regiments from the north was a big blow to them and I had hoped that their King would consider retreat. But despite the fact that the army was now significantly smaller than ours, they decided to march to Harappa. Their army reached the battlefield at night and their engineers spent the whole night setting up camp. We heard the sounds of hammers and saws throughout the night.

There was the customary 'pre-battle meeting' between Sage Shunahotra and King Vishtaspa and the opposing generals in the middle of the battlefield to discuss the rules and regulations for the battle. The start and finish times of the battle and the signal for the start and end of the day was agreed on. Both sides agreed that no medical personnel would be attacked.

Shushun knew a lot about battle formations, strategies and counter strategies. He explained to me the different battle formations and their pros and cons. I soon knew of formations called the Wedge, the Lotus, the Falcon, the Phalanx and the Double Wedge. He predicted that Sage Shunahotra would use the Falcon formation on the first day and he was right.

The beak was the infantry, the head was made up of elephants, the body was full of archers and the wings the fast cavalrymen swooping down from the sides. When I saw this huge formation, I wondered how the enemy had any chance against the might of this Harappan army. As predicted by Shushun, the Avestans countered with a Lotus formation. They had the chariots forming the centre with the petals alternating between infantry, cavalry and the archers.

The idea was that the infantry would spread out as they approached the enemy to let the chariots race up against the beak of the Falcon. We watched from a vantage point close to the edge of the copse.

The Avestan soldiers wore colourful uniforms. The infantry had brown trousers tied at the ankles and cream coloured loose shirts tied at the waist with red cummerbunds. The Cavalry were impressive with red trousers and violet shirts and red turbans with a tail, which waved in the breeze when they galloped. The chariots were mostly two wheeled and extremely fast. The wooden wheels with spokes had pointed brass studs on the side, which made them lethal.

The infantry in front carried the standard of Ariana - a winged disc. They had tall brass tipped spears with an Avestan flag at the tip. The flags over the chariots also had the emblem of the winged disc. They were an impressive sight. There were drummers beside each phalanx with very large kettledrums. The tempo of the march was decided by the captain and relayed by the drums. The drums sounded ominous and set the heart thumping. The standard bearer was also in charge of the Conch shell.

The Harappan soldiers, on the other hand, were all dressed in white dhotis tied up at the back and white shirts. Their hair was tied to the right side and they wore no headgear. The captains and generals wore a turban rolled up over the head with a tail that dropped down on to the right. The turban was also white. The Harappan standard was carried by a standard bearer separately for the infantry, cavalry and the elephant regiment. It was a white flag with a fire-breathing falcon in gold. The shields of the soldiers carried the same emblem, as did the chariots.

I watched the two mighty armies march towards each other as soon as the standard bearer blew on the conch. They came head to head and started the verbal and psychological war before the physical battle commenced. Both sides hurled abuses at each other and the drums tried to drown out each other.

The Harappans yelled, "You mountain dwellers, uncultured brutes! We'll teach you a lesson you'll never forget!"

"Cattle thieves!"

"You are all bastards of unknown fathers!"

The Avestans responded with, "Cow worshippers!"

"Weaklings! One of us can eat ten of you!"

"Underdeveloped freaks!"

The sound of the kettle drums, conchs, bugles and thumping feet was deafening, and I must admit, frightening. The elephants, which made up the rear of the charge behind the beak, stomped steadily forward. They wreaked havoc among the enemy foot soldiers. The archers had their bows loaded with poison tipped arrows. The sergeants of the platoons started a menacing sounding chant in tune with the drums.

The Avestan infantry marched aggressively towards the Harappans and as they neared the beak of the falcon, they suddenly separated sideways leaving an open path for the chariots to rush forward. The chariots would have succeeded, but they were slowed down by the slight slope of the ground. Thus, at the end of the day, when the final conch was blown, the battle was evenly poised. There were a large number of casualties on both sides. The first of the wounded began to arrive at the field hospital by lunchtime and we were busy for the rest of the day till well after dusk.

It was late on the second night of the battle when I saw it first. We had retired into our tents tired after a day of fixing broken bones and patching up gaping wounds. The three of us were sitting in front of the hospital tent when I heard it. It was slow at first, a deep rumbling kind of sound. Whoever it was, he knew his rhythm. It became louder, but kept the same pace. We stopped talking and stared in the direction of the sound.

It was Shushun who broke the silence with, "Oh dear."

"Why? What is happening?"

"Come, you have to see this."

The drums had become louder, but the rhythm stayed the same. It was dark in the field and we could see the fires in the Avestan camp. The Harappan soldiers were patrolling the periphery of the field. We had to first get past our guards and then avoid the Avestan guards. Shushun knew exactly where he was going. He ducked behind the rocks on the edge of the copse along the line of trees in the darkness.

We crossed the field to the west bank of the river where the music was coming from. Fortunately, monsoon clouds were beginning to gather and we waited until a particularly large cloud covered the moon and made a dash for the other side of the field towards the river.

Parthava brought up the rear and kept saying, "We will be caught and beheaded by the Avestan soldiers."

"Stop being so pessimistic, Parthava. Think of it as another adventure with me," I said, smiling.

When we reached a cluster of large boulders overlooking the river a rather disturbing sight lay before us. On the only flat part of the bank on the western side was a row of fires. Several men carrying burning torches were going round the row of fires chanting something softly. A small group of women sat around the fires at a little distance from us on the left.

As we watched, from our hiding place behind a large rock, the men knelt down on the far side of the rows of fire and doused their torches in the river. Despite the several big roaring fires, the whole place became very dark. There was no breeze and the fires spouted high into the sky with dancing tongues that seemed to touch the low clouds. I could make out the men sitting in a row on the far side of the fires now. The women suddenly stood up and started to walk towards the fires, slightly swaying side to side as they walked in a line.

The drummer increased the tempo and a new sound joined the beats: Dhung Dhung..Dhring Dhring…Dhirim Dhiri... Someone was playing a wind instrument a rather soulful, extremely low-pitched melody. The woman in front started to sing. Initially she was so soft that we could not hear her, but as she neared the row of fires, she became louder and louder. She started off with a monosyllabic sound, almost a wail, before breaking into a song. As soon as she started to sing, a string instrument joined in. It was slow and gut wrenching music. I could only make out a few words as the Avestan she was using was more Median than Avestan.

"It is a long time since I have heard that language. It is from the westernmost part of the country, the district of Carmania. This is their funeral service," Shushun whispered.

"What is she saying?" Parthava wanted to know. He had tears in his eyes even though he had not understood a single word.

"She says that he was like the birds on the trees which brought love to her life and disappeared with sunrise, he was like footprints on sand which disappear when the tide comes in, he was like the snow on the mountains which melt at the sight of the sun. They are fabulous musicians and write soulful songs. She is obviously mourning her paramour who has died in the battle today."

As we watched, the women went round the row of fire once and did something strange. Each of them stood in front of one of the fires and took off all their clothes and dropped them on the fire. They just stood in front of the fire with arms raised before them. One of the men stood up and sprinkled something over their heads chanting something.

"Are they going to jump into the pyre?" Parthava whispered agitatedly.

"It is none of our business. Just watch and don't make any noise unless you want all of us killed," whispered Sushun sternly.

They did not jump into the fire as Parthava and I had feared. They just walked into the river one by one and kept going until we thought they would drown. I almost got up to run and save them, but Shushun held me down.

"The two of you are going to get us killed. Keep still."

They stopped when they had gone neck deep. I do not know how the current did not whisk them off their feet. They were still singing. Then they came back and sat in a row in front of the fires. A man stood up and threw some powder into the fires. There was a lightning flash and a bright yellow tongue of flame shot high up in the sky and came down as quickly and went out.

It temporarily blinded all of us. He repeated it at all the fires. When the last of the fires went out, it was pitch black. I could not even see my friends who were lying next to me. It was still and quiet for a moment and then the chanting began again. This time it was a low pitched and slow with just the drums keeping up the beat. It was the men who were singing praises of the fallen soldiers in chaste Avestan.

One torch was lit and the men started walking slowly back towards the Avestan camp. The women followed behind, now wrapped in white clothes. The voices trailed off as the procession disappeared into the night. I felt emotionally drained and more tired now than after a full day's work at the field hospital. We walked back in silence. As soon as we reached the camp, Parthava had thousands of questions for Shushun. The two of them sat talking till the early hours of the morning.

The next day brought more of the same fights and similar injuries. The general tried the new lotus formation with long-range archers in the middle and elephants and the infantry forming the alternate petals. According to the spies, the Avestan general, Parviz, was going to try his famous double wedge formation.

The Lotus would be the ideal counter attack. There were a lot of sword and arrow injuries along with burns from the fire arrows. The casualties were high on both sides. This went on for the next six days with neither side showing any signs of winning or giving up. The casualties mounted every day. We had to transport some of the most seriously wounded soldiers back to the city on bullock carts once they were stabilised.

The field hospital was hectically busy. Shushun was a great help. When he rolled up the sleeves of his long jacket and worked on wounded soldiers, it was easy to forget that he was the prince of a large country. He was particularly skilled in treating chemical burn injuries caused by magical arrows. Parthava tirelessly provided us with supplies. The three of us became much closer to each other than before.

On the seventh day, Sage Shunahotra took charge of the battle. He went back to the first day's formation of Eagle. This time the cavalry made the beak, the elephants the head, the infantry the body and the wings were made up of archers with cavalry archers at the edge of the wings. Shunahotra was in the front with the General on his white steed looking regal and rather fierce. I knew he was going to use his yogic powers to unleash invincible arrows each of which could destroy a whole platoon.

As soon as the conch blew the start of the day's proceedings, he let loose a barrage of arrows at the tip of General Parviz's double wedge formation. It was soon obvious that the Avestan army was no match for his powers. The combined onslaught of the Sage's power and the thundering elephants routed the Avestan army. The casualty was very high with bodies piled up everywhere. As dusk approached and the end of the day's battle was sounded, an eerie silence descended on the battlefield. The soldiers withdrew and I went in with the medical team to pick up the wounded survivors from the field.

It was a scene of ghastly, gruesome carnage. There were battered, broken bodies everywhere. Severed limbs lay strewn across the field and the earth was soaked in blood. Our feet sank into the soggy field as we walked carefully to avoid stepping on dead bodies and on the nearly dead injured. Our torches threw flickering shadows over dead soldiers and horses. The stench of burning flesh from the fire arrows was overpowering and the thin dhoti end covering our faces did nothing to stop it.

I felt sick and full of the age-old questions: was this carnage necessary? What would we achieve that was worth so many lives? A wife, a sister or a mother in a distant land, just like my Lopa or Nivya or Mother would be waiting for a son, a brother, a lover or a husband to return. Children would wait in vain for their fathers. The sheer waste of precious human life appalled me.

It was very late at night when we had brought all the wounded soldiers back to the field hospital. We spent the rest of the night patching them up. We had to send many of them back to the city as the field hospital became full, half way through the night.

When the cockerel announced the daybreak, both Shushun and I went to the end of the gully to look at the battlefield before retiring. Parthava joined us just as the sun came up over the hills in the east. The Parushni was still in darkness and we could not see much of the field. But as the sun rose in the sky, it was swathed in bright yellow light. The field had been cleared of dead bodies and other debris. A new battle formation would be set up again bringing the same dead bodies, the same lost lives.

I sighed deeply and said, "I don't know about you, Shushun, but I hate war. It is completely meaningless and unnecessary."

"You are right. Unfortunately, given the nature of human beings, this will never end until the day humanity destroys itself. The great sage Utnaphistim from Sumeria has predicted that humanity will destroy itself one day. He also said that a messiah will come and resurrect the world and there will be peace after that."

We were about to turn around and leave when Parthava called out, "What is that out there?"

Half a dozen riders were coming towards us from the direction of the Avestan camp.

"We better warn the General. They are Avestan soldiers," he said.

"They are indeed Avestan soldiers with a flag of truce," Shushun said. "They are carrying the white standard with a dove insignia."

"Does that mean they are surrendering?" I asked.

"No. They are asking for negotiations or settlement of the war. It seems they are either on the verge of losing or they expect reinforcements and are playing for delay."

"How do you know all this?" Parthava asked, forgetting that Shushun was a prince from a country that had fought several wars with Sumerians.

"Well, I have been involved in one or two skirmishes with Sumerians," he replied with a smile. "I am sure we will find out soon enough." Surprisingly, he showed no signs of tiredness despite having worked continuously through the night without any rest or sleep.

I was fast asleep the minute my head hit the pillow only to be woken up by Parthava shaking my shoulders vigorously.

"Leave me alone. I have just gone to sleep."

"No, Upaas. It is nearly noon. You have been asleep for several hours now."

I sat up.

"What? Why didn't you wake me up earlier?"

"There was no battle today and the nurses are managing the wounded quite well without your help. But you have been summoned to the royal tent. Sage Shunahotra wants you there."

I washed and changed quickly and ran across the copse to the royal tent. The large tent was full of people. Sage Shunahotra sat at the head of the gathering dressed in his royal robe with the crown on his head. The General, most of the Council of Elders and Sage Vishwamitra stood on either side. To my right were several Avestans I did not recognise.

I bowed and spoke without lifting my head, "My humble apologies Sage Shunahotra. I was busy all night with the wounded and did not go to bed until this morning."

"Do not apologise, Upaas. We are grateful for all the work you and your team have done to save our soldiers' lives and limbs," Shunahotra said. "Let me introduce you to King Vishtaspa, the lord of Ariana."

I turned to King Vishtaspa, bowed my head and said, "My greetings, Your Highness. It is my pleasure to make your acquaintance."

"I have heard a lot about you, Master Upaas. You successfully escaped from our soldiers and stirred up a hornet's nest," King Vishtaspa replied.

"We are negotiating a truce and an end to this unnecessary bloodshed, Upaas. There are a number of Avestan soldiers with serious injuries who will not survive the long journey back to Ariana. I have agreed to have them treated in Harappa. The King has graciously offered the assistance of their physicians, who will stay back to help you with the additional work your team will have to do. I need your opinion."

I had to think fast. It would be a boon to have the help of the Avestans and I could learn a lot about their methods of treatment.

"I am grateful for the offer, Sage. The help of their physicians will be invaluable and there is a lot we can learn from them," I replied.

Just then there was a commotion outside the tent and the guard came in and announced, "The prisoners are here, Your Highness."

Two people with their hands tied behind their back were brought in. The one in front was a tall man dressed in black. He had a long angular face with a pointed nose and a greying beard. His jet black eyes appeared to be staring into the distance. The one behind was much shorter and slightly stout. He wore a dhoti like the Harappans and a mask covered his face. He had his head bent down and walked slowly dragging his feet.

King Vishtaspa stood up and said to the Sage, "Here are the two prisoners, Your Majesty. I hope you will treat them according to the laws of your land."

He turned to the soldier and said angrily, "How dare he keep his face covered in front of the King? Take that mask off this instant."

The mask was ripped off with alacrity. There was a gasp from the Sage and everyone else. Unfortunately he had his back to me and I could not see him. So Sage Shunahotra's words came as a great shock: "Ubhaya! How could you do this? After all the city of Harappa has done for you and your family? You came here as destitutes. Your family was given a place to stay, a job and you were well looked after. Is this the way you repay your hosts?"

I was deeply shocked. Ubhaya just stood silently, staring at the floor and then he snorted and spat on the floor.

The general pulled out his sword and stepped forward saying, "Why, you ingrate!"

The Sage stopped him from hacking Ubhaya down.

"Take him away before one of us decides to finish what the General was about to do."

The soldiers dragged Ubhaya out of the tent. I seethed with anger. This ungrateful coward had caused so many deaths and so many soldiers had been maimed in an unnecessary war.

Sage Shunahotra then turned to Matriya and said, "As for you Matriya, what you have done is unforgivable. You will be tried before the Great Council and a just punishment will be meted out to you."

The soldiers dragged the Magus out of the tent and marched him into the stockade. It was much later that I learnt the terms of the settlement. The Avestans had suffered severe losses and expected no reinforcements. To continue fighting would annihilate the rest of their army. So, they had agreed to withdraw into their country and make reparations in precious stones, copper and olive oil. Sage Shunahotra had agreed to supply them with a limited amount of Soma, just enough for their Yasna, on a regular basis until their own crop recovered. It was a face saving deal for King Vishtaspa.

We made our way back to the city the following day. I was full of doubts and questions -- why did Ubhaya betray Harappa when the city had done its best for him? He was given a chance to become a physician, a most rewarding occupation. Was the Magus justified in doing what he did? Did the end justify the means? He was prepared to sacrifice thousands of people to achieve notoriety and acceptance by his peers. Why did King Vishtaspa not negotiate before the war? With the loss of two regiments even before the battle started, he should have known that there was no chance of victory.

"It is no use wondering about what has happened, Upaas," Shushun broke into my thoughts. "I know what you are thinking. There is a wise sage in Sumeria who I am going to visit. They tell me that he knows the answers to all questions. Why don't you come with me?"

"I have never heard of this sage. Is he better than our great Shunahotra, Vishwamitra or Vasishta?"

"No. He is not better. But I am told that he is a wise man and he knows the answers to all the questions, including the question of mortality."

A visit to Sumeria was something to look forward to. But first, I would go back to Harappa, to Lopa, to my family. I would go back home.

❖

Further Reading:

1. ***Gods, Sages and Kings: Vedic Secrets of Ancient Civilization*** by Dr David Frawley. Passage Press, Salt Lake City, Utah.
2. I***n Search of the Cradle of Civilization*** by Georg Feuerstein, Subash Kak, David Frawley.
3. ***The Penguin History of Early India from the origins to AD1300.*** By Romila Thapar. Penguin India.
4. ***Mesopotamia: The Invention of the City*** by Gwendolyn Leick. Penguin UK.
5. ***Ancient India.*** By R C Majumdar, Motilal Banarsidass Publishers Ltd.
6. ***Modern English Translation of Rigveda Samhita*** by Prasanna Chandra Gautam.
7. ***Myth of the Aryan Invasion of India*** by David Frawley.
8. ***The History and Culture of the Indian People;The Vedic Age*** edited by R C Majumdar. Published by Bharatiya Vidya Bhavan.
9. ***Underworld: The Flooded Kingdoms of the Ice Age*** by Graham Hancock
10. www.ajaonline.org
11. www.ancientindia.co.uk
12. www.archaeologyonline.net
13. www.asi.nic.in
14. www.harappa.com
15. www.indiahistoryonline.com

Printed by Amazon Italia Logistica S.r.l.
Torrazza Piemonte (TO), Italy

12941008R00146